Émilienne

BOOKS BY PAMELA BINNINGS EWEN

Émilienne
The Queen of Paris: A Novel of Coco Chanel
The Moon in the Mango Tree
Secret of the Shroud (Walk Back the Cat)

THE AMALISE CATOIR SERIES
Dancing on Glass
Chasing the Wind
An Accidental Life

NONFICTION
*Faith on Trial: Analyze the Evidence for the
Death and Resurrection of Jesus*

PAMELA BINNINGS EWEN

Émilienne

BLACK STONE
PUBLISHING

Printed in the United States of America
Originally published in hardcover by Blackstone Publishing in 2023

First paperback edition: 2024
ISBN 979-8-212-87681-0
Fiction / Historical / General

Version 1

Blackstone Publishing
31 Mistletoe Rd.
Ashland, OR 97520

www.BlackstonePublishing.com

"Émilienne? The grand cocotte!
I liked her. She was the best girl in the world."
—Gabrielle (Coco) Chanel

PROLOGUE

On this cool, fall day, the day of Le Bal des Quat'z'Arts, Émilienne d'Alençon awakens early. She pushes up against the pile of satin pillows behind her, yawning, stretching, listening to the churches of Paris tolling the bells at noon. Sunshine streams through the bedroom, and looking about, she spots the culprit who has disturbed her sleep.

Lily, her maid, smiles, delighted she's awake.

Only eight hours before the show.

Émilienne eats a hearty meal to sustain her until midnight, after the performance—a café au lait, soft-boiled egg with toasted and buttered wheat bread, thin slices of cold veal, and half an orange. Afterward, Lily helps her into her afternoon dress, and Émilienne then retreats to a quiet corner in the salon downstairs. There, she reads a story, sipping chocolate, sometimes drifting into daydreams of the show this evening, something Paris—no, *Europe*—has never seen before. And she also smiles thinking of the dress she shall wear to Maxim's after for celebratory drinks.

At exactly five o'clock, Lily calls the carriage around and they head for the Folies Bergère theater. Giant posters by artists Jules Chéret and Henri de Toulouse-Lautrec—friends and competitors—line the streets, announcing Le Bal, an annual scandal that captivates, shocks, and brings out all of Paris. But this year's show, starring Europe's most notorious courtesan, Émilienne, promises something special, promises to reach new heights.

And so, for one time only, Le Bal is renamed—Émilienne au Bal des Quat'z'Arts.

At five thirty they arrive at the theater and hurry to Émilienne's dressing room just over the stage. Tonight, she is the *étoile,* the star. Already bouquets—roses, carnations, gardenias—cover every inch of the room. Lily and Émilienne are forced to watch their steps.

No orchids, Émilienne notes. Good.

Quickly, she changes into practice clothes and dancing slippers. Hurrying down the stairs to backstage where the barre stands, she warms up her muscles, quietly counting time in her head.

When she is in her dressing room again, with two and one-half hours until the show—two hours for makeup and hair and a half hour more for the costume—she sits down at her dressing table with greasepaint and colors. She is a playful artist, working magic on her satin complexion so it glows, painting her lips red, lining her big golden-brown eyes. Then Lily releases her long strawberry blond curls, brushing them out and letting them tumble loose over her shoulders.

For this performance, for the first time, Émilienne will wear a bodysuit, a translucent costume of silk that tricks the eye. Appearing nude from the stage, it fits like skin. In a world where good girls cover even ankles and wrists until their wedding nights, this shall light a spark. With a wink for Lily, she writhes into the suit, long sleeves covering her arms, tights down to her ankles.

Lily places a garland of pink camellias on Émilienne's head. She hooks a triple row of diamonds around her neck and a thick, flat diamond bracelet on each wrist.

Monsieur le Directeur comes to wish her luck. This evening the house is packed with kings and princes, dukes and earls, he says. Both the highest and lowest members of society, here together. As the musicians test the instruments below, Émilienne imagines the curtains parting, the audience gasping at the transformed stage with the backdrop of glittering stars in a dark sky, the silver trees, the snow.

Now she hears the cue. Lights fade as she arrives backstage. The audience waits in silence as her music begins. Émilienne takes her pose, center stage, a sculpture among the white landscape. Slowly, the curtain opens as she stands motionless in streams of pale light and rising mist—a queen of the night.

When at last she moves, gliding forward, the cheers begin. She gazes at the audience with wicked delight. But, reaching downstage, at the high footlights, something far, far away gleams, catching her eye. Émilienne halts, standing still. She looks off and steps through space and time, drifting back . . .

Her small figure walks down a long street lit only by the moon and gas lamps on corners. Her old wooden clogs click on the cobblestones, breaking the silence in the hills of Montmartre. In the distance comes a foghorn from the river Seine below.

The air is frigid. She pulls her worn red coat around her. The gray woolen gloves she wears miss a finger, but there is no one here to see. Here, at the top of a curving, descending street, Paris spreads as far as the eye can see. She is filled with joy at the sight. She is just a girl. One day . . . one day everyone in the city shall know her name. Kicking up one foot, she throws her arms wide and spins, once, twice, spinning on down the street.

Paris is at peace. Prussia and Napoleon's wars are over, the Revolution, the Commune riots. This is the beautiful time, the Belle Époque. A girl can do anything now if she tries hard enough. Tonight, Paris seems to hold its breath, waiting for Émilienne.

Part One

CHAPTER ONE

She is a young girl from the hills of Montmartre, and when she walks down the street, heads turn. Barely eighteen, Émilienne André understands the value of her beauty, how to use it, and more important, how to charm anyone at any time. Anyone but Maman.

Maman hates her, she is certain. She never misses a chance to remind Émilienne of her own heavy burden, bringing a girl into the world. Maman says if Émilienne had never been born, Papa would still be here—why, after he left she was forced to work from sunup each morning until midnight to feed herself and a hungry girl.

Now, a girl who is no longer a child.

Émilienne used to believe that she remembered him—when she was young. She used to picture a strong man with eyes that smiled, a man carrying her in his arms as he sang, dancing around a room. She used to think that Maman was wrong—that Papa loved his girl.

Now? She's not so sure. She has never seen the man.

Maman says she is a worthless dreamer, and perhaps she should be out on the streets. At least that way she would have to work.

But Émilienne works too! She cleans the lodge where she and Maman live together in the small, cold room—scrubbing the stone steps all the way to the top floor where the seamstresses sew until her hands and knees are red and raw. She also cleans the lodgers' rooms and washes their clothes in the cellar. All without pay, which the lodge owner gives Maman, and she keeps. Maman is the concierge here and for another lodge over on the rue des Martyrs.

Why does Maman hate her so? Other people seem to care. Why, doesn't the bookseller smile when she slips away from her work and into his shop? He lends her good books, the ones she will learn from, he says. When she opens those books, it seems she leaves Montmartre and Maman's red, angry face and all this world behind. He lets her read in a space behind the rows of shelves, and Maman never thinks to look for her there. In turn, Émilienne dusts his bookshelves once a week.

And doesn't the old man with the ragged beard sitting on a chair outside the entrance of the café Le Faisan Doré—oh, that lovely place—doesn't he slip her sweets when she comes around to listen to the music, to peek inside when the door opens?

On this January night in the new year, Émilienne crouches on a flat stone in an alleyway alongside the lodge. Maman stumbled home a couple of hours ago, carrying a large bottle of wine and dragging along a filthy drunk from the street.

The man, spotting Émilienne, stopped just inside the door. Swaying, squinting, he waved his arm in her direction, spitting, "Here! This is more like it."

Maman flew into a fury. Émilienne shrank back into a

corner, but it was already too late. Out came the strap, and while she ran—ducking, darting toward the door with Maman striking her legs, her back, a hip—the drunk laughed. Only when the front door slammed behind her and the damp air outside sank into her bones did Émilienne realize she had left her coat. Even in her thick wool blouse and skirt she's freezing. Soft flurries of snow fall tonight. Huddling in the alley, she wraps her arms around herself.

Perhaps the man tonight will pay Maman enough to buy some sausage for the bread tomorrow morning. Her stomach growls.

Leaning against the wall, Émilienne brushes away the tears. She reaches under her skirt, rubbing the stinging cuts on her legs, still bleeding. When Maman's in one of her furies, no one can guess what she will do. Maman will do almost anything for a few francs. She has threatened to sell her girl more than once—not a threat to ignore in Montmartre.

Just threats, but still.

Shivering, Émilienne curls into a ball on the ground, hugging herself against the icy cold. She peers up at the windows on the top floor where the seamstresses work, but all is dark now. Sometimes they work past midnight. No luck, not tonight. If only she thought earlier to run up there before they left, perhaps she could have slept in their workroom—a place Maman never visits. The seamstresses have hidden her from Maman on many nights like this, from the time she was a child.

They hear. They know.

A smile flickers through, thinking of those women, of the sweets they used to keep for her when she was small. Of the lovely bolts of smooth silks and satins—such pretty colors!— they would show her and the intricate lace and embroidery and the delicate rosettes. Fine things made for great ladies. Now that she is older, the seamstresses allow her to listen when they talk of love and stories of their customers, the beautiful coquettes of Paris and the rich men who love them.

Oh yes, she is old enough to understand *les belle horizontales*, the courtesans who seem to rule the hearts of Paris far below the butte Montmartre. Butterflies, all of them. She dreams of becoming a butterfly, too, rich beyond dreams and free from Maman and the leather belt and living in a tiny, crowded room. Even now, hiding in this alley, she watches them in her mind, glittering up and down the Grands Boulevards where no pretty girl who knows how to laugh, to smile, to flutter her lashes goes hungry or cold. Some dance in cabarets, some sing onstage, and Suzette, her favorite seamstress, says, some are just too pretty for any man to leave behind. These are girls who know how to flirt.

Émilienne understands the worth of flicking your skirt, lowering your lashes, a slow smile, and more. She's no dum-dum. She learned two years ago, when she was sixteen and hungry enough, how to give pleasure to a boy for money enough to fill her belly when there is no other way to eat. But she's no grisette, to settle for a drunk and few sous—like Maman.

A loud noise comes from above, Maman's voice shouting. Émilienne freezes, listening. A man roars. Laughter. Then silence.

Soon Émilienne will find a man who knows her worth, a rich man who will care for her and keep her always warm. Doesn't everyone say she is beautiful? She will leave behind Maman and her shabby room with one wood table and one broken chair and two old mattresses on the floor and the thick glass window that hides the light. She shall leave these hills for the streets of Paris below. She shall dance onstage like the butterflies and own jewels and dresses in every color of the rainbow, and slippers instead of clogs.

But that little voice whispers inside—*When? How? Already you are eighteen.*

For years, Émilienne has practiced dancing on backstreets in the hills when no one is around to see, molding stories with her body, holding her back straight, her head high. She practices for the day when she dances in the theaters of Paris, perhaps even dancing down the glittering boulevards, too, later in the night.

Not long ago, Émilienne mentioned her dream of dancing in Paris to Suzette. And Suzette nodded, looking her up and down. "You are pretty enough," she said. But then she took Émilienne's hand in hers, and, holding her eyes, she leaned close, whispering, "You must leave soon, little one. I believe your maman plans to sell you, child. Here on the hill pretty girls disappear all the time. Get out, away, and quick."

Even Suzette knows the threats.

Émilienne heard the words, and she understood, but still, she'd waited. Perhaps Suzette was wrong. Now, in the alley, she knows the threat is real. She swallows, feeling cold. She must leave. Where will she go? What can she do to eat, to live?

You will dance, a small voice whispers inside.

She has always loved to dance.

❀

Émilienne sits on the steps of the lodge the next morning. Maman is still upstairs. A shaft of sunlight almost seems to warm her, and she's drifting off when the sound of footsteps on cobblestones startles. Blinking into the sunshine, she rubs her eyes, watching a tall, slim woman with flaming red hair seeming to float toward her. At once Émilienne recognizes her from the posters hung all over Montmartre.

She sits up straight, realizing she is in the presence of

Countess Valtesse de La Bigne, known as the Valtesse, the grandest courtesan in Paris. The Valtesse must be coming for a fitting. Émilienne follows, tiptoeing past Maman's room to the floor where the seamstresses work.

Émilienne stands in the doorway, gazing speechless as Suzette and the women greet the star. She watches each move as the Valtesse slips off the long white gloves, flinging them onto a nearby shelf and lifting her hat. Suzette takes these treasures, placing them carefully on a table. Émilienne admires the great beauty. Her shining red hair winds in loose braids around her head. A few curls fly free around her face, giving a soft look, softer even than a pompadour, and Émilienne swears she shall remember this trick when she is rich and bold.

Turning, the grand courtesan, painted by great artists and adored by men, fixes her eyes on Émilienne. "Have you been following me, girl?"

But Suzette spoils the moment, turning Valtesse around to examine a fine piece of lace already cut and on the table. "Ah, you have found it, Suzette. The Alençon lace I have longed for." She claps her hands together. "Have you more?"

"Yes, of course." With a frown at Émilienne, Suzette waves toward a bolt of lace on another shelf. "Over here, mademoiselle."

Émilienne's eyes follow the trim figure as she moves. "Yes, exactly!" the Valetesse cries. "This I must have for my new gown."

"It's lovely lace, but very expensive," Émilienne says. Again, Suzette looks at her with a frown. Valtesse smiles, taking a seat at a table, where Suzette now places the bolt of lace. Émilienne crosses to the table and sits across from the countess. "One day I hope to have gowns made of this lace."

Valtesse looks up. "If you are smart you shall. Pretty girl. What are your dreams?"

"To dance onstage in the greatest theaters . . . in all Europe, if dreams come true." After a slight pause, she adds, "I would have rich lovers, too, like you Madame Valtesse, and Paris would know my name."

Everyone laughs. "This is Émilienne," Suzette says. "She lives in the building."

The countess holds her eyes. "You are called Émilienne?"

"Yes, Émilienne André."

She sits back with a sigh. "I suppose your first name is good for the stage. But the surname, André? No, I think not. It is too dull." She looks off as if thinking, then down at the lace.

"Of course. This is it! We shall change your name to Alençon, *chéri*." She tilts her head, smiling. "How do you like this, Émilienne d'Alençon? It's an important name, with an aristocratic sound."

"Change my name?"

"Dreams sometimes come true. You must prepare for when the time arrives for dancing. That is not far off, I believe." Under lowered lashes, she adds, "And Alençon lace is quite expensive."

Everyone laughs, all but Suzette. "Mademoiselle, she is young for jokes."

"Not so young." Turning to Émilienne, she lifts a finger, fixing her eyes on her. "She understands. Now, look here, girl, with your eyes and hair and that cute little nose, you must change your name at once. With d'Alençon behind you, I predict you shall engage a successful career."

When the Valtesse has gone and the others return to their work, Émilienne rises, ready to leave. Suzette takes her arm and whispers in her ear. "Why do you stay, Émmy? I worry. You are old enough to leave the nest, such as it is." Her hand tightens on Émilienne's arm as they reach the door. "I wager you've got strap marks on your back again."

Émilienne nods.

With a glance at the others, she adds, "Mademoiselle was right. You go off and dance in Paris and you will do well. Listen to what she says."

Émilienne nods again. As she starts to close the door, Suzette whispers, "Émilienne, you must run."

❧

A week has passed since that morning and every waking hour Émilienne has thought of Suzette's warning. She must leave. When she walks through the neighborhood streets now, it seems the stench of poverty hangs even deeper over Montmartre.

With one franc and three sous in her pocket, today she is on a special errand. Uphill on rue Lepic, she waves to a farmer resting at a fountain. He nods, leaning against his cart while the horse drinks. A young man passing gives her the eye as he drags his leg behind him. Behind him several lorettes, prostitutes reeking of patchouli, cluster before a wooden building, guarded by a muscular man. One, a thin girl with dark circles beneath her eyes and bones protruding from her chest, shivers from the cold as she stares at Émilienne.

Quickly, Émilienne looks away.

Pulling her coat tight around her, she walks on, passing the general store. Here the hill rises on a steep slope. She passes her washhouse, the bookseller, Father Salomon's jewelry store, and an artist's studio. Monsieur Toulouse-Lautrec, that strange little man, sits before a window, painting. He looks up but does not seem to see her.

Up and up she walks, feeling the strength of her legs. She passes Café Lapin, quiet this afternoon—come Sunday it will fill with people in the neighborhood: prostitutes, seamstresses, laundresses, fruit sellers, workmen, all dancing and listening to music. The road winds now, left to right, then streams up, past a row of small shops, past the popular cafés—the Lune Rousse, the Truands, the Ciel—past wagons filled with vegetables just in from farms, and past a baker's shop, which makes her stomach growl, her mouth water.

Rounding a corner, then straight ahead, she comes to the place du Tertre in the shadow of the cathedral, Sacré-Cœur. Here, the colorful square, surrounded by more shops and cafés, is bustling with artists and their sketchbooks—so many today—women picking vegetables from crates just arrived on trucks, and men lounging on benches, drinking wine. Children, dogs, and some goats run underfoot through the square.

Suddenly, above the noise of voices, a lovely sound reaches her ears, one long trembling note, followed by another. She turns in that direction to see a man with a violin in the far corner of the square. He stares at her as he begins to play—a gypsy, perhaps. Those dark eyes are tempting, as is the music, but she has a purpose and turns away, scanning the crowded square again.

Church bells toll eleven o'clock—already! She looks up at the cathedral. The morning is almost gone. No time to linger. Émilienne heads for the cobbler she seeks. She has some money in her pocket, thanks to a pretty boy from down the hill, from the city.

Scanning the shops ahead, she spots the cobbler, just a few steps away. He sits at his table in a three-sided hut, pounding a piece of leather on his bench. Émilienne takes a deep breath, fingering the coins in her pocket, and strolls over to him.

"I hear that you make dancing slippers, monsieur. The ones with soft leather and no heel?"

He nods without lifting his head.

She sets her hands on her hips, staring down at him. "I am here to buy."

At that he glances up. He gives her a long look. "Are you a dancer, then?"

She smiles. "Yes. Yes, I am."

Setting down the hammer, he rises. "Then come, sit on the stool over there. I must measure."

Following him, she takes a seat. "How long will it take to make the shoes?"

"Take off those clogs."

She does as he asks. When he finishes, he takes out a tablet of paper. He writes the measurements, her name, and beside her name, the words—two francs.

"Two!" She tilts her head, lowers her chin, and, looking at him under her lashes, begins to bargain. It won't take long. She shall have the slippers—already she feels them on her feet.

CHAPTER TWO

Two weeks later the dancing slippers are in Émilienne's hands, and she knows it is time to leave, but still, she lingers. How fast time passes. She cannot go, she cannot stay. Cannot make up her mind. But every day she sees them, girls like her all over the hills, working fifteen hours a day scrubbing floors on their knees, others patrolling the streets, wide eyed and hungry, no longer pretty, looking for a man with a few sous in his pocket.

That is the life ahead for her, or worse if Maman's threats are real—unless she leaves.

One evening, when Maman has gone off, she stands in the center of the room, cold, even inside, thinking perhaps this is the day. Perhaps this is the day to leave. Her eyes land on a box in a corner where Maman stores secret things that Émilienne may never touch.

Gathering courage, she walks to the box and sits down beside it. Inside, she finds a pretty scarf, a photograph of a younger Maman with some strange man, and a small, cracked mirror. She remembers this mirror set on a dressing table in the room long ago. She remembers Maman sitting before the mirror each morning, combing her hair, gazing at her image.

Without a thought, Émilienne picks up the box, sets it on the only table in the room, and pulls out the broken mirror. She sits down and looks at herself.

A stream of light from the window turns her hair red gold when she moves a certain way. Pulling pins from her hair, letting it tumble over her shoulders, she watches the effect of the light on the color. If only she owned a ribbon! She runs her fingers through the curls, longing for a life of ribbons and lace and laughter and books. She longs for days filled with joy.

Not life here in Montmartre. Not with Maman.

Strange how sometimes a thought strikes, and one thing leads to another, changing the course of a life. It is in this instant that Émilienne makes her final choice. She leaves the mirror on the table and walks to the front of the room where her coat lies on the floor. Feeling the new inner pocket that Suzette sewed to hide the slippers, she picks up the coat, pulls it on, and leaves.

As she reaches the bottom step of the lodge, she longs to run but fears slipping on the icy stones. Trembling, Émilienne hunches, tucking her hair into her coat as she hurries along, listening for footsteps behind. Her head fills with worry as she turns onto rue Lapin, the long road that descends into the city below. Where will she sleep? Without even one sou in her pocket, how shall she eat tomorrow, or the next day, or the next?

From below, music rises in the night. She knows a concert café with dancing girls just ahead at the place Blanche on boulevard de Clichy, a favorite of the men of Montmartre.

She has heard the men there throw coins into a hat for the dancing girls. Perhaps they will let her dance on the stage for an hour or two.

It would be nice to enter the heart of Paris with a few francs in her pocket.

By tomorrow she will be safe from Maman. She will disappear into the city.

The place Blanche, at the edge of Montmartre, is a little less than halfway down the hill. When she arrives at the café, the old man sits at the door as always, chair tilted back, eyes closed, dreaming his dreams. Passing him without a word, she enters the small, crowded room, aware of heads turning, feeling eyes on her.

"Émilienne!" She hears the voice and stands on tiptoes peering through the smoke.

A hand grabs her arm, and she swats it away. Turning, she finds Gaston reaching for her again. Troublesome boy, but still, a friend for all her years. "It's about time you showed up here, my girl." He nods in the direction of a table near the stage, surrounded by boys she's known since they wore short pants. "Come this way."

"Wait a minute!" She stops, and he turns. "I came here to dance—on the stage, I mean. I want to dance."

"Not tonight. That's only on Friday and Saturday nights."

She stares, shrinking back. She'd counted on coins from the hat. She looks about for the first time. The walls of the small dark place filled with drunken men seem to close around her. What now?

Someone pinches her round bottom, and she jumps, moving close to Gaston.

He turns, taking her hand, and pulls her on through the boisterous crowd. Soon they arrive at the crowded table. Gaston stops, and, relieved, she looks around at the familiar faces. She is safe here.

Gaston calls out, "Look! Émilienne has arrived."

She can hardly hear over the noise.

"Émilienne, you are mine!" Lucien calls out.

"Whoop! Maman lets you out at night?"

She laughs. With yelps and whistles, the boys all move, making room, and Gaston pulls up another chair. Someone gropes her thigh underneath the table, and she slaps it away, laughing.

Just then the noise around her fades as a young man struts out onto the stage. The same violinist she saw at the place du Tertre, when she bought the slippers. He carries a large black case, which he sets down, then he disappears behind the curtain again, returning with a small three-legged stool.

Tall, thin, with dark hair curling at his neck, he is the most handsome boy she has ever seen.

She holds her breath while he opens the case, pulling out the violin and his bow. Cradling the violin against his shoulder like a mother would a child, he holds up the bow. He tests the strings, once, then twice. Closing his eyes, he dips his chin— the crowd falls silent.

As the music comes, she cannot take her eyes off the violinist. The noise, and the boys' laughter around her, all fade. So intent is he that not even once does he look up. Watching every movement of his hands, his fingers, the expressions crossing his face, she realizes that to him she is invisible. He thinks of nothing but the violin, seeming unaware of anything or anyone around him. He hears only the music.

She shivers, feeling the music, too, each note singing in her veins.

This one is a rebel, she decides. Nothing like Gaston and

the other neighborhood boys she's grown up with. This one is a man.

"The gypsy draws a crowd here every night." Gaston leans close, whispering in her ear.

Maman says the gypsies cast spells. But Maman is not here.

Gaston turns, waving to someone across the room. Then, pushing back his chair, he leaves.

Soft and slow the music comes, surrounding Émilienne, wiping away her fears, all the uncertainty, and instead filling her with joy—new, sweet feelings, like nothing she has felt before. Closing her eyes, she listens in darkness, and when she opens them again, she finds him looking right at her.

In this crowded room, this boy has found her, and she cannot look away. His music lifts her now on waves of pleasure, carrying her to another place, one of possibility, a new beginning. Everything before this moment slowly disappears—the crumbling lodge, Maman's hard face, the slop mops and scrubbing clothes, and living hard—in the music all that is gone.

Already she feels free of Maman. The thought almost stops her breath.

Perhaps this boy—this man—is meant for her. Perhaps he is the one who will care for her, take her down into the city, dress her in lace, as in the stories Suzette tells of the butterflies, the courtesans of Paris.

At last, the music fades. She sits silently while the gypsy violinist packs his instrument in the case and disappears behind the curtain. He will come for her, she knows. Once again, the room fills with the noise of men's voices. She turns at a burst of laughter behind her to see two women entering, staggering into the room. A chair falls, and a bottle is thrown against a wall, shattering.

Gaston returns now, shouting to friends at the other end

of the table, when the violinist touches her shoulder. Turning, she looks up into his eyes. He holds out his hand. None of the boys seem to care or even notice when she leaves, moving with him to a table near the other end of the curtain.

He says nothing until they sit down, as he pulls out the chair for her. She looks at him, practicing the look she is certain the Valtesse would give if she were here.

His eyes hold hers. "Did you like the music?"

She nods.

He takes her hand. "I saw you and knew at once, you are the woman I have been looking for all my life."

His fingertips are hard, but his hands are soft. In the moment she feels a strange connection between the two of them. He smiles as if he knows her thoughts.

He orders wine for her, absinthe for himself—the green fairy, people say. Late into the night, they sit together, and he talks of music, his dreams, the famous places he will play his violin.

She sits silent, entranced as he goes on. When her glass is empty, he pours more, even though she shakes her head. He drinks his glassful, then hers, and then he asks her name.

"Émilienne," she says, watching his lips.

"You are beautiful," he says. He sits back, running his eyes over her. "You provoke me, little one."

She lifts a shoulder. "Good."

His name is Roland, he says, leaning close. "Come with me."

"Where shall we go?"

With a short laugh, he takes her hand.

She hesitates, though already she knows the answer. He offers a place to sleep on this cold night. Her feet are still on the rocky hill of Montmartre, but her mind and her heart are free. He lifts a curl of her hair, touching it to his lips. When he stands up, holding out his hand, she takes it. He leads her around the stage, then behind, weaving through piles of dirty blankets, cartons, wine barrels, bottles, chairs, and an old man sprawling on a torn red quilt. Together they step outside, through the back door, and into the night.

Roland takes her to a room in the back of a small house built on the edge of a cliff carved from a hill on the butte Montmartre. Here the earth seems to fall away. Her eyes gleam at the sight of all of Paris below. With the little house perched as it is only a few feet from the edge of the cliff, she steps lightly when she enters.

Roland smiles. "Don't be afraid, it won't fall off."

Just inside the door, she stops, looking about. He places his hands on her shoulders and turns her around. His eyes are dark, almost black. He holds her against him, one hand pushing into her back, the other moving down over her hips.

Before she can think, or speak, he kisses her, his tongue probing, and a feeling she has never felt before ripples through her. His hands move, his breathing comes shallow.

He lifts her into his arms, carrying her to his bed, and as he places her atop the mattress, he says, "You belong to me, little one."

His voice, his words, suddenly annoy her. Sitting up, she swings her legs over the edge of the mattress, pressing her hands against his chest. "I belong to no one but myself," she says.

Looking down at her, he smiles. With a gentle touch, he brushes curls back from her forehead. Curiosity holds her tongue as he leans over her again, hands touching either side of her body. "I like spirit in a girl," he says.

She must remember this.

She stills, barely breathing as he watches her while loosening her blouse from the tucked skirt, slipping his hands underneath, cupping her breasts. She knows what comes.

But, for some reason, this time is different. Always before she'd hurried, hungry and tired, just waiting for the coins to touch her hand. And never has she allowed a kiss. But now, as Roland's lips cover hers, she closes her eyes and sinks against him.

She wants to learn how to love. She wants to know.

※

When her eyes flutter open, Roland is gone. She lies motionless, letting time pass, remembering, recalling last night. Perhaps she drank too much wine—she doesn't remember. Last night is gone, and, really, none of it seems real.

Frowning, she pushes up from the bed. Swinging her feet to the floor, she sits there, silent, looking around.

What might have seemed a love nest in the dark is a shabby, cluttered room in the light, with a dirt floor, not one made of wood. The shutters on the window are cracked and broken. Roland's things are strewn about, and in one corner, his clothes are piled halfway to the slant of the ceiling. A wood table near the door and a chair with a broken arm are the only pieces of furniture, other than the bed.

She rubs her eyes. This place is worse than the lodge. The Valtesse would never set foot in this room. Why is Émilienne here?

Fragmented memories of last night flood in. You are mine, he said.

Not so pleasant after all. No man will ever own her.

Her stomach tightens. She must leave before Roland returns. Never again will she fall into the hands of a man who lives like this. From this moment on she vows never to spend her time with a man with dirty hands and dirty floors. She will never love a man who is not wealthy and not possessing of a generous heart for a girl like her.

A noise outside startles her. She freezes, holding her breath as a wave of fear rushes through her. But she hears nothing more.

After a moment, she breathes again and looks about. Where is her coat? She is wasting time. So many people saw her at the café last night. What if word gets back to Maman and she comes searching?

Shooting up from the mattress, she hunts for her clothes, now scattered. Here, her shirt tossed to the end of the bed, and there her clogs, not far from the door. With an urgent feeling, she moves fast, dressing while listening for the sound of footsteps, a hand on the door—Maman's or Roland's hand, either one.

As she pulls on her skirt, reaching down for the shoes, the old, uncomfortable wooden shoes, she slips them on and picks up her coat. In daylight, it won't take Maman long to find her. What a fool she was not to have continued on down the path yesterday—she could be in the city now. Thoughts of Maman turn her mouth dry.

Opening the door, she peeks out. Then lunging into the road, as a feral cat jumps when cornered, she runs from Maman, Roland, and all of Montmartre. At the end of the street, she turns a bend, flying down the path, down and down toward Paris below, past the cemetery, and—closer now—down again toward new life and away from Émilienne André. She runs toward the lights, the boulevards where luck can strike for a girl, where pretty girls with money in their pockets and clean hands and fitted dresses play and laugh. They are safe, loved.

At the bottom of the hill, she gazes at the long, wide street before her. Already early dusk veils Paris in a pink glow, and as she walks, the gaslights are like stars guiding Émilienne forward. She thinks again: Where will she live? How shall she eat?

She's faced these questions before; they are not new. In this moment, all Émilienne d'Alençon sees before her are the glittering lights. Turning, she looks back up at the dark hills of the butte Montmartre.

With a shiver, again she runs. Not once does she look back.

CHAPTER THREE

PARIS, 1889

She makes her way across Paris toward the place de la Madeleine in the 8th arrondissement. Having lived in the shadow of Sacré-Cœur all her life, the famous La Madeleine is her first thought. And indeed, standing before it now for the first time, the old church's presence in the pretty square is comforting. After all, Sacré-Cœur protected her for all her years so far. Now, perhaps La Madeleine will spread her cloak over one more homeless girl. As she slips into an alley across from the church in the square later that night, a thought comes—despite the cold, at least here she is safe from Maman.

The next morning she wakes to the pleasant sounds of birdsong and the soft voices of a choir singing in the church. Stretching, she smiles. The crowds here do seem more settled, more serene, surely because of the looming presence of the church. She will sleep here until she finds a stage and wages, she decides. Until then, she will dig food from wastebins behind restaurants and cafés.

But after almost a week of searching for work up and down the avenue des Champs-Élysées and in the small winding streets behind the roundabout at the Arc de Triomphe, eating whatever she can find in alleyways, she has had little success. Most girls seem to dance at the same cafés each night, holding their places. They've grown friendly with the men who choose the dancers, leaving little room for strangers.

Although today, an old woman counting coins at a small concert café does suggest she return at six o'clock tonight to take her chances with the other girls.

Six o'clock—so with time to wait, but not to waste, Émilienne heads out to an area ripe with promise, she's been told, the street along the far side of the Seine, just across the Pont Neuf. Her skirts by now are streaked with dirt. But her hair is easy, tumbling over her shoulders as usual. The old woman at the café, seeing her rubbing her cheeks, has pity, and gives her a damp cloth to clean her face.

Walking along the Quai d'Orsay, Émilienne's spirits sag. Art shows and shops and bookstores are everywhere on this side of the river, but she finds few cafés, and even those are not rowdy nighttime places. Instead, they draw quiet crowds. They've no need for dancers to entertain.

Turning around, she realizes the Pont Neuf is far away. She lifts a shoulder. The next bridge will do as well, and perhaps it is even closer to the café. If she hurries, she can arrive by six, in time to dance—if she is chosen. She picks up her pace.

A strange, acrid smell drifts toward her. Smoke? She stops, lifts her nose in the air, sniffs, then continues on. But as she walks the smoke worsens, becoming dense and thick with ash that hangs in the air. She rubs her eyes and covers her nose and mouth, straining to see the next bridge.

Instead, a vortex of black smoke rises. She turns, then turns again. Too late to walk back, she fans smoke from her face and hurries along the quay toward the bridge ahead, longing for fresh air.

Squinting through the smoke, suddenly a silhouette of something becomes visible. Images in the dust. Machines? Perhaps people? She hears noise signaling men working—clanging and pounding, and voices shouting, all seeming to come from every direction at once.

With her nose and mouth covered with one hand, she holds the other out ahead, gasping as she walks toward what she thinks may be the entrance to the bridge. The stench of hot tar brings on a cough, and she reaches out for something to hold as she can barely see.

A voice comes from right beside her. "Hey! Look out!"

Without thinking she jumps back, and strange hands catch her around the waist.

"Merde!" she shouts, straightening, her voice raw. "Leave me be. Get your hands off me!" Whirling, she slaps a face, a man's face looking down at her own.

The hands pull her away from the thick smoke, into air that seems almost clear. She takes a deep breath as he releases her, laughing. "Well now," he says, rubbing his jaw. "That's no thanks!" She is five feet and an inch, and he looms over her. "For a kitten, you can fight." He crosses his arms, still smiling.

She glares at this man who has a square jaw and lines crinkling at the corners of his eyes. Laughter in his eyes gives him a pleasant look. Broad shoulders, big hands blackened with smoke, rolled-up sleeves, tattered pants, battered boots, and a cap—he is one of the workmen.

"That's quite a spirit you've got there."

She looks about. "What's going on here?"

"Still no thanks?" He takes off the cap and nods, looking

behind her. "If I'd not got to you in time, you would be buried under the next pile of dirt."

Glancing over her shoulder, she sees a deep hole where she'd been walking.

"It's right deep enough," he says in a cheery tone. "And you're awful small. Without me you'd have disappeared down there." Pulling a red bandanna from his pants pocket, he reaches out, wiping her chin. "Didn't you see those?" He jerks his chin, and she turns, spotting the pile of steel beams.

She gasps, turning back.

"This here's construction for the Exposition." She hears the note of pride in his voice. "We're working on the tallest building in the world."

She starts at the sight of the tower beyond the clouds of smoke and dust—and she stares up. Still . . . tallest in the world? Looking at him, she shakes her head. "That's some kind of imagination you have."

"Well, come back when the party starts and see for yourself. Then you can tell your friends you know the man who built it."

She laughs at this. Workmen swarm over the site. "I see you're not building it all by yourself."

"Just about."

"How tall is it?"

"Three hundred meters when it's complete."

"Three hundred!" She shakes her head. "I don't believe you."

"It's not quite finished up top, but it will be in a few months, just in time. People will come from around the world to see the Exposition."

"You think you'll finish in time?"

"Sure. We're already building cafés inside, too, even up top. Imagine—while you sip you can look out over the rooftops of Paris. All the way across the city!"

"That's a long way to climb just to eat."

"Oh no, we'll have lifts to carry you to the top." He runs his eyes over her. "I guess you're pretty enough. When it's finished, I'll take you up."

Here is something to brag on—even Maman would be impressed. But right now, she must stay focused on finding work and not be pulled into imaginings. She twists her long hair behind her neck, tucking the ends into the fold of her collar. She must hurry to get to the café across the river by six.

Turning toward the bridge, she stops—rubble still blocks the entrance.

Émilienne groans. She had forgotten. Now she must walk back to the Pont Neuf, and she will probably be late.

"Lost?" Slapping the cap on his head, the workman takes her arm in a gentleman's style. "I'll show you to the other bridge."

She pulls away and turns. "I know exactly where it is. I just came from there."

"No matter!" Walking fast, he hurries behind, then walks alongside her. "Foreman's gone. I need a break. And it looks to me like you need a friend."

"How do you know that?" She glances at him from the corners of her eyes as she picks up her pace.

His lifts his brows and grins. "It's written all over you, little kitten."

She likes this fellow and cannot help giving him a smile. She has spent the last five days, since coming down the hill, playing up to slick men at the smaller concert cafés. It's nice to be in proper company right now, even though he is not a real gent. As they walk, he tells her about his work building the tower, the Eiffel Tower, he says.

But when the bells of Notre-Dame ring six times, she stops, then runs toward the bridge she crossed to get to this side of the river in the first place.

Behind her, he shouts, "Hey, wait!"

Turning, she faces him, walking backward.

"What's your rush?"

"I'm late. I dance, and I'm late." This is almost true. Even though she has not yet been given a job, sooner or later she will dance onstage.

In her mind she turns the phrase—she loves the sound of the words, *I dance.*

He picks up his step, and reaching her, he plants his hands on her shoulders, holding her on the spot.

"Hey!" She pushes him away. "I must go."

Holding up his hands, he says, "Tell me where you dance, and I'll come watch."

She cannot help smiling. "I dance at Les Bonnes Filles." Perhaps by luck it is not yet too late for tonight. It cannot hurt to try. And, if not, she will return tomorrow. She adds, "Just ask for Émilienne."

Then she picks up her skirts and runs.

From behind he calls, "By the way, I'm Henri!"

Henri. A nice name.

Through the café windows, she watches the usual crowd of men already soused, with a few pale, blank-faced girls among them. A stench wrinkles her nose as she enters the place—the smell of cheap wine and smoke and sweat. First thing, she looks for the musicians right near the very small stage. Not a bad group, a piano, drums, a saxophone.

She takes a deep breath and holds it as she works her way through the drunken men, heading for the door to the right of the stage. All concert cafés must be the same, she guesses—loud, rowdy, festering in the same foul stink. In the days since she left Montmartre, she's not earned a sou, but she has learned a thing or two. Swatting off the groping hands, she twists and turns through the crowd.

Pushing through the stage door, she enters a room lit by a lantern on a table. Right away she stops dead, swallowing disappointment. Through an open door to an alley, she sees girls practicing steps, getting ready for the show. Of course, she is too late. Sinking back against the door, she curls her fists, thinking of the night ahead searching out scraps of food.

She shakes her head. It was that man, Henri, who made her late. Tallest building in the world? Not likely.

Still, she will not leave without a try. As the music strikes up another tune, she straightens and moves toward the table. There, the old woman still counts coins. Resting her hands on the table, Émilienne leans forward, raising her voice as she speaks. "Good evening. I am here to see Monsieur Tally. I am one of his dancers tonight."

"Not no more you ain't, girlie." Without looking up, the woman flits her hand in the direction of the alley door. "You're too late. Them out there are the ones for tonight."

Émilienne straightens, staring at the door. Smoothing her skirt, she looks about, feeling hopeless—and angry. Again, she leans on the table, until at last the old woman looks at her. "Listen, madame," she says. "I must dance tonight."

As she speaks, her own words bring tears. She blinks, forcing them back. "Please. I must dance."

The woman merely stares.

Émilienne holds her gaze. "If you take a chance, I will split my coins with you." When the old woman frowns, she steps away and spins, flinging out her arms. "Look at me, madame. I shall bring in coins every night. Just give me a chance."

She catches an expression crossing the woman's face, a flicker of something good. But the moment passes, and with a little shrug, she looks down, counting again. "Sorry, *chéri*. You are too late."

Her stomach growls, and Émilienne blushes. The woman looks up, lifting her brow.

Feeling weak, Émilienne turns and leans against a post, closing her eyes. One second. Then she will leave with a smile on her face and find a drunk man to pay a coin for a kiss or two.

Her stomach growls again. How long has it been? Last night, a hunk of bread.

"*Chéri*."

She turns at the sound.

"Come back tomorrow night," the coin counter says. "Get here early enough and I'll see that you dance." Émilienne's eyes widen as the woman slides a small coin from the uncounted pile to the edge of the table. Their eyes meet, and the woman nods.

Again, tears pool. Hurrying to the table, she sweeps the coin into her coat pocket. Two sous, enough for a bowl of soup and perhaps a slice of bread.

"I will not forget this, madame."

The woman nods and ducks her head. Already she's back to counting coins.

❧

Outside the café she stops, turning the coin in her pocket, looking right, then left. Which way to go? She's freezing, and the church of La Madeleine now seems far away. With a shrug, she sticks both hands in her coat pockets and, hunching against the wind, turns left. The street is dark, but the moon is high, and the stars are bright. As she passes alleyways near the concert café, she scans them up and down. She must find a safe place to sleep.

She spots a small shop with lamps still burning inside. Just ahead, a group of men huddle around a fire. They look up at her approach. Scuttling around them as they call to her, she hurries on to the market.

A bell rings as she enters. A young boy sits on a high stool behind the counter. About twelve years or so, she guesses.

"Have you hot soup?" She presses her arms over her stomach as it grumbles.

He shakes his head. "We are closed, mademoiselle."

Her eyes land on several loaves of bread. She points. "How much for a loaf over there?"

"Two sous for a half a loaf."

"Two for half! That's robbery."

He shrugs. "Maman sets the price, not me." His eyes dart to the doorway. "You can take those carrots over there if you want. I was going to throw them out."

Without a word she lifts a loaf of bread from the bin and three sad-looking carrots in the next, bringing them to the counter. At least she shall fill her stomach tonight. She hands over her coin. The boy slices the loaf in half and wraps the bread and carrots in a thin sheet of brown paper while she waits.

He follows her to the door, locking it behind her. The men still hunch around the fire, so she continues in the same direction as before. Two blocks down, she finds an alley with stone stairs leading to a door. She shall hide behind the stairs to sleep. With a glance over her shoulder, she slips into the alley, clutching the bread and carrots in her arm.

As she approaches the stairs, she hears a noise—a small whimper. Perhaps a dog or cat? She walks carefully now, quietly, thankful for dirt rather than pavement under her wood shoes.

Right at the steps, again she hears the soft noise. She peers around.

A small face looks up at her. Large dark eyes in a thin, pale face surrounded by a shaggy mop of brown hair. The moon lights the boy curled into a corner where the wall meets the back of the stairs. There he huddles, shivering, arms wrapped around his knees, saying nothing while he waits.

"Ah . . ." she whispers. "And who are you?" The child cannot be older than five or six years.

He merely stares.

"I had meant to sleep here," she says.

He struggles to stand up and falls back down.

She sits on the steps, placing her feet on the ground before him. "Have you a home?"

He shakes his head.

"No? No maman, no papa?"

Again, he shakes his head. As he looks up, the moonlight catches tears in his eyes. Reaching out, she touches his head. His hair is soft as silk. Ah, she knows how it feels to be alone. Unloved.

"Stay. We shall keep each other warm tonight."

His eyes drop to the package she holds, the bread, the carrots.

Smiling, she ruffles his hair. "I shall sit with you, and we can share this meal." Hiking up her skirts, she sits down beside him, leaning against the wall. Opening her coat, she pulls him close. He's so small the coat covers both. The boy snuggles against her, eyes fixed on the bread. Beyond the alley, out in the city, a carriage rolls past, and voices come, then fade.

"Now, we eat." She tears the loaf, handing half to the boy. She nods, and he bites into the bread, as does Émilienne. When the bread is gone, they shall still have the carrots left. Chewing, he gives her a shy smile. She plants a kiss on his forehead and slides her arm around his shoulders. He is all skin and bones as she pulls him to her. Together they will provide some heat.

Still holding him close, she tells him that in the morning,

they will share the last carrot for breakfast. "Such a sweet flavor in these things, don't you think?"

"Yes," he says in a small voice.

"We are lucky tonight, enfant chéri. Who would have thought a carrot could taste so good."

When the child slumps against her, asleep, she looks down at him, studying his pretty face and wondering who he is, remembering her nights in the alleys of Montmartre and the fear a child's imagination can conjure.

Perhaps she shall take him with her tomorrow night while she dances. Perhaps he shall stay with her a little while.

But when she wakes in the morning, he is gone, along with the carrot.

The next evening, Émilienne arrives at the concert café well before six o'clock. She breathes a sigh of relief as the old woman at the table spots her and nods. She pulls a writing pad from a drawer. "Your name?"

"Émilienne."

She picks up a pen, dips it into the well. "And your family name?"

"D'Alençon," she adds, remembering Valtesse and her prediction of success.

The woman gives her a quick look before her head dips over the writing pad. Émilienne catches her slight smile. "D'Alençon," she repeats, writing. "Aristocrat, are we?"

Émilienne holds her breath, waiting.

"Right then." She looks up. "You are on tonight. Curtain at seven, be back here at six. If you are one minute late, you're out. After the show, our girls split the toss."

A chance, at last. "I'll come on time."

Émilienne drifts through the empty room in front, which still stinks of old beer and sweat, and out into the sunlight. Her luck has changed. Tonight, she shall fill her empty stomach with her share of the coins, perhaps with some left over. She is a dancer now.

Just then the bells of Notre-Dame toll. She smiles. This is the start of her new life.

After sitting on the street outside the café so as not to be late again, Émilienne arrives before the old woman at six o'clock sharp. The girls practice their steps in the alley behind the café for an hour before the show. Everything is new to Émilienne, but the choreography is simple, and excitement gives her energy. The dancing shoes feel fine, and she is quick to learn. It turns out the woman counting coins is also the instructor. She says she must be addressed only as *Madame*.

Only five girls were selected to dance, with Émilienne first on the list. "Just flirt with them," the girl behind her whispers while they practice. "If the men see what they like, we'll have a full hat."

Before the show starts, Madame has Émilienne cross the stage to place a bowler upside down in the far corner for the coin toss. Cheers explode in the room as she appears. Making the most of this occasion, she lifts her skirts, swishing her ruffled petticoats, showing her ankles, giving the crowd a wink.

But when the old woman hisses her name, she goes running back.

At seven o'clock, a signal from the musicians calls the girls into line. When the music strikes up and the girls enter onstage, Émilienne leads. The room fills with a crescendo of applause, louder than last night.

Émilienne has danced down the streets of Montmartre,

danced for herself all her life. Here, with her dancing slippers
on, and the lights and music and noise, this is something different. As the drum rolls and the girls flirt with the crowd, she
draws every eye. Suddenly, she spots a familiar face, the workman from the tower, Henri. Laughing, she gives him a high
kick, before moving on through the set.

At the end of the routine, each girl dances to the edge of
the stage for her curtsy and shouts her name. When Émilienne
takes her bow, the crowd chants, repeating her name over and
over, and a hand brushes her leg from below. Like the other girls,
she twirls just out of reach. The audience joins her laughter.

Why did she take so long to come down from the hills, she
asks herself. What fun! What joy! They even called her name
at the end! Even better, she shall eat tonight. How different
this night seems, compared to her life so far in Montmartre. It
almost seems she has stepped into another world. Thinking of
Maman's bitterness, she basks in the love she receives tonight.

But she shall think no more of Maman or what is past, nor
even of the cold, not on this lovely evening. Bless these rowdy
men. As the line exits stage right, the girl behind plants her
hands on Émilienne's shoulders and, leaning forward, asks her
to teach the spinning turns she used just after her curtsy.

"Of course!" Émilienne gives the girl a smile.

"I'm Claire," she says, squeezing her shoulder.

"Émilienne," she replies with a wink.

Afterward, Henri bursts backstage, and without thinking,
she flings her arms around his neck. Here is a new, old friend.
He waits, chatting with Émilienne and Claire, while coins are
counted. As the old woman drops a franc and two sous into
her hand, Émilienne stands very still, looking down at the first
money she has ever earned by dancing. She was right to come
down from the butte. Clutching the coins, she closes her eyes

for a few seconds, enjoying the hard feel of her own money, the sense of power surging through her.

This is just the beginning. Ah, what a night!

Later, Émilienne, Claire, and Henri sit together at a table, talking. Henri tells Claire of the tower he's building. He buys a bottle of wine and passes it around while the musicians play.

It seems Claire has danced at every concert café in Paris for the last year. She knows the rules of these places—how to get around them and how to keep a job.

"But one day I shall dance at the big theaters and cabarets." She looks at Émilienne under sleepy lids. "That's my dream. What do you want most in life?" she asks Henri.

He throws back his head, as if thinking. Then he says, "A pretty wife and five babes." He smiles. "Four boys, to help with the work. And a girl to keep us happy."

Claire nods. "Sensible man." She turns to Émilienne, "And you? What are you looking for?"

"Me?" She yawns, sliding down in the chair and stretching her legs, hands clasped behind her head. Strange, she thinks of the crowd tonight, how they loved her. But when she answers, she says, "Right now, a place to sleep."

She glances at Claire. "Will you be here tomorrow?"

"I suppose." The girl nods and stands. "If you need a place to sleep, you can come with me. I have a room with some other girls, and we can squeeze in one more, if you like." She smiles. "It's not much, though it's cheap."

Émilienne perks up at the offer. "Thanks," she says. "Any place is better than an alley." Turning, she holds out her hand, pulling Henri up as well.

With Henri in the middle, his hands curled around their waists, they stumble from the café together, making their way down the street. Gaslights glow in the early morning fog. At

the corner, Henri drops back. "I'm off to build a tower, girls . . .
I shall see you soon enough."

Claire's room is on the ground floor of a broken-down old
wood building, two stories high, squeezed between rows of leaning shacks. The girls sleep on old blankets on the floor. Claire
whispers just before they enter on tiptoes, "Keep your money in
your pocket, and lie on the same side." With a glance over her
shoulder, she adds, "You can share my pallet if you like. Until
we find another."

Pulling her blouse loose from her skirt, Émilienne sinks
down onto the blanket, followed by Claire. Barely room for
two and the room is cold, but she is warm compared to sleeping
in alleys. She smiles. Last night the hat held a two-franc coin,
and the old woman said she has never seen this happen, never
before. Not until Émilienne came along to dance.

CHAPTER FOUR

This afternoon Émilienne waits for Henri at a sidewalk café on boulevard Saint-Germain. Customers crowd the café inside. But out here a brazier burning coal nearby keeps her fairly warm. Today is Sunday, and he is off work. The sun shines. For the beginning of March, this is an almost perfect day, and she's got a few francs in her pocket too. She dances at cafés all over Paris now, and Henri shows up from time to time.

She has made clear to Henri that she only wants a friend. Of course, she would never say this aloud to him, never hurt him—but she cannot afford a man with empty pockets. Also, she must be free to grab opportunities as they come. Since she has learned the rules, she plans to move up in the world, and fast. Soon she will dance at the real theaters, and she shall become a courtesan, one of those women with carriages and four horses, jewels and rich gents. Hands as white and soft as snow. She shall own dresses made of silk and linen and ribbons and lace.

With a sigh, she smiles to herself. Despite the cold, she is no longer hungry. She is making her way forward, free of Montmartre and Maman and fear. When the waiter approaches, she asks for a bottle of red and two glasses. She pays with coins from her own pocket.

Sipping wine, she watches carriages roll past, then shifts her gaze to a shop across the street where bread and sweets are sold. It must be closing time, as the baker leans against the doorframe just outside, gazing about. His eyes light on Émilienne, and when she waves, he does, too, then turns around and goes inside. A moment later, the baker emerges holding a small package in his hand. He closes the bakery door, crosses the street, stops at Émilienne's table, and sets down the package.

"For you, sunshine."

She looks at the slick brown paper and then back up at him. "And what is this?"

Lifting a shoulder, he smiles. "A few small cakes. You are young and lovely, and I see you have got two glasses there on your table . . . so . . ." He spreads his hands. "I am closed for the afternoon, and there is no one else to eat these but you and your friend when he appears."

She points to a chair. "Come along and sit with us. Enjoy the afternoon."

He shakes his head, but she insists. "Come, now come!" She catches the waiter's eye. "Over here. Another glass, please."

The cakes he brought are delicious and light, filled with vanilla fluff. Closing her eyes, she takes another bite. "Almonds," she says, licking her lips. "I have never tasted anything so good."

The baker leans back in the chair, crossing his arms over his chest, gazing down the boulevard. "This is the life, is it not?" When the waiter appears with another glass and fills it to the top, he lifts it to her. "Here's to luck, my lady."

Lady. A word she longs to own.

She takes another bite. She would have never tasted cake like this up in the hills.

"I will bake these for the great Exposition," the baker says. "I shall line up my cakes in colorful rows on a long table each day, in a shaded spot just behind the new tower. They say people will come from all over Europe to see the Eiffel Tower. And I shall make my fortune in its shadow."

She lifts her face to the sun, listening as he rambles.

He taps the table with his fingers. "The icing on the cakes will be the colors of France . . . Perhaps I shall put three stripes of colors on each cake."

She takes the last bite, licking white icing from a finger. "Perhaps you can sell cakes in the tower café, and one day we shall look out over the city while we eat them."

"Wait until you see the tower." Just then a hand rests on her shoulder. She looks up to see Henri. "*Bonjour, mon beau ami!*" she cries.

"Hello there, my boy." The baker's tone is jovial as he pushes back the chair and stands. Turning to Émilienne, he bows. "Enjoy the sunshine. I must close the shop."

Henri grins at the baker as he sits. "Were you trying to steal my girl, monsieur?"

"Certainly. What else can a man do in the face of such beauty on such a day?"

Émilienne blows a kiss goodbye and then pushes the box of cakes toward Henri. "Taste these, they are delicious."

Henri looks at Émilienne as the baker strolls off, his eyes shining. "Listen, I have news! I hear the city is sending a troop of dancing girls through Europe to spread word of the Exposition. And auditions are this week."

Émilienne's eyes grow wide.

"Where? When?" What luck. What news! "Can you find out?"

Henri smiles, looking pleased. "I know more than that, kitten. I have found the man you want to see. In fact, I already told him of you."

"Yes?" She leans forward, holding her breath.

"He writes for a magazine. Comes around the tower sometimes to watch the work, says he's writing all about it. I've helped him out a time or two."

"And so . . . ?"

When he sits back, arms over his chest, she swats him. "Come, don't tease!"

He laughs. "Oh, all right. He's the one who told me about the dance troop. And . . . he's also the boss, putting the troop together." He pauses, then adds, "So, I happened to say I know the most beautiful dancing girl in Paris."

She takes a deep breath. "Where shall I go? What must I do?"

He pulls a slip of paper from his vest pocket. Unfolding it—*so slow, he is*—he pushes the note across the table. "Charles Desteuque. He writes for a magazine called *Gil Blas*. Have you heard of him?"

"*Gil Blas!*" Of course, she knows *Gil Blas*. Claire has told her all about Charles Desteuque. He writes about the theaters and dancers in Paris, the gossip as well as reviews. Every dancer in Paris knows the man and the magazine.

"Auditions will take place in the little park behind the tower. I'm to bring you to him tomorrow."

Unable to sit still a moment longer, Émilienne jumps up, flinging her arms around Henri. Laughing, he pulls her down into his lap and reaches for a kiss. She turns her head aside, resting it upon his shoulder instead. Henri is a good friend. But, after Roland, she understands what life could be like with a man without money.

"Meet me tomorrow at the tower, tomorrow afternoon at

three thirty," Henri says, stroking her hair. "We are to meet
him at four."

With a sigh, Émilienne rests her hand on his chest, still
leaning on his shoulder and feeling light as air. Tomorrow she
will meet the man behind *Gil Blas*!

"And another thing . . ."

She sucks in her breath. "Yes?"

"They pay the girls to dance, pay for rooms and meals . . .
and you will even ride on a train."

She pulls back, looking at him, almost speechless.

Oh, how she loves Paris.

Oh, how she loves the world. Not even thoughts of Maman
could ruin this day.

⚜

The following afternoon, having spent the entire day preparing for this audition, Émilienne swings along the Quai d'Orsay
toward the construction site where Henri waits. Claire has lent
her only good dress for the occasion, a stylish gown of bright-red
satin. It is just too bad she has to cover the dress with the
coat. Still, she looks quite stylish, Claire said. And she loaned a
red ribbon, which Émilienne has wound through her hair and
pinned atop her head in the latest style. It is her misfortune to
wear an ugly pair of shoes today, but, except for her dancing
slippers, these are her only ones—Claire's feet are too big. A
cloth bag hangs on her shoulder, containing the slippers, for
when she's asked to dance.

If only she had a hat—one day she will have shelves full of
lovely hats.

Thoughts of what will come if she succeeds to win over
Monsieur Desteuque spin through her head. She will travel all

through Europe. She will shine, and everyone shall know her name, the newest star in Paris. She will own an apartment on one of the Grands Boulevards and a carriage and four. And she shall have as many gowns as her heart desires—not the copies for which Suzette is famous. She loves Suzette, but she shall have the real thing, gowns by Charles Frederick Worth, the great designer.

As she gets close, Émilienne bends back her head, staring up at the tower, the work of art. Henri was right. It looks almost complete to her—lovely, really, if you look past the dirt and grime at the delicate iron lace Henri and the men have built. This iron lady is strong. Henri told her how each steel beam in the tower required so many small rivets to hold it together. And each rivet required four strong men like Henri. First, they heat the iron. Then they let it cool until at last, it swells, expanding inside the beam and becoming a part of the tower.

Better than magic.

As she nears the site, she searches for Henri. From high above the workmen call down to her, whistling, laughing. They flirt—they think she's Henri's girl.

Let them think it, he says, a girl like her can make a fellow's name.

As if conjured, Henri's hand slips around her waist. He follows her eyes up the structure, then takes her arm, pulling her along, saying that they must hurry. Behind the tower, a colorful village spouts—large pavilions with flags of every color for every country in Europe flying at their peaks; small shops with shuttered doors, tents, small three-walled huts, some open fires; and artisans, merchants, workers, and peddlers swarming around them. They only just dodge two husky men pushing wheelbarrows filled with boxes as they hurry past.

She wonders if the baker of the delicious vanilla cakes has

already staked his spot. Just then Henri steers her through the crowd to the edge of the bourgeoning village. She grips the bag holding her precious dancing slippers.

"Look ahead, kitten."

She follows his eyes to an open stage with girls milling about. "Must be over a hundred girls," she says.

"More. I saw them up top, on the tower."

"This could take days!"

He turns to her with a wink. "Not for us." Suddenly he stops.

She looks up at him. "What?"

"Those shoes, Émmy."

"What's wrong with them?" Of course, she knows. Her clogs are made of wood. In Montmartre, no one ever noticed. Everyone wears them there, but here, they don't escape the eye. "These are all I have . . . except for my slippers."

Her stomach tightens as they draw closer to the crowd of hopeful girls ready to audition—plenty of competition. But Henri circles around them, surprising her as he veers away. She stumbles, and he pauses. "Look over there." He nods in the direction of the trees, and she turns to look.

"Right over there," he repeats. "Standing under the tree."

She hesitates, spotting him now. A short man, not much taller than her own height waits in the shade. He's slightly slouched, one hand tucked inside his buttoned vest, the other in a pocket. He wears a bowler hat, gazing at all the audition girls from afar. "Is that *Gil Blas*?"

"Yes, Charles Desteuque." Henri yanks her arm. "He's the one we want to see. Don't stand there like a stone, keeping him waiting."

Émilienne pulls her arm free and smooths her hair. Claire combed it into a soft pompadour this morning. She pulls out loose strands of curls about her face. "Don't you worry." She gives Henri a coquettish smile. "I know how to handle men."

"Oh, yes?" He takes her hand, pulling her along. "Then use those pretty eyes because if he likes you, you're in."

Monsieur Desteuque has turned now, spotting them. Aware of his eyes on her, she lifts one foot, pulling up her skirt just enough, then, with two quick kicks, the old wooden shoes fly through the air, landing on the grass. He turns, looking at the shoes, then back to her.

Pulling her hand free, she strolls barefoot across the lawn, eyes fixed on Charles Desteuque as she grips the bag with her dancing shoes. He puffs on a stub of a cigar, watching her approach. The ground is cold, but this is worth it. Reaching him, she looks up, wearing her heart-shaped smile. "Good morning, Monsieur Desteuque. I am Henri's friend."

He nods without a smile, although his thin curled mustache gives a twitch. His nose and ears are red from the cold. His round, dark eyes look sad, but as they sweep over her for a quick look, he takes a step back and nods. "Mademoiselle . . . ah . . . d'Alençon?"

"Émilienne will do."

Henri, hurrying behind her, interrupts. He has taken off his cap, she notices. "You see, here we are on time," Henri says. "I would never have thought I could keep such a promise while pulling a woman around."

Monsieur Desteuque greets Henri, then turns back to Émilienne. "I have seen you dance, my girl, once at a café. You are more beautiful in the sunlight. I never could have guessed." He slaps his hand on Henri's shoulder, never taking his eyes from her. "Thank you, my boy."

"Henri is building the tower, monsieur."

"All alone?"

"I suppose he has a little help."

"And you, mademoiselle?"

"I am not building the tower."

Henri lets out a laugh.

"I am a dancer, and I wish to join the Exposition troop. I want to travel and dance." She tilts her head. "You will see more of my talent when they call my name in the audition."

Monsieur Desteuque takes a long look. Lifting her hands, she releases the red ribbon, then the pins in her hair, and as it tumbles down, she shakes her head. Sunlight turns her strawberry hair to gold, she knows. She runs her fingers back through her curls. She twirls the red ribbon now as he inspects her.

He lifts his brows. "In your case, an audition shall not be necessary, *ma chéri.*" Reaching out, he touches her hair, then draws back. "You are quite lovely, you know."

"Yes, I know."

"And saucy too." He takes the cigar from his mouth, tossing it onto the ground. "Then France calls upon you, Mademoiselle d'Alençon." He pulls a small notebook from a pocket and a pen from another. "I must take your information—for the records, for the list, of course."

Can this be true? Does it really work like this? She looks at Henri, and he smiles. She states her name and age, giving him her address at Claire's place, and he writes all of this down in the notebook. And she names each café in which she has danced—and then she stops, realizing that this is the beginning. Her life is split in two, between her years in Montmartre, and her new life, with better years to come in the city.

When he is finished writing, he sticks the notebook back in his pocket. "Fine. We shall sort out pay, expenses, such things later."

Joy, sheer joy, surges through her. As if he understands, he smiles at her. Little does he know that she would have taken this job with no pay, just to have the start. Glancing at Henri, she gives him a look of thanks. She shall travel, she shall dance. Soon all of Europe will know her name.

Monsieur Desteuque interrupts her thoughts. "Will you dine with me?" His eyes hold hers.

"Now?"

"There's no better time."

She hesitates. "But what about the auditions?"

"In your case, that is not necessary." Looking over her shoulder, he adds, "My assistant is handling the other girls."

Between them, Henri frowns.

She tilts her head, understanding. "I will come with you." With a laugh and a quick glance at her bare feet, she adds, "If you don't mind my ballet shoes." Before he can answer, she reaches into her bag and, pulling out the slippers, she puts them on—lifting one foot, then the other.

He tips his hat, then with a look at Henri, Monsieur Desteuque takes her arm. Together they stroll across the lawn, leaving Henri behind. She glances over her shoulder, and Henri has her clogs in his hand. He sticks up his thumb and nods.

As she walks on, she's aware that her luck has turned in the past few minutes. She looks about, memorizing the scene, the bare forest of trees, branches just budding against the clear blue sky, and on her right, the small wood houses crowded between the park and the road and the Seine. Oh, she will never forget this moment, she tells herself. She is a real dancer now, not just any girl dancing for coins.

And she holds tight to this powerful man, this man who can change her life with a snap of his fingers.

"My carriage is right over there," he says, pointing. "We shall have luncheon at a small place just off the Champs-Élysées."

"I love good food, and I am hungry too."

He pulls her close, laughing. "A woman who likes to eat! Most women won't admit to a good appetite."

Her hunger at the moment may be due to the disappearance of her last coin yesterday morning, in exchange for a bite of fish from an old woman's cart.

"How are you connected to the troop, monsieur?"

"I promote the venture. In my column, in *Gil Blas,* I shall write about the troop and the dancers." He steers her around a muddy spot.

She smiles, clinging to his arm. Every dancer in Paris knows *Gil Blas.* So, this is he—the man to make a girl's career. All the great courtesans and dancers try for mentions in his articles.

He chatters on, mentioning names of girls she knows. He will make her known, he says. That is what he does when he likes a girl. He will get her out onstage and, with his column, let her shine.

"Just call me Charles," he says in the carriage, resting his hand on her knee.

❧

After weeks of practicing until her bones ache and muscles burn, toward the end of March, the Exposition show is on the way. They shall tour several cities, returning in two and one-half weeks.

The girls are driven to the train station in carriages with posters plastered on the sides, and ribbons and balloons, and everyone shouts and waves as they pass by. At the station, a crowd surges around the girls, curious. Already steam rises from underneath the train, and as they march toward the assigned carriage, men hang out the windows calling down to the girls.

"Twenty girls, twenty!" The conductor shouts, hurrying them along. "First stop, Brussels."

Monsieur le Directeur of the troop has ordered rehearsals tomorrow afternoon. Monsieur is certain that this show will cause every man to fall in love with France and dash to Paris to view the Exposition in September.

As they approach their carriage, a porter stores Émilienne's travel bag in a closet, along with those belonging to the other girls. She climbs on board, carrying her vanity case. A velvet pouch tied around her wrist contains two francs, lipstick, and a card identifying her as a French citizen and a member of the troop.

Halfway down the aisle, she stores the vanity case on a shelf above two empty seats and slides in toward the window. Odors of musk, sweat, perfumes, and smoke seem to saturate the interior of the train. Reaching for the window, she lifts the glass and takes a long breath of fresh air.

The train whistle toots, the first warning. Another burst of steam rises from under the carriage, and with another toot, the car shifts, then moves.

"Are we allowed to open the windows? I thought it was against the rules."

Émilienne looks up at the girl sliding into the seat beside her. "Ah, sit down. These rules were never meant for us."

"But . . . monsieur said . . ."

With a sigh, Émilienne closes the window but for an inch at the bottom. This one, Jacqueline, is sometimes a bore. Closing her eyes, she mutters, "Listen, if you catch the porter's eye, ring for champagne."

Hours later, she awakes, and, realizing where she is, sits up straight.

"Almost there," Jacqueline says.

She looks out over green pastures, gardens, forests, cottages here and there, farmers' wagons waiting at the crossings. They have left the crowded streets of Paris behind. They pass a small village, and suddenly wood buildings two stories high appear, with laundry strung on lines outside between the windows.

The train whistle blows. Émilienne glances at Jacqueline. "Not long now. I'll bet some soldier boys will be waiting for us at the station."

The train slows as the whistle blows a second time. Émilienne closes the window fully and pats her hair. As the porter appears through the forward door, she rests her hands in her lap to hold steady. When she sets her feet on the ground, she won't be in France!

Now, as the train rolls into the station, she sees French flags hanging on the walls, along with Exposition posters announcing the troop's arrival. "Welcome" is written above each poster.

As they chug to a stop, heads turn on the platform—mostly men, seeming to move as one, looking for the dancing girls, she realizes. Jacqueline leans over her shoulder, struggling to see.

"There must be a hundred men out there."

Émilienne raises the window again and leans out, waving. At the back of the platform, workmen turn, gaping, while gentlemen raise their hats, cheering the pretty girls from Paris.

Soon everyone rises, and Émilienne does, too, picking up her vanity case as she joins the line to the exit. Cheers rise from the station platform as each girl descends. Moving slowly toward the door, she tells herself this moment is only the beginning. When she appears in the carriage doorway, looking out over the cheering crowd, the sound flows right through her, pumping blood, and she does just what any girl would do.

Dropping her case, she smiles down over the waving men, then, swinging to one side, she strikes a pose—hand behind her head, hiking up one knee and skirt, showing a froth of red, white, and blue petticoats in the colors of France, revealing a few inches of her leg and the new ankle boots.

The crowd explodes.

As the men surge toward Émilienne, she reaches down for her vanity, exposing her décolletage. Porters appear, coming from every direction. Policemen push their way through as she descends to the platform, surrounding her, while all around the men close in, stomping, whistling, clapping their hands, just having a time.

"Your name, mademoiselle?" One young man yells. "What is your name?

"Émilienne!" she shouts, her heart singing with pleasure and pride. "Just call me Émilienne."

"Look at that gold hair!"

"Welcome to Brussels, Émilienne!"

"Hey, you, there! You with the little snub nose, give us another look. Give us a smile."

And she does just that as she moves toward the pile of bags and the other girls standing there, mouths agape.

"Step back, step back!" A policeman shouts. Still they call her name, chanting now—*Émilienne, show us some more!* And suddenly she worries. No one else made such a show. What if she is sent back to Paris for breaking rules?

Wrinkling her nose, she moves with the troop toward the exit.

"What a mess," someone says.

With no time to think, she stumbles, falling, still holding onto the vanity case. A hand reaches down, and a gentleman helps her up, takes the case, and with his arm around her shoulders, plows her through the crowd, leaving the mob behind.

Outside the station, she stops, overwhelmed and trembling. The kind gentleman hands her the vanity case with a smile. She gazes about for the troop carriages.

The last carriage with three girls already seated waits.

She boards it quickly. Turning, just before she sits, she cries out, "Wish me luck?"

The gentleman smiles, stepping back through the thinning crowd. "You don't need it! You already have more than your share."

CHAPTER FIVE

On the first evening, Monsieur Desteuque shows up. Yanking Émilienne aside right before the curtain rises, he peers down at her with his red eyes.

"Sounds like you started a riot this afternoon, Émilienne."

She cocks her head. "Better a riot than boredom."

He studies her, then shakes his head. "Never seen anything like it."

She shrugs, praying he does not send her back to Paris. "Things just happen, Charles."

He sticks his thumbs in his vest and rocks back on his heels. "See you do it again, girlie. Every night if you like." He smiles, tips up her chin. "You've got spunk. You'll sell tickets."

Somehow, he seems to see her as his own ticket to the future. She wonders about Charles Desteuque. He is a bit morose underneath his bluster—a powerful man, but perhaps lonely.

From the first night until the last, at curtain call, the crowd shouts for Émilienne. And, each night, Charles stands in the wings, watching her, studying the audience. Sometimes, leaving the stage, she gives the corner curtain a little tweak, just a quick flash of her petticoats when the other girls have gone—one last reveal from Émilienne.

Charles chuckles. The Paris Exposition is all everyone talks about in Brussels. Seats for the traveling show sell out every night.

From Brussels to Lille, Amiens, Rouen, and returning to Paris. Weeks of packed theaters, and in that time, Émilienne learns the secret to success for a girl like her. No matter what you are ever told, just keep the spotlight on yourself.

And Charles seems to agree. On her return to Paris, Claire presents her with three columns in *Gil Blas* mentioning the Exposition tour and the troop's rising star, Émilienne d'Alençon.

By the time she is back on the city streets in April, the Eiffel Tower is complete, lifts and all, and ready for the opening of the Exposition. It is a man-made wonder for the world to ponder. Henri takes her up in the lift. She clings to him as it bounces about. But at the top, at last, looking out over the roofs of Paris, she realizes this tower will change the city. No longer are Parisians bound to earth. Why, from the top of the Eiffel Tower the whole city can be seen at once!

The Exposition opens on the fifth of May, and Paris is the place to be.

Émilienne is in the right spot at the right time, Charles says. With her beauty and his column, she shall conquer Paris—as long she follows his advice.

Until she is a star, she must sleep at night, not all day as the girls sometimes did on the tour. His voice is stern. This is the time directors look for dancers and when dancers must rehearse.

She must wear gowns that reveal her curves, and she must learn to bind a corset. He spares no expense in creating his vision, and, except for that first night with him just after they met, he seems to expect nothing else in return. This is his life—*Gil Blas*, making a girl, turning her into a star. Did he not make the reputation of Liane de Pougy? And Gabrielle Dorziat, and La Belle Otero, the youngest and most fiery courtesan in Paris?

Slowly, she begins to understand Charles. Charles Desteuque is alone, a man who longs to mark his place in the world—to be remembered. The girls he creates are his glory. Perhaps he basks in their reflections. Perhaps, even, he believes his creations will, like children, stand as his marker when he is gone.

Either way, she has grown fond of him, and she recognizes her good luck. Charles will baptize her into the glittering world of the demimonde, his girl with the laughing eyes, as he says. He pays a dresser to cut her hair, just a bit here and there to loosen the curls. He pays for everything, even someone to teach her proper speech—how to speak like a society lady—telling her she should stop using terms like "dum-dum." He sends her to the finest seamstress in Paris, Madame DuBois, whose talent includes copying in minute detail the latest fashion designs.

And Émilienne must wear paint at night—makeup for the stage to heighten her beauty, even on the small stages at the concert cafés. And, like a lady, she must wear a hat and gloves when she goes out, even in the daytime. She must stand straight, holding her head high when she walks. Even offstage, a girl must shine!

One day, Charles takes Émilienne to Longchamp on a Sunday for the races. Everyone must be seen at Longchamp, and Émilienne must learn to enjoy the horses.

When his carriage enters the gates and veers off to the right, to the grass along the track, she looks about, spotting friends—Claire, girls from the troop, girls from the concert cafés—everyone in carriages or sprawling on blankets laid out on the grass, picnicking, drinking cheap wine and good champagne.

Familiar faces, gaiety, and laughter warm her. Girls like her—the world of the demimonde, Charles says. Suddenly, Paris feels like home. She has never felt this way before, so connected to the people around her, even the ones she does not know. It's as if she has found the place where she belongs. A place where she is loved, appreciated, sought out—at least for this day. Here, Maman and her indifference do not exist. Peering around, Émilienne wonders if this new world, compared to the one she fled in Montmartre, could be a dream.

No! Dreams disappear.

Émilienne clinches her hands into fists, even while she smiles at something Charles just said. She must hold on to this connection and these feelings. No matter the cost, she must do everything in her power, anything Charles suggests, to hold on to this dream.

Charles leans toward her as he lays out a blanket on the lawn. "How do you like this party, kid?"

She shines on him. "Longchamp is delightful." Turning, she looks back toward the entrance, past the gate, and peers at rows of seats covered with blue-and-white-striped canopies above, shading them from the sun. There, gentlemen in top hats and ladies in fine gowns sit in comfort.

"Who are those people?"

She nudges him, and he turns, following her eyes.

"Ah, those are the aristocrats. Those seats are saved for gentry, society. The stands and the stalls behind them, too, are all private. The area is called the enclosure. You cannot sit there." He lifts a bottle of champagne and pours her a glass. "Not without the right escort."

She frowns, taking the glass. With another look over her shoulder, she turns back to him and shrugs. "I prefer our picnic."

But she dips her head, hiding her burning face under the broad rim of her hat, suddenly longing to sit in those seats.

"Émilienne, are you all right?" Charles's voice is too loud.

"Of course!" She lifts her head, forcing a smile, and looks past the enclosure to the right, to a crowd of men gathered under an old oak tree. "And over there?"

He follows her eyes, then shakes his head.

"Many a good man has been brought down by those fellows. They are betting on the horses. Betting is not for girls like you."

Later, before the races begin, they stroll back and forth before the stands. Émilienne's parasol provides shade from the sun. She spots the sea of long white gloves on ladies sitting in the enclosure and silently thanks Charles for the ones she wears today—shorter in length, but elegant. Even better, she notices that strolling with Charles on her arm sets the chatter going. Of course—*Gil Blas* is here! The men stare while the ladies look off, pretending not to notice the newest great beauty.

This girl is one to watch.

She glances at this crowd in the special seats from the corners of her eyes. She knows what those men want and what the women whisper behind their fans. She lifts her chin, ignoring the gawkers. That pleasant feeling of belonging, that connection she felt before, is gone now. One day she will claim the stage at the Folies Bergère, and every woman's husband in the stands will be there to see her.

But will she ever be allowed to enter the stands?

Maman's face rises before her, laughing. The thought brings a sour taste to her throat and swirling in her stomach as she walks along with Charles. She has no aristocratic roots. She is the seed of a maid and a man she barely remembers.

Never, Maman growls, swinging the strap.

The trip to Longchamp with Charles showed Émilienne how important it is for a girl longing to dance in the big theaters of Paris to draw attention, to get noticed. This is why he applauded the ruckus she caused on arriving in Brussels, why he escorted her to Longchamp, parading her back and forth before the enclosure.

She had not given this much thought before, but when he invites her to the grand opening of a new theater called the Moulin Rouge, suddenly she realizes. Charles could have asked any of his other girls—Liane or Caroline or Gabrielle, and so many more. But all of them already stand in his glow. Émilienne d'Alençon, on the other hand, is his newest challenge.

On the evening of the grand opening, Charles has a special request. She must wear a little more makeup tonight, more than just lipstick and powder. "The paint you girls used onstage when you were on tour. Though perhaps a bit lighter." And she must wear her evening dress, the one with décolletage that Charles bought her.

When she skips out to the carriage, he looks her over, makes her turn around, then nods. "Lovely," he says as the driver helps her inside.

She laughs, giving the driver a wink. But as she sits beside Charles, a smile hovers over his face. "Perfect, in fact," he says.

Her corset feels too tight this evening, and in the carriage she yanks on the bottom until he covers her hand with his and shakes his head. "The silk will tear if you are not careful," he says. His eyes linger on her breasts exposed in this new gown made of delicate gold silk. Claire gasped when she helped Émilienne into it earlier, turning her around for inspection.

"You will kick up some dust in that," she said.

The carriage rolls through the city. The night is warm, the sky is clear, and across the river the Eiffel Tower shines with the new arc lights—silver shimmers rise on the beams, seeming to reach for the very stars. Most boulevards, too, are now lit with the new lights, casting black shadows between the lighted posts.

"Where is this place?" Émilienne asks.

"In Montmartre," he says. "On the boulevard de Clichy."

Her heart jumps. She ran from Montmartre once, why come back? She ducks her head, covering her eyes while her heart pounds. And Clichy of all places! What can be good about Clichy?

Charles does not seem to notice. "This inauguration tonight is the place to be seen. Everyone in Paris who counts will be there."

She turns to him now, wide eyed. She knows the neighborhood, every square inch of the streets, and she knows this new cabaret is dangerously close to Maman's lodge. What if Maman spots her, out on one of her nightly prowls?

Surprising her, Charles gives her a knowing look. He covers her hand with his. "Your old life is dead, my darling girl. You have reached a turning point. This is something new, and here you must be seen."

Memories flood her mind, and, once again, she is the hated daughter cowering in the alley. She closes her eyes, tightening her hands into fists. She must not let the fear take hold, especially not tonight. With deliberation, she brings up the image she saw in the mirror tonight before joining Charles in the carriage. That girl is strong. That girl left Maman behind, traveled throughout Europe with the Exposition troop, is written about in magazines, dines with gentlemen. That girl is brave and free.

Charles pokes her arm. "Forget all that now. Stick with me, and in a few months every music hall and cabaret will fight to claim your name on their posters." With a sideways look, he adds, "Including the Folies Bergère."

The Folies! She takes a deep breath. "All right, but I need a cigarette."

"Ladies do not smoke."

"This one does."

"Look here." His tone turns strident. "Some girls have luck, some have help. You've got both, girlie. Now do you want to get to the top, or not?" He clucks his tongue. "I'm creating a goddess, and what does she say?"

Émilienne sighs. He is right. She pats his hand. "Sorry, Charles."

They turn into the square where she used to hang around when she was small, searching for loose change, lost clothes, sometimes even food. Dark, almost abandoned, this is where Gaston and all the boys were found at night, and where a girl, slipping out late when her maman was fast asleep, could flirt without whispers floating around.

But tonight, the seedy square has disappeared. Everything has changed.

The boulevard de Clichy blazes with lights and color. Ahead, in a fantastical setting of electric lights, the old wooden building that used to stand here is gone. In its place, a glorious, fiery building rises in gaudy splendor, queen of the hill, a huge cabaret painted red with a windmill on top silhouetted in lights. Everything is red, gold, and black, as if risen from an artist's laudanum dream.

On the square and pouring from side streets in all directions, it seems all of Montmartre and Paris gather for the show. Carriages jam the streets; men, women, and children whoop and call to one another; musicians play on every corner.

Émilienne peers out at the hatless women with untamed hair and no gloves—these who scramble for every sou, for each slice of sausage and bread as she'd have had to do if she'd not fled. Prostitutes, concierges, laundresses, seamstresses—what has become of Suzette? Suzette cared for her when she was small, hiding from Maman. Had Suzette not warned her to run, she, too, would be in this dreary, tragic crowd. Suzette gave her the courage to find a new life.

Charles taps the roof with his stick, impatient, and Émilienne starts, then sits up straight, looking away from the crowd. Minutes pass, and then the carriage rolls to a stop at the entrance to the Moulin Rouge. Émilienne smooths her gloves, while a man in a frock coat opens the door and helps her out. Fixing her eyes on the entrance, she hurries toward the door with Charles just behind. Someone calls her name, and Charles grabs her arm, pushing her inside while the theater's guards push back the crowd.

Inside, they take a breath, gaping at the high ceilings and strange architecture, at the long balconies, silhouetted in electric lights—and again red paint glaring, and gilt dazzling against the black. Music blares in the packed room as dancers on the floor to her right churn with the beat. She turns, her eyes skimming the walls covered with colorful paintings, expanding the room, expanding the joy. She stops, peering at alcoves carved into dark corners, then lifts her eyes to the high stage, lined again with those bright white lights, and up farther still, to the gilded red arch overhead.

Charles nudges her, and they move forward together. The floor seems to vibrate as dancers gyrate, swinging along with the music's spell. Clusters of sparkling chandeliers under the high curved ceiling look like stars in the night.

At the edge of the dance floor, a waiter guides them to an empty table, removing a sign that reads, "*Reserved—Monsieur Desteuque.*" There, seated at last, Émilienne exhales a long, excited breath. Then they look at each other and laugh.

"Impossible," she says, leaning close.

He nods. "True. None of this is real."

The orchestra starts a rascal tune, which makes her long to dance, but already Charles is off for the bar on his own.

"How d'ya get that old goat to drag you along everyplace he goes?"

Émilienne looks up, recognizing a pretty girl she sees around from time to time, already making her name, one of Charles's girls. Near her own age, she supposes, the girl already dances at the Folies and other fine theaters and cabarets, hanging around with the great beauties, the courtesans. And it is clear, too, that she is young, fresh fruit.

Before she can get out a word, Charles's girl sits down.

"I'm Liane de Pougy, by the way."

"I know," Émilienne replies. "Charles has mentioned you." She likes the look of this girl, so she quickly tamps down a few jealous thoughts.

"They call him the empty bottle, you know." Liane leans close, smiling. "Do whatever he says, Émilienne. He's chosen you, and you will dance at any place you choose soon enough."

Straightening and looking about, Liane lifts a finger, and the waiter hurries over.

Charles told her how he made Liane, found her in a concert café on the wrong side of the river Seine. Took her in hand, just as he did with Émilienne. Sure enough, Liane de Pougy will soon be a star.

"Why do you think he does it?"

Liane gives a little shrug. "Who knows. Maybe it makes him feel better about himself, you know, like looking in a mirror and seeing what you want to see, instead of what is real."

She once had the same thought. Émilienne turns, looking for Charles. He's stopped at a table across the floor, talking to a man, an artist. She has seen him around, sketching dancers at different theaters and cabarets. "Who's that fellow?"

Liane scans the room. "Oh, Monsieur Toulouse-Lautrec. Strange man. Get to know him though. He paints posters for us girls."

She nods, remembering the artist in the window near the place du Tertre. "I have seen the posters . . . So that's the fellow."

"One of them."

The waiter arrives, pouring the champagne. As he steps back, waiting, the two girls toast. "To the empty bottle," Liane says. The orchestra switches to a new key now, a number with a harder, faster beat, and a man shoos everyone off the dance floor.

"I hear they're opening with the quadrille, but it's something special tonight," Liane says, shouting through the music. A large, yellow circle of light appears before them on the dance floor just then, and an announcer moves to the center.

"Ladies and gentlemen . . ." he begins, and then his voice disappears in the yips and yowls of eight dancers skipping into the light—four girls wearing white cotton blouses slipping off their shoulders, red-and-gold-striped satin skirts, and long black tights. The men dance in white shirts with matching red-and-gold-striped vests and intriguing black tight pants.

"Ladies, gentlemen, and . . ." the announcer begins again, but laughter and hoots drown his words as the music rises and the dancers mimic behind him. With a wide smile, he bows deep, spreading his arms to encompass the room. " . . . And everyone else too—welcome to the newest show in town, the Moulin Rouge, and introducing . . . the Can-Can!"

As the music strikes a lively, steady beat, his voice drowns in the roar. Émilienne joins Liane, laughing, as the music rises to a fiercer pace and dancing girls lift their skirts, swishing ruffled white petticoats above the knees, showing their long black stockings, even garters too—and applause rings out and joyful shouts. Never has Émilienne seen such abandoned, wild fun. The girls kick right on beat, legs reaching new heights, then they break into a spin.

They jump, flip, turn cartwheels, shouting when the men move in, while the horns wail to a crescendo and the drumbeat goes on. The girls are now mere swirls of red and gold, and she and Liane sit back with the champagne, as if tomorrow shall never come.

Liane leans close. "Have you ever seen anything like this?"

"Never," she shouts, still clapping hands as the audience reaches a rhythmic beat.

"Scandal! Fabulous!" someone nearby yells. Glass crashes on the floor around them, and someone calls for a waiter, and someone else shouts to *sit down over there*.

"*Aiiiiyaiii!*" Liane suddenly yells as before them the girls turn together in one smooth move, flipping up their skirts, baring bottoms to the world—bottoms encased in nothing more than ruffles, ribbons, and lace—and now they slide into a split while the music rolls to one triumphant blast.

Liane turns to Émilienne, her eyes shining. "In my years I have never . . ."

Émilienne nods. "I know that red-haired girl, looks a bit like a rooster. Louise Weber. We danced together just months ago."

"They call her La Goulue. She is one of Charles's girls. Her posters will soon be all over Paris. He will see to that."

La Goulue's loose blouse exposes her fleshy, bouncing cleavage as she steps from the line, taking another bow for the cheering crowd calling her name. Suddenly her partner lifts her, throwing her up as she flips, landing on the floor in a double spin, sliding into a split. The crowd roars as she throws back her head and howls.

Then the girl jumps up, strolls right toward Émilienne and

Liane. Picking up Liane's glass, she drinks down the champagne in one long slug. All eyes turn to their table, and with a wink for Émilienne, La Goulue smashes the glass on the floor before running back to her partner.

"Charles did this," Liane says into her ear. "This will be in *Gil Blas* tomorrow, with our names. He planned this little bit, I just know."

Émilienne, still laughing, fixes her eyes on Louise, the glorious rooster strutting. Charles did this? *Oh, life is a beautiful play*, she thinks, wiping tears from her cheeks. She loves this place, and Charles, and Liane, and even La Goulue. She loves the glitter and music and, especially, the champagne.

She shall play like this for the rest of her life, she swears to herself. Never shall she grow old and tired.

As the dancers disappear and the house calms down, Émilienne pulls a cigarette from her wristlet. "Did you see the man with La Goulue? The one with no bones?"

"Valentin le Désossé."

Émilienne lights the cigarette from the candle on the table.

Liane gapes, resting her hand on Émilienne's arm. "Mind, Charles will not have this," she says, glancing around.

She drops the cigarette on the floor, remembering as she rubs it out. Rules.

"Ladies do not smoke," Liane says. "At least, not until we are known. Not till we are stars."

"I shall never become a star if I don't find a job, and soon."

Liane sits back. "Listen, you are just beginning. Charles has plans. That is how he operates. Don't mess things up."

She looks off.

"I hear Cirque d'Été needs someone."

Émilienne snaps her head around, eyes wide. "Yes? Oh, tell me!"

Liane holds up a hand. "It is not much, you know. But they put on a good show—elephants, tigers . . ."

"But I'm a dancer . . ."

"Hold your horses. They want a rabbit dresser, I hear. Someone to train the little furballs to jump through hoops and such."

She knows nothing of rabbits. Though she can learn.

"Of course, I don't know what Charles would think . . ." Liane says, lowering her voice. "He likes to hold the stick."

Émilienne smiles, excited. "I can handle Charles."

As she speaks, the man himself appears, pulling up a chair between them. "Ah, my two favorite ladies. Glad to see you get along."

A waiter slips a glass on the table before him. Clamping a cigar between his teeth, Charles picks up the bottle and pours for all three. Émilienne lifts hers, toasting him before she drinks, though her mind spins with thoughts of training rabbits—of a show all her own.

Everyone loves a sweet rabbit.

"Here is to luck," Charles says, sipping the champagne. He leans back, spreading his arms over their shoulders. "But, with me, you don't need luck."

The next *Gil Blas* edition issues a glittering report of the new cabaret, the Moulin Rouge, raving over the arresting performance, especially of the firecracker La Goulue and the spectacular sight of the Paris beauties attending. At the top of the list—Liane de Pougy and Émilienne d'Alençon.

CHAPTER SIX

The next afternoon, Émilienne waits in front of the main entrance of the Cirque d'Été on the avenue Champs-Élysées. Posters on the doors and surrounding lamp posts announce the theater's reputation in matters of haute equestrian art and fearless horsewomen; its trained elephants, wild tigers, and other such majestic giants of the animal kingdom; and its world-famous acrobats, clowns, and great dancers.

True to the gossip Liane heard, at the bottom of the posters, the Cirque pronounces an amazing new show in the works, featuring dancing rabbits onstage. The fabulous, funny performance shall commence on a day soon to be announced.

Her heart slows as she reads. *Is she already too late?*

She pushes on the door again, but of course at this time of day it remains locked. At last, tired of waiting, she walks around through the alleyway to a door in back. Two men drag large metal cans down one side of the alley. She scoots past them, and now—*voilà!*—she has luck.

The door is open, braced with a third can of waste, and without any hesitation, she slips inside. The director's name is Franconi, Liane told her. Rumor has it that a man from Brussels was first hired for the show and then decided to leave.

Not wanting to irritate Charles by keeping it a secret, Émilienne mentioned the idea. Surprising her, he said if she gets the job and trains the rabbits, he will do the rest. He'll take her home to glory in *Gil Blas*.

She follows a long hallway toward the sound of voices near what she believes to be the front of the theater. She has dressed to impress, just in case, wearing her plain day dress, but with the tightest fit of corset she could manage, taking inches off her waist. She feels fine and knows she looks her best. And this afternoon, before she left, Claire swept her hair into lovely swirls of gold, with ribbons curling down on one side.

New shoes, bought with her first pay from the dancing troop, carry her quietly along as she peers left and right, seeking the director. She shall find Franconi today—or die!

She moves down one hall and then another, heading for a dressing room up the stairs, where a couple of workmen claim to have last seen Monsieur le Directeur. She finds a tall, thin man wearing a curling mustache, standing in the middle of a dusty room.

"Monsieur Franconi?"

Startled, he looks her up and down, then frowns.

"Mademoiselle. You do not belong here. I am busy." He waves his hand in the air. "Go away."

She steps across the threshold. "Monsieur, if I may have a word . . ."

"Go away, go away. I have things to do."

She tilts her head, peering from underneath her lashes. "But Charles *Desteuque* sent me. He says you need someone for your rabbits."

"Unless you've come to clean this mess, get out. Get out!" As he shouts, he hurries toward a corner of the room, toward a pile of dirty towels. Stooping, bracing his back with a hand as he straightens, he mutters, "Merde! What shall I do with these?"

Émilienne hurries over, taking the towels from his arms. "I am here to help."

This time he looks at her. Over the armload of towels, she gives him her heart-shaped smile. "I shall place these just outside, and when I leave, I shall take them to the laundress."

Swaying toward the door, feeling his eyes on her, she drops the towels in a pile near the doorway and quickly turns around. "I have come to train the rabbits, well enough to take them onstage."

He presses his hand to his forehead, staring at her now. "Who sent you?"

She leans against the doorframe, hands behind her back, showing her curves to her best advantage. "As I said, Charles Desteuque . . . *Gil Blas*."

"Ah." The closed room has trapped a rancid smell. Moving to the window, he opens it and sits down on the sill. He crosses his arms, one corner of his lips turned down as he looks at her again. "What did you say your name is?"

"Émilienne. Émilienne d'Alençon."

"*Gil Blas*, eh?" He smooths his mustache, looking her over. She can see ideas turning in his mind. Why, with a beautiful girl and rabbits, and *Gil Blas* promoting the show, she might do. "Have you experience training rabbits?"

"Yes, of course. Why would I have come?" She does not recall ever having touched a rabbit in her life, but, remembering Liane's words at the Moulin Rouge, she continues. "I am a rabbit dresser, monsieur." When still he waits, she adds, "Rabbits are funny little things, and I have an affinity for the rascals. Did you know they are very smart?"

Seconds pass. And then he nods!

"I understand you need someone right away, Monsieur Franconi. And I'm ready to start today."

With a relieved sigh, he heads for the door. "You are pretty enough. Well, come with me. Five francs a week, and I shall give you a try." She follows him from the room as, over his shoulder, he adds, "I shall see how you do, what the audiences think. If you do well, we will up your pay to ten."

Ten francs a week! But when he stops, turning, inspecting her again, she says, "Fifteen, after I show what I can do, and if the audience likes what they see."

From where did those words just come? Now what has she done? Still, she stands before his eyes, as if either way she has naught to lose.

"Fifteen, but only after the third week . . . if ticket sales increase."

She rolls her tongue in her cheek. "Five for the first week, ten for the second, and if I do well, fifteen francs a week from then on."

He chuckles, his eyes grazing her breasts, her waist. "All right, but not a sou more. And fourth-place billing, if you last."

"Done," she says.

He smiles. "I like your spirit. Come, I'll show you where you dress and then introduce you to your rabbits." She follows, turning behind him down a flight of stairs, then on down again, below the level of the street. No windows here. The area is dark, lit only by occasional gas lanterns hung on the walls.

"Plan for twenty minutes onstage, every evening but Sunday," he mutters.

He stops on the step before her, and she almost runs him down, catching the rail just in time. "But listen here, girl. You have three days to prove your worth or you are out. I shall stop by then to check your progress with the rabbits . . . Mademoiselle . . . ah . . . d'Alençon."

She nods, wondering how long it takes to train a rabbit.

He opens a door to a small room. Inside, four tables, each with a mirror and a chair. "This is the dressing room. You will share with three other girls."

Behind him, ladies' costumes hang from a wire strung between two walls. Émilienne sniffs; already she loves the smells of the backstage room—a hint of sweat, the scent of powder and paint, and something more, something sweet. A lingering smell of dead flowers? Or perhaps the fragrance of four girls' mixed perfumes.

Walking inside, he fingers a purple skin suit with long sleeves and legs, together with a matching skirt reaching just to her ankles.

"Is this all?" She turns, looking toward the director.

He nods, spreading his hands. "Just make it work."

The pay, if she succeeds, is a fortune. She can eat every day. And after all, her body will be covered, even if the suit is awful tight.

"All right," she says. A scandal is coming up. Almost anything to get a girl noticed is all right, Charles says. "Well, I guess it's time for me to meet my rabbits."

He gives her a surprised look, beckoning with his finger. "Yes. Come along."

She hurries behind him, down the winding hallway again, until he stands before a door. In the center of the room, she sees several cages holding rabbits. Here, light filters into the room through a high window, the glass thick with dirt.

Monsieur Franconi waits in the doorway as she walks past him to the cages. "They are fed every morning. And they do love their carrots." As if impatient, he adds, "But you know more of these things than me."

Two months ago, if the carrots were here and he was not, she would have eaten them all in one minute.

The cages for the poor little beasts make her cringe, filthy as they are—three cages, nine rabbits. Stooping down onto her knees, she peeks at the rabbits, wondering how long they have been locked in this storage room. "This place won't do at all for training, monsieur. It is too small. Too hot." Her voice is firm and sure, as any rabbit dresser would object, she is certain.

He shrugs. "I cannot have rabbits running about."

Turning, she glares at him until his face flushes red.

He stares back, then shrugs again. "I suppose you are right. Use the large room behind the stage during the day for training."

"Does the room have windows?"

"No, I thought they would do better in the dark where you cannot see them."

She laughs. "If someone can find some carrots, I will get to know them now. Tomorrow morning I shall begin the training."

Monsieur Franconi nods, turning to leave. "Three days, remember. Oh, and . . . over there, a pointer. The fellow who fled, leaving us without a show left it here." He looks back. "You do use a pointer?"

"Yes, of course."

At last, he smiles. "I think you will do, mademoiselle. The audience will pay little attention to the rabbits with you onstage."

But she watches him go with dread. She knows nothing of rabbits, nothing at all. Where does she even begin?

After the director has gone, Émilienne looks at the rabbits, and they look back at her, one black, the rest white with splashes of dark spots. When she opens the cages, they slip right past her, seeming to multiply while she reaches for one, and another.

One hour wasted, stumbling, swearing, rounding them

up—back into the cages. Almost June and the room is hot.
She drops to the floor, sits cross-legged, and looks down at her
captives, studying them. Church bells toll, three o'clock, then
four, while she ponders the question of training. Sometimes
the little creatures venture to the edges of the cage, looking up
at her. And then an idea comes. Lifting the latch on the door
of a cage, she takes out the nearest rabbit, sets him in her lap,
and strokes his fur.

One at a time. That is how she will begin.

By the end of the second day, the rabbits know her voice, her
scent. She's become fond of them. Rabbits are smarter than she
knew. Using rewards and the pointer, a short stick with a small
ball attached to the end, first she teaches circles—running in
circles on command. After a while, they seem to like the game.
Or perhaps it's the scent of food on the ball of the stick that
keeps them going.

They seem to want to please her. After much holding and
petting and cuddling, most of them learn to comply with two
hand signals—forming a circle and running for a carrot on cue.
They each have a special personality, she realizes. Already she can
tell them apart, and she names them in her mind. The smartest, solid black, she names Emperor. Already he is her favorite.

By the third day, they obey four hand signals—circling,
running, hopping, sitting on command. And at the end of the
third day, absorbed in the work, she feels a definite connection
with her little pets.

"Mademoiselle?"

His voice startles her. She did not hear him open the door.

"Close it please, Monsieur Franconi, before they all run out!"

Entering the training room, he quickly shuts the door, and she looks up. *Three days, already?* This is the test.

Pulling out his handkerchief, wiping sweat from his brow, he takes a long breath. "Well now, let us see what you have accomplished." The shutters are open, but the window opens to the alley. Inside, the air is warm, and perspiration gleams on his face.

She has rehearsed the rabbits for this moment, teaching them to link the patterns on command. Each time they go through the paces, she gives out carrot bits.

Her success and the heat win the day. "Good enough for three days," he says, still wiping his brow. "You will do." As her mouth drops, he turns on his heels, slamming the door behind him.

For an instant, she stares after him. She has got the job. True, she is not dancing yet, but she shall be rich, and everyone will know her name. Scooping up Emperor, she hugs him to her breast. Charles will be thrilled.

The Exposition dancing troop and Charles Desteuque gave her this start. No more sleeping on the floor in one room with a crowd of girls. Turning, she gives a fond look to the white rabbits down on the floor.

Rabbits. Who would have dreamed?

CHAPTER SEVEN

When the news of Émilienne's performance is announced in the Cirque revue, the newspapers pick up the story, savoring the irony of rabbits at the Cirque among the elephants, tigers, horses, and other large beasts. The debut of the Cirque's beautiful new rabbit dresser also intrigues every journalist in the city. Most have seen Émilienne—at the Moulin Rouge opening and around and about   and now, they talk of little else. She is thrilled. Interest is so high that Monsieur Franconi hires an artist to paint and print posters of her with the rabbits. Her first posters.

Hanging on walls all over Paris is Émilienne, wearing her costume, complete with bunny ears. Kneeling with elbows down in front and her chin propped on one hand, she gazes back at each viewer with a mischievous smile, her round bottom lifted high, with one white rabbit perched thereon. Gentlemen of Paris stop to look on corners and in windows, and ticket sales increase by the day.

When opening night arrives at last, Émilienne d'Alençon's debut in the demimonde of Paris is the most talked about event. Now, the curtain is closed, the orchestra tunes up, and she waits onstage with seven rabbits in cages out of sight. Two are perched on the limb of a backdrop tree behind her.

As someone signals from stage left, she adapts a jaunty pose, lifting the pointer and resting it on one shoulder, like ladies hold their parasols. The audience is filled with royalty tonight, Monsieur Franconi says—the Duc d'Ange, the first duke of France; François d'Orléans, the Prince of Joinville; Princess Marguerite, and more. Peeking from behind the curtain earlier, she'd recognized several gents from the best journals, magazines, and newspapers as well—with *Gil Blas,* her Charles, seated right before the stage.

Franconi steps up, resting his hand on her shoulder. "Stage fright? Don't worry, do your best, and it will soon disappear."

Stage fright? She's given that no thought. She's too excited.

He claps his hands twice. "Curtain," he calls to the announcer in the wings. Wearing a tall, black top hat, a frock coat, and a white, high-collared shirt with a bright red cravat, the man pushes through the edge of the curtain, stage left.

"Ladies and gentlemen!" he shouts, and the orchestra strikes a long, harmonized chord. "For the first time ever, this evening the Cirque d'Été presents onstage our newest sensation . . ."— and here the trumpets blow—"Presenting, our beautiful Émilienne d'Alençon, and her amazing rabbits!"

The rowdy crowd applauds, whistling, stomping, and slowly, the curtain opens, revealing a wooded scene. Émilienne stands center stage in a circle of light wearing the bodysuit, skirt, and bunny ears on her head. As the house turns quiet, a strange feeling of power courses through her, a feeling of holding almost magical powers.

But the spell breaks as the music strikes and someone in the private stalls hoots and calls out to her. In the instant, a group of handsome young men, aristocrats she is certain, rise to their feet, chanting her name. With a wink just for them, she laughs and turns toward the two rabbits placed behind her. Plucking them from the branch on which they perch, she spins around again, strolling to the footlights.

"Ladies and gentlemen," she says, and the audience, silenced and curious, waits. "We welcome you, my little rascals and I. We are happy to see you are here." And after a beat, she adds, "And more important, that you've arrived on time. As you will learn, we have two rabbits onstage at last count, but you never know when they shall multiply."

Quick laughter invigorates, and as the musicians strike up a new, brisk tune, backstage workers free the remaining rabbits from their cages, all hopping onstage to the music, moving toward her in two straight lines led by Emperor. The sight is too much. Émilienne cannot help laughing, and again the audience joins the fun.

"So sweet, so loveable," a voice calls out.

Then another, "Look! Already they multiply!"

"They must be yours, Marcel!" And with this, spectators catch fire.

"You take the rabbits. The dresser is mine."

"Bastard, have you no manners?"

And the rabbits do entertain—running in formations, jumping through hoops, hopping over burning candles, forming circles, squares, and pyramids while she circles her hand in the air each time, slipping them their rewards. Why, her little ones do love her! Despite the noise, the hilarity—they tend only to her commands.

And now, the main trick. Her throat seizes. *Will this work?*

The orchestra plays the lead-up, and then the music hits a certain beat. She taps Emperor's tail with the pointing stick. A stagehand walks to center stage, placing something on the floor—a wooden stand with a pistol propped thereon. The audience gasps, and as he retreats, the black rabbit separates from the group. Emperor hops over to Émilienne and stands still beside her.

As the drum rolls, Émilienne juts out her hip and twists to one side, showing her curves, a pose designed to draw every eye while she sweeps her hand over Emperor. Before her, the black rabbit now sits behind the pistol. As the eyes of the audience follow her hand, she hears a little scream.

Émilienne halts, turning toward the audience. "Don't be afraid," she says, smiling. "This is the one with the lucky foot."

The music strikes up, drowning the laughter, and Émilienne lifts the pointer high, while eight little rabbits gather around her too.

In total silence, the audience waits. She taps the stick on the floor—once.

Twice.

Three times. Emperor jumps toward the pistol, landing on a wired trigger invisible beyond the footlights.

Only a pistol, but in this vast and crowded room the shot sets off a roar—a woman screams. Émilienne lifts the little Emperor up into her arms as the music morphs into a lovely waltz. In triumph, she moves toward the footlights carrying the black rabbit. With a mischievous smile and a flick of her brows, the audience comes to life.

Émilienne beams her smile out over the crowd. Success! Chaos reigns in the high seats as ruffians scramble toward the stage while others fight to hold them back. Some push their way into the stalls, but the music drowns their voices. Standing straight as a queen, as Charles has taught, she gazes out over her subjects, taking bows. The feeling of power surges through her again.

Émilienne holds her pose, squeezing the last bit of homage, while Emperor sits quietly in her arms. Flowers rain down around her, joy sings through her veins. Emperor jumps from her arms just then, and she turns, watching until he reaches a stagehand, and she turns back to her audience. She shrugs, laughing as she spreads her arms wide, and dukes, princes, kings, and everyone else out there rises, chanting her name—*Émilienne, Émilienne!*

Yes. At last. Tomorrow all of Paris will know her name.

After seven curtain calls, Émilienne heads for the dressing room, working her way backstage through the hands waiting to congratulate her and up the stairs, squeezing past Madame Tournou, mistress of the tigers, with her own dressing room, while Émilienne shares with three. But that will change.

At a quiet little restaurant off the main beat that night, she has dinner with Charles, celebrating. He looks at her with those sad eyes, even while he smiles, lifting his glass. "I knew you would come to this, Émilienne."

"Come to what?"

"You are on your way to great success." He leans forward, holding her eyes. "And I made you, just as I said I would. You and Caroline, who you shall meet soon, and Liane, your sweet friend, Liane, and others." He calls for a bottle of champagne and leans back, looking pleased with himself as he puffs his cigar.

"Sixty years in our cellar, monsieur," the waiter says when he returns.

Charles nods while the waiter pops the cork and fills the glasses.

"Here is to my Three Graces, the most beautiful women in Paris."

"Three Graces?"

"To you, Liane, and Caroline Otero." He looks off, and the smile dies. "To the Three Graces, to the last."

"Why do you say, 'To the last'?"

Taking another sip, he studies her and nods. "We are in a beautiful age, my darling. Even decades from now, when these halcyon days are gone, when the skies grow dark again, as they always do from time to time and Europe weeps, still they will talk of you three."

Sipping his champagne, he smiles. "Perhaps they shall remember me too?" He lifts a shoulder. "One never knows. But, for each of you three, the best of my girls, I have made you stars."

"Here is to life and joy!" Émilienne says. "And to you, Charles, the magician."

❧

"A New Star Rises over Paris," *Gil Blas* writes the next morning. "Émilienne d'Alençon, rabbit dresser at the Cirque d'Été, is the newest phenomenon in Paris, perhaps in all of Europe. You have never seen a rabbit trainer with curves like this. Even the rabbits stick around. Do not miss this show!"

Crowds wait at the door of Cirque d'Été each night, demanding to see Émilienne and her rabbits—and soon, tickets can no longer be found. Of course, Monsieur Franconi is delighted, increasing his new star's wages almost double on the spot.

She must find a new place to live and soon. A lovely set of rooms someplace, on a busy boulevard. She must shop for new hats and dresses, shoes made of soft leather, and silk stockings.

Why, just yesterday, Franconi moved her to a new dressing room, one of her own.

Émilienne, the girl from Montmartre, is now Cirque's new *étoile*. The rabbits changed her life, and she loves each and every one.

CHAPTER EIGHT

A few months later, Émilienne winds her way through the back-stage barriers—past old furniture and boxes and bits of various sets—toward her dressing room, still listening to the raucous cheers below. The rascals were spectacular tonight, each remembering the routines. Eight curtain calls this evening—eight! The stage is covered with roses.

All the best courtesans love roses.

Just as she enters her room, her new girl, Lily, calls—"Watch out, mademoiselle!"

But the warning comes too late. Something catches Émilienne's foot, tripping her, and down she goes, the room spinning, Lily hurries toward her, crying out.

Émilienne pushes herself up to sit, feeling her legs, her arms—no broken bones. Reaching down, Lily takes her hands, helping her to her feet. They push through a sea of flowers toward the dressing table. There Émilienne sits, still stunned as she looks about at the mass of flowers covering almost every surface.

And . . . she wrinkles her nose. Most are orchids.

She has never liked these pallid blooms, brazen with their almost phallic look.

Yet, here they are, covering her dressing room, looming everywhere—in baskets, boxes, vases, pots, bouquets in corners and on her dressing table, bouquets covering the floor, each tied with white satin ribbons and bows.

Turning to Lily, she lifts her brows. "What in hell is this?"

Lily is new, soft spoken—a shy girl, no older than herself.

"They just arrived, mademoiselle," the girl says, handing over a cream-colored envelope. "They came with this note. Ah . . . Monsieur Franconi had the hands remove the other flowers . . . to make room for these."

"Well, get rid of them after I leave, please." With a glance at the signature on the note, Georges-Auguste d'Ange, she adds, "An old man, I suppose. Only very old men send orchids." Sweeping the flowers from the dressing table onto the floor, she catches Lily's eye in the mirror. "Do not worry, my girl . . ."

"But mademoiselle, Monsieur Franconi . . ."

"I shall take all the blame when he comes around. Now, help me out of this costume, and hand over the robe."

Once she is free of her costume and comfortable again, she reaches for the cream, removing greasepaint while watching Lily in the mirror. "Please have the room cleared, Lily. Or just push the old things out into the hallway for now. And, in the future, remember I prefer roses and gardenias."

Leaning close to the mirror, she wipes away the last of the stage makeup and inspects her face. She's to meet a new gentleman this evening at Maxim's. Her hand freezes—*What was his name?* She cannot recall, but once there, Hugo, the maître d', shall assist in the matter. He is quite useful in things like this, Liane says.

"Orchids are expensive," Lily says, bending to lift a pot. "They cost ever much more than roses."

"Yes. Too expensive to waste, you're right." Lifting the bunny ears from her head, she sets the band aside. "Charles says I should get to know other dancers and performers in Paris." She turns toward the girl. "Let's send some of these"—she sweeps her hand over the flowers nearest the door—"to the other girls performing here tonight. I know most girls love orchids. Let's see . . . send the rest to La Goulue, at Moulin Rouge, and some to the girls—the stars, like Liane de Pougy and Caroline Otero and others at the Folies Bergère too. Just add a brief note to each one with my name."

Pleased with herself, Émilienne sits back while Lily combs her hair, imagining the surprise the girls will enjoy when her orchids are delivered. A knock at the door interrupts her thoughts. She draws her brows together. No one comes up here without Monsieur Franconi's consent.

"See who this is, Lily. If it is the old man who sent the orchids, tell him I have already gone."

But when Lily opens the door, a young man pushes past her, sailing into the room.

Émilienne looks up to the most handsome man she has ever seen, a man with the face of an angel and a bit of the devil in his smile. Removing his hat, he stands before her staring. Then his eyes roam over the room. He turns in a circle, observing the flowers toppled on the floor, kicked aside for a trail to the dressing table, others crushed together in corners, and on tables and chairs. Turning back to her, he wears a look of sheer disbelief. "You have murdered my orchids!"

She hides her smile. Facing the mirror again, she pretends to smooth her brows. This one is no old man. From the corners of her eyes, she studies him in the mirror. Despite his slender body, with that firm jaw and fine blond hair and mustache, and those laughing blue eyes even as he complains, he might be a fine gentleman to know.

She picks up a narrow brush from the table, dipping it into a jar of crimson paint. "I dislike orchids, monsieur."

After a pause, he drops his hands, still clinging to the hat. "I . . . I can think of nothing to say. To my knowledge, every girl loves an orchid."

"Not this one." Leaning toward the mirror, she paints her lips, ignoring him.

"Then I shall send peonies next time."

"Roses will do."

He lifts his brows.

Turning to him, she breaks into laughter.

"Very well. Roses next time." He gives a slight bow. "Georges-Auguste d'Ange at your service, mademoiselle."

Setting the paintbrush down on a platter, she recalls his name on Franconi's list of prominent guests this evening—although she does not remember if he holds a title. But orchids are always a bad sign.

"As you can see, I am not prepared for company."

"Please forgive the intrusion." His tone is friendly, light, and easy, with no sense of superiority or arrogance or worry. "What have you got against them? The flowers, I mean."

He is so calm, so mannered. "I could give you a long list. Though here are two." She ticks off two fingers. "They are rather pale, and the flowers have no scent. Not much, anyway."

"Perhaps the rabbits would like them." He looks about.

She motions to Lily, handing her a comb. "Excuse me, now. I have an engagement this evening and must prepare." She watches him moving toward the door. He is quite handsome. "I am sorry about the flowers," she adds.

He stops, turning back. "My grandfather grows them, you see. So, I have learned to love them. Orchids are his passion. All of these come from his hothouses down south." After a beat, he adds, "These particular blooms are quite rare. Like you, Mademoiselle d'Alençon."

When she lifts her brows, he smiles like a boy. Such a gentleman, after her rude remarks. He is not shy, like a boy. No, she already knows he can hold his own.

"Besides, I may as well tell the truth. I know it is late for this . . . but I have come to ask you to dine with me this evening."

She shakes her head. "As I said . . ."

"Of course, I understand. Besides, when I saw this"—he sweeps a hand over the room and his fallen flowers—"my hopes were dashed."

She says nothing. Lily moves behind her, combing her hair, twisting it into the pompadour she usually wears at night.

Still, he waits. "However, I do have a table at Maxim's, if you would consider doing me the honor, Mademoiselle d'Alençon."

She's curious enough to go with him—he is handsome, probably rich—but another gentleman awaits. And, besides, she knows that it is best not to seem too easy. A star at the Cirque d'Été cannot accept invitations merely at the drop of a hat.

"I am sorry, Monsieur d'Ange."

"Tomorrow then."

She hesitates.

"Tomorrow is Sunday. I shall come for you in the afternoon. We will drive through the Bois de Boulogne and stop for dinner."

Oh, to be seen on Sunday parade in the Bois. *She must accept.*

She gives him a cool look. "All right. I shall meet you here, as I work with my rabbits on Sunday afternoons." A blatant lie, but better than showing him the shabby place she still shares with other girls.

"Two o'clock, shall we say?"

"Make it three." She does not rise till noon. "And one thing, monsieur, no more orchids, please."

He slaps his hat on his head, smiling. When he has gone, she turns back to the mirror. Perhaps she could get used to orchids, perhaps she could get used to him.

Georges. Already the name sticks in her mind. When a knock comes again at the door, her heart jumps. If he has returned, perhaps she shall allow him to escort her to Maxim's this evening after all.

When Lily opens the door, only Franconi stands before her. Émilienne picks up the hare's paw, brushing powder over her cheeks as he steps in. "*Mon Dieu*!" he blurts, coughing and looking about. "What has happened here? Did you and the young duke engage in battle?" With a worried look, his eyes jump from one spot to another, following a trail of trampled orchids.

The young duke?

She stammers, "No, no . . . I just don't like the things." She tosses the powder aside, glancing at him. "You say he is royal?"

"As royal as a man can be in France after the revolution. He has the money, make no mistake. Young d'Ange is the first duke of France. His father died not long ago, and the son has assumed the title. He commands a great estate."

Émilienne stares at him, speechless. Not long ago she danced for coins. Now, she earns a fortune, and tomorrow afternoon she shall ride in the carriage parade through the Bois de Boulogne, and all of Paris will see.

Monsieur Franconi grips his lapels, turning to leave. "My

compliments little rabbit dresser. Georges-Auguste d'Ange is a man to watch."

When he is gone, she catches Lily's eyes in the mirror, and both girls smile.

"Georges," Émilienne says, trying out the name. A good strong name.

CHAPTER NINE

At three o'clock sharp, the duke's carriage stops before the backstage entrance of the theater. Of course, Émilienne will not go down to him and waits until he appears at her dressing room door and knocks. At the sound, her stomach tightens. She shall ride through the Bois de Boulogne this afternoon with a royal—a real duke. What should she talk about? How should she act?

Men do not mind stupid girls if they are pretty.

She may be from Montmartre, but she does not want to be known as a stupid girl. She must think of smart things to say to the Duc d'Ange. She loves to read. Despite Maman's disinterest, she learned from the books in the bookseller's shop in the hills—especially about travel, adventures in foreign lands. Perhaps she could bring up the books she has read?

But when she opens the door, immediately she forgets those worries. Because she sees it in his eyes—it is he who worries. And well he should! Why, Liane's borrowed gown fits perfectly to her curves. Embroidered with colorful tiny flowers, the pale-yellow dress is just right for a summer afternoon. The jacket bodice pulls in her waist, displaying her décolletage to her advantage— she catches his quick glimpse and smiles to herself. Thin lace sleeves compliment her creamy skin. And she wears long kid gloves, a gift from Charles for this occasion. A lady always wears gloves, he repeats.

Now, Georges takes her hand, bending to kiss it, then stands aside while she dons her hat and picks up her parasol and fan. When she is ready, he pulls her arm through his, guiding her down the stairs as if she were blind and made of porcelain.

Emerging into the alleyway, she almost stumbles when she sees the young duke's landau, painted gold, touched with black—and, on the door, the family crest. Four sleek black horses wait in harnesses. A coachman stands aside, then helps her up into the open carriage.

As they drive out into the streets, through the avenues and boulevards of Paris, Émilienne opens her new parasol. She loves the feel of sunshine on her face, but Liane advises her never to allow the sun to touch her skin, rather to rest the open parasol on her shoulder instead. Again, like great ladies do.

Georges turns to her. "What will the rabbits do for the rest of this afternoon?"

"They are granted a holiday."

"Why are all but one white?"

"That's how they came. But I may dye some of them pink and promenade them down the boulevards one day."

"Then you must wear the costume as well."

"Perhaps, though I would be arrested."

"I would pay your bond."

"That could get expensive, monsieur."

He takes her gloved hand in his. He is a man with a fat wallet. "Please call me Georges."

She looks into his eyes and nods. "Émilienne."

Someone waves from a passing carriage. Caroline, La Belle Otero! The gift of orchids did the work—Émilienne lifts her hand and nods.

"That reminds me." Digging into his pocket, Georges produces a small velvet box wrapped in satin ribbons and holds it out to her. Startled, she hides her surprise. Her first gift ever. Maman never gave her anything. Émilienne holds the box carefully, unties the ribbon slowly, while her heart thunders. Inside, a gold-and-diamond bracelet sparkles against black velvet. Lifting it, she dangles it on a finger, watching sunlight spark the facets of the stones.

"May I?" he asks, setting down her parasol. He takes each hand and gently removes the long gloves, placing them beside her. Georges clasps the bracelet around her right wrist without a word. Again, she lifts it to the sunshine, watching the diamonds flash.

A moan from the back of his throat sounds like sheer delight. He leans close, whispers in her ear. "Better than orchids, yes?" But, before she can speak, he takes her hand, kissing the underside of her wrist.

She turns to him, and he meets her eyes.

"It seems already I have fallen in love, mademoiselle."

"Émilienne." Her reply comes out a whisper.

With a tender smile, he traces her lips with his finger. "You have captured my heart, Mimi." His eyes hold hers, and she finds she cannot look away. "Émilienne . . . such a long name for a small girl. May I call you Mimi?"

"No, yes . . . no."

"Between the two of us. A name just for me?" Seconds pass, then he adds, "And you must call me Georges."

Dropping her hand into her lap, she nods.

On this Sunday afternoon, the sky over the Bois de Boulogne reflects the light of pure white clouds, the whitest clouds she's ever seen. Only a few streaks of blue break the glare. Heat shimmers on the pavement along each side of the boulevard, but spreading oak trees provide plenty of shade for children's games while their mamans and nannies sit and gossip. Near the forest edge, old men lounge, smoking their cigars and watching the parade.

From the opposite direction comes a familiar landau. An older woman, a once-famous courtesan, still beautiful, but alone. Liane pointed her out at the Moulin Rouge. Now, the woman lifts a glass to her eye, inspecting Émilienne as the carriages pass. *We two live in the same world now*, Émilienne thinks. But will she also be alone someday?

She dismisses the thought, smiling to herself. She is young and carefree this afternoon, riding along in a carriage with the first duke of France. It is her turn now. Why, it is her own colorful posters hanging all over Paris.

Émilienne flicks open the fan from her lap. The day is hot. On the right, the cool forest beckons.

"Is there a pathway through those trees over there?"

He follows her eyes. "Yes. It's a nice walk."

Georges directs the driver to stop. "Wait for us at the lake café," he says.

Émilienne places her hat and fan on the seat with her other things—enough of society's rules. Georges jumps out and lifts her to the ground. As the carriage moves off, they stroll toward the forest.

Once in the cool shade of the trees, she takes a long, deep breath of the fragrant air. Here they have some privacy. Ancient oaks surround them, hiding the wild forest beyond where grass and vines grow thick and high.

A patch of violets along the shaded path catches her eye. Georges picks a small bouquet and tucks it behind her ear.

"Here, for you. A smaller hat."

The flowers remind her of the unfortunate orchids. "Please, I ask your word that you shall never mention the murder of your orchids to anyone, Georges." She frowns. "Especially not to your grandfather."

He waves off her words, pulling her close. "He would only laugh. Grandfather likes a woman with spirit."

"And you?"

"As do I."

She lifts her face to his—their first kiss, soft and sweet. He rests his hands at her waistline, and she steps back. His hands are gentle, and in her days with the boys of Montmartre she has felt rougher. But this is all too soon.

He cups her face in his hands. "Do you not understand? Already, I love you, Mimi."

"Come, let's walk."

Soon the lake comes into sight, and they stop, watching water cascade from high rocks on the other side, stirring the water below.

"I hear music!" Émilienne twirls and reaches her arms high in the air.

Georges laughs as she grabs his arm and pulls him along toward the café in the distance.

As they walk along, he tells her a little of his life and of a group of friends he calls the Princelings, old friends from childhood days. "We studied together also, at the Sorbonne."

She says nothing, listening.

"The duchess . . . my maman . . . thought it best I learn with other boys when I was young. We had our own schoolyard. Studied together with our tutors." He shrugs. "And we have stuck together ever since." He traces a finger down her bare arm. "You shall meet them soon."

"I would like that."

"But what of you?" He takes her arm, pulling her closer. "Did you grow up in Paris?"

Georges will never hear from her that she comes from the streets of Clichy and the butte Montmartre. Nor will she claim Maman—neither the drunk who is her father. She hardly knows him. Shed his name, André, when she shed her life on the hill. Never shall Georges know her past—a woman without a sou, of the days and nights without food or a place to sleep.

"My life was dull," she says. "The usual stories small girls tell. My father was a surgeon. He died when I was twelve, and I miss him still. He read stories to me, giving me the love of reading."

"Reading, a fine gift for his little girl. And how did you learn to train rabbits?" He chuckles.

She smiles while answers spin in her head. "An uncle, Maman's brother, has a farm. When the weather was too hot in the city, Maman would send me to him. I caught a rabbit once, and when he saw my love for the little beasts, he allowed me to keep them there." With a sideways glance and a smile, she shrugs. "Training them for tricks is easy when you have a carrot in hand."

Turning, he pulls her into an embrace. "You were a sweet girl, I imagine. And you are still today."

When they reach the café, they choose a small round table on the shaded terrace near the water's edge. A piano man plays a light melody, something romantic and flowing. While Georges entertains her with stories of his band of friends and their adventures, they drink champagne and nibble Russian caviar, and Georges feeds her fleshy, cold oysters from Saint-Vaast with a wonderful nutty flavor. It isn't until sunlight turns to silver on the lake that Georges finds his driver, and the carriage comes around.

He takes her to his rooms at the Maison Dorée. She strolls to a large window looking out over the now quiet street. He comes to her, standing behind her, wrapping his arms around Émilienne as she leans back against his chest, looking up at the stars and dreaming. When at last he lifts her into his arms, carrying her to his bed, Liane's advice to make him wait is forgotten. Georges's kisses are tender, raising chills. As they make love over and over again, he swears he is hers forever.

They wake at noon with all the bells of Paris ringing in the day. Georges hikes up on one elbow, brushing hair from her forehead. "Are you hungry?"

"Yes, famished."

He bends, kissing her. "I shall take you across the street to one of the best places in Paris, Café Anglais. The chef has a special dish with scrambled eggs and crayfish à la Bordelaise. You will think you are in heaven."

She yawns and stretches, looking about. This is a man's room—large and dark, too dark. Émilienne seeks light. Long windows with heavy draperies stretch across two corner walls. She longs to pull the draperies back, letting in the sunshine. Still, even in the weak light the wood floors gleam. A fireplace faces the bed. Ah, a fire in that would be cozy on a winter night.

Georges's room is surprisingly neat. No wonder the man was shocked at the state of his orchids in her dressing room.

Rising, she stands beside the bed. Long curls tumble over her shoulders. She lifts her hair with both hands, then drops it, turning, seeking a mirror. "I must look a mess."

"Never." He points to a door across the room. "In there."

Crossing the room, she stops to peek behind the drapery, looking out the window over the busy boulevard. "After we eat you must take me home."

"No, never." He sits up against a pile of pillows, clasping his hands behind his head and watching her.

"But of course, you must." She swings around, smiling. "My babies wait at the Cirque. We run through the routines before each show." Then, looking down, she adds, "We are second this evening. Will you come?"

"Of course. And I shall bring my rowdy friends. We shall all go out after!"

"Oh." She had almost forgotten. "Georges, my time is claimed tonight."

He stares. "Another man?"

She nods.

"Well then, stand him up."

"I cannot at this late date." He is a wealthy and important gentleman from London after all.

Walking over to her, Georges places both hands on her shoulders, his eyes bore into hers. "Listen, Mimi. Things are different now. Tell him that. Tell him . . ." He throws up his hands. "I don't know . . . tell him you have fallen in love with someone else. He's out of luck."

She pulls back. "He's just business, Georges."

Slowly, his frown disappears. "Ah, well then, get rid of him!" He takes her hands in his, lowering his voice as he moves close. "I shall take care of you, Mimi. Come, I love you. We must make arrangements."

Liane had said this time would come. Émilienne is a demi-mondaine, and a star now. She dips her chin, watching him from under her lashes. "I have expenses, you must understand."

His face lights up. "We shall find a place together, right away. An apartment on a lively boulevard."

Her heart races, though her tone is cool. "Perhaps." She looks off. "But if we do this . . . I shall continue my show, and dancing."

He plants a kiss on her forehead. "You shall continue dancing, and whatever you want, you shall have."

"As you said, arrangements are required. And the apartment must be mine, Georges. I must own the place if it is to be my home." Again, Liane's advice comes rushing through her mind as she tries to remember everything that she was told.

He nods. "Of course." Gazing down into her eyes, he adds, "But, my darling, we must be discrete. At least at first. Only our friends may know."

Surprised, she watches him in silence.

"Otherwise, Maman, the Duchess d'Ange, will interfere. She has ambitions . . ."

"What sort?"

"Ah, you must understand, Mimi. Maman is stuck in the old days, when titles were important, not merely . . . decorations."

"Your maman is a royalist?" She frowns. "France is a republic now."

"Yes. But she does not like change. Maman would go back in time if she could. A republican government is messy. She believes a lack of law and order was responsible for our loss in the war against Prussia. And she never got over France's humiliation when the Prussian Army took Alsace–Lorraine and then paraded their victory down our streets of Paris."

Émilienne clucks her tongue, stepping back. "What has that to do with us?"

For a moment he hesitates. Then, "Nothing." He throws up his hands.

With a forced smile he takes her into his arms. "You must not worry over this, my love. I will wait for you this evening after the show. We shall talk more about our arrangement then."

She purses her lips. "Perhaps. We shall see." She is no street girl to be locked away from the world. She has choices now. "In this arrangement . . . I must be free to come and go as I please."

His brows draw together. But then he says, "Of course. Lovers do not need chains."

She holds his eyes. Memories of their lovemaking last night, of Georges's pledge, his love, the promises he made, calm her mind. He places his hand over his heart and the other over hers.

Her own skips a little beat.

Feeling certain now, she says, "All right, my darling. I shall inform the gentleman this evening that I am otherwise engaged."

Later, as the carriage rolls away from Café Anglais, she stares through the window unseeing, thinking of their conversation. Does she really love Georges? She has never been in love before.

The next thought comes quickly. *Think of what he offers. Does love even matter?*

But that question flicks away as she relives the moment Georges placed his hand over her heart, and she flutters all over again. What a difference there is between a lover like Georges and the boys she knew in Montmartre. This feeling for Georges is so strong, so urgent. This must be love she feels inside. Yes, she decides.

But what of the duchess, Georges's maman?

Yes, a mother holds great power over a young, unmarried man, even one with a title. But not enough to sear their love.

She leans back, feeling content. Love will win in the end.

CHAPTER TEN

It took some time, but the apartment Georges purchased for her on avenue des Champs-Élysées is a charming place, with tall windows that let in a wash of light. Georges chose well. Émilienne stands on the balcony outside their bedroom on this cool fall evening shivering, rubbing her arms. Tonight is her last show with the Cirque, which is open only from the spring until fall each year. Already she's received offers from other theaters, though the one she longs for, the Folies Bergère, has not yet come.

Charles is thrilled. He would have her accept the offer from Les Ambassadeurs right away. Still, she shall wait a few days before accepting to see if an invitation comes from the Folies. This is her decision to make.

Looking up and down the avenue she notices the horse-chestnut trees are beginning to shed their leaves. She leans on the balcony rail, looking down, admiring the gold and yellow leaves on the pavement. A smile comes as again she realizes, this is her home. Her own home.

Turning, she walks back into the bedroom, looking about, letting herself see the room as if this is the first time. Georges furnished her home with the best—only the best for his Mimi, he says. Standing just inside the glass doorway, her eyes touch each beautiful thing he has bought for her—the art, the hand-carved furniture, an enormous bed with fine silk sheets and satin quilts. The walls are covered in pale green silk, just as she dreamed. Georges calls this room Émilienne's boudoir. Perhaps because she requested the black velvet stripes on the green silk walls.

She had thought to put her finishing touches to the place, but with her schedule at the Cirque and Princeling romps through Paris after every show, it seems there is barely time for sleep in the lovely apartment. The parties never stop.

Now that her contract with the Cirque is over, perhaps things will change.

Soon they shall marry, Georges says. She smiles to herself, remembering. When he said those words, he handed her a gift, a single black pearl on a golden chain. "This shall prove my eternal love," he said. The pearl was ancient, valuable, handed down through the family for generations. "Every d'Ange woman has worn the black pearl when she married, Mimi. It is yours now. Think of me when you wear it."

Thoughts of Liane's dry smile when Émilienne first repeated his marriage promise to her friend almost ruin the moment. Liane can kill with that certain smile.

But, fingering the lovely pearl, her joy returns. She trusts Georges. He means what he says. He has given his pledge, his vow.

Besides, she has no time to worry now. Émilienne is sought after by almost every theater in Paris—some offers arrived even from the South of France, on the coast.

How she would love to dance in Monte Carlo.

Everything is on the table.

❧

In her dressing room after her last show at the Cirque, Émilienne seems to hover inches over the floor as she prepares for
the evening festivities Georges has planned. He has promised
this will be a night she shall never forget. She gazes at the silver
dress hanging to her right, a gift from Georges to celebrate.
Then she picks out three long strings of pearls to wear, gifts
from a gentleman in the audience last week whose name she
cannot recall.

Lily sets a small diamond tiara on Émilienne's head—another gift that Georges says proves his devotion. It belonged
to the duchess. Émilienne turns this way and that, watching
herself in the mirror, admiring the sparkling stones. The diamonds turn to fire in her golden hair. Tonight, when she walks
into Maxim's, everyone will understand that the Duc d'Ange
and Émilienne are together, that he is her patron and protector.

"What will your maman say? That is, if she hears of this,"
she said to Georges when he gave her the tiara. The words had
slipped from her mouth before she caught them.

"I'm the heir," he replied. "The Duc d'Ange. The family
jewels belong to me." Smiling, he took her in his arms. "But
with this, we must still be discrete . . . for now."

Sitting here before the mirror, for a split second, thoughts
of the formidable woman for whom she must remain discrete
force Émilienne to close her eyes. A small voice deep inside
warns that the duchess is not likely to celebrate marriage between her son, the great heir, and a dancing girl, a woman who
could one day take her place.

Downstairs over raucous noise the announcer calls for the next act.

With a glance around the dressing room, Émilienne knows she shall miss this place, and the rabbits. Tonight, the little rascals received extra treats—they, too, are stars. Now they are trained, they are valuable to the Cirque. Monsieur Franconi swears he shall take good care of them, that the new rabbit dresser shall be kind.

She leans closer to the mirror, slicking on lip paint. Behind her, Lily moves about, arranging Émilienne's belongings to be picked up the following day. Watching the girl in the mirror, she realizes she has become fond of Lily. What will happen to her now that the show is over? She sits back and sets the brush down on the table. What if Lily ends up on the street?

With this, Émilienne turns. "Listen, Lily, this is just the beginning. Why not stick around with me?"

Lily stops and turns. "Yes?"

"Yes! You shall be my lady's maid." She likes the turn of that phrase. "My apartment has rooms."

Lily looks at her for a long time.

"Stay! Five francs a month, a home to live in, and meals, of course."

Lily's shoulders drop, and her hands fly to her face. She weeps! Surprised, Émilienne rises. "Come, come, Lily." She slips her arms around Lily's shoulders. "Did you think I could leave you behind after all we have gone through together?" Steering her to the small couch, they sit while Émilienne wipes away the tears.

When Lily looks up, her eyes shine. "Mademoiselle, I was afraid. I didn't know where to go or what I could do after we part."

Tipping up the girl's chin, Émilienne smiles. "Now you may stop the worries."

With a pleasant little shudder, Lily nods.

"Good, then it's settled. Have you family here in Paris?"

"Nearby, just outside of Paris."

"Well, you shall live with us, but first we both need a little rest. Go and visit your maman and papa. Georges and I leave for Deauville tomorrow afternoon, and you can come to us when we return." She cocks her head. "Yes?"

"Yes, mademoiselle."

"And this too—you must call me Émilienne. We are friends?"

Blushing, Lily smiles. "Yes."

Downstairs, the audience breaks into applause, and Émilienne remembers Georges waits outside. As she jumps up, hurrying to the mirror, the door opens and Caroline, La Belle Otero, steps inside. Such style in that blue linen gown against the girl's pale skin and the high, feathered hat.

She leans back against the door, frowning at Émilienne. "Look at this! Not even near dressed, and already we are late! I shall walk down with you when you are ready, Georges insists." Wandering into the room, her eyes travel to the tiara. "Such a lovely one, Émmy. A gift from Georges?"

"Of course," Émilienne gives her a sardonic look. "And from his maman, although I doubt she knows." With a laugh, she rises, and Lily helps her into the silver dress.

"I hear the duchess is a terror."

Émilienne turns, and Lily begins the task of buttoning in the back. "I haven't met her. I suppose Georges shall solve that problem."

"Don't count on that. I hear her spies are everywhere."

"Hush!" Émilienne tamps down rising anger. "Don't spoil a good evening."

Caroline tosses her head, taking a seat on the couch while Lily finishes.

Émilienne turns to the mirror for one last look. Then, with a glance at Lily, she says, "I will send for you when we return."

She lifts her skirts, moving toward the door. "Come along, Caroline. Let us go tame the rogues."

Linking arms, the two hurry down the back stairs, but as they reach the ground floor, Caroline pulls her in the direction of a corridor leading to the front entrance instead of the alley where Georges usually waits. In the grand hall, the audience sounds like thunder through the walls.

As they reach the entrance, Caroline steps aside, flinging the doors wide. Confused, Émilienne stops, then follows Caroline's eyes. Below, she sees a vision—it could be nothing else.

Before her, in the street, a long, low open landau awaits. Painted in sparkling silver with red-and-black trim, the carriage shines under the gaslights. A bloom of swirling flowers, thousands of flowers—garlands of roses, lilies, gardenias—wind together around the carriage and horses. But the horses and driver are nowhere to be seen.

Instead, the Princelings, harnessed with silver, await.

Along with Georges.

Émilienne stares, her eyes wide, mesmerized by the mystic scene. In a flash she understands that Georges has given her the one thing she has longed for—his proof of love. Someone loves her! He will always keep her safe, always protect her—feelings she has never felt before. Georges does not take, he gives. He treats her with tenderness.

This is her new world that Georges offers without conditions.

Caroline screams with delight, shattering her thoughts, and the men below burst into laughter—cheering, stamping feet, huffing, and snorting as waiting horses will do. The gleeful two-legged horses are bound to the carriage by silver ropes and leather and rows of tiny bells. These rich and powerful royals from another era call for the girl from Montmartre on this chilly fall night. No longer monarchs, now they only play.

She turns, calling Caroline, but La Belle Otero has disappeared. Still laughing, Émilienne dances down the steps to the carriage. The theater doorman helps her up into the driving seat, then places in her hands the reins and a whip.

There in the night, from the driving perch she looks over the royal heads. But she wears the diamond tiara—she is royal too! Joyfully she snaps the whip in the air. "Go!" she commands. "Go! Race down the boulevards. I shall show no mercy till we arrive at Maxim's!"

CHAPTER ELEVEN

Just awake, Émilienne pulls the soft quilt closer around her. Turning her head on the pillow, she sees that Georges is not here, then gazes around her own room in her new home. She must have slept late. Yawning, she clasps her hands around the back of her head on the pillow. Smiling up at the ceiling, she thinks of last night, of making love. Georges's wild nature calms when they're alone and he holds her in his arms, almost a different man than the one who takes her out at night with the Princelings.

The press follows them everywhere, which Georges dislikes.

But Charles is happy, and so is she. She is noticed. Besides, Charles is the one with knowledge, the one who makes the girls.

In a few hours she leaves for the theater, Les Ambassadeurs. Although she still longs to dance at the Folies, no offer came after she left the Cirque. At the time, she had planned to visit the Folies director before accepting one of the other offers in hand. But Charles held her back, insisting she accepts Les Ambassadeurs.

Let the Folies come to you, he advised. A star never begs.

The Folies will come round soon enough, Émilienne knows. Meanwhile, Les Ambassadeurs treats her like a star. And why not? Why, the theater has been sold out every night for her show since she began. Even the standing area in the promenade under the stalls is always full.

Throwing back the quilt, she rises, saunters to a window just as the clock strikes half past two. Lifting a small blanket from her reading chair, she throws it around her and steps out onto the balcony, breathing in the cold, fresh air. Low, dark clouds cover the sun. December. Perhaps snow will soon fall.

The avenue is quiet for this time of day. Two young lovers huddle together as they stroll past. Across the street, workmen gather around a drain.

Below, a coach stops at the building entrance. She watches as the coachman climbs down from his seat and hurries around. A gentleman in a frock coat, well tailored, and a top hat, steps out. His high, stiff collar and briefcase mark him as a man on business this afternoon.

Émillenne retreats into the bedroom. This building houses only private apartments, and she wonders which the courier will visit. A bell rings downstairs, and then she hears Georges's voice and a stranger's reply. She opens the bedroom door, listening. But the voices are low. Strange. She has never noticed Georges having any interest in business before.

Two hours pass before Georges enters the bedroom. She's dressed, prepared to leave for the theater, and had almost forgotten the man downstairs. "Who is the visitor, my love? He looks important."

Georges wanders through the room, stopping before a

window, where he stands, looking off. She hears the coachman's whip snap and horses pulling the carriage away.

Turning back to her, a short smile comes, but still, she sees a flash of something in his face she does not understand. "A messenger from Maman," he says. His voice is tight.

She picks up her gloves and pulls them on, watching him. "Is it trouble?"

"No." He shrugs, walking toward her. "Nothing to worry us. Though I must make a short trip to London, at Maman's request."

"London! Are you going alone?"

"Philippe, ah, the Duc d'Orleans is already there. The Earls of Paris and Haussonville, and the Marquis of Lasteyrie, will come with me."

Most of the Princelings. Royalists all, she realizes, having never thought of this before. But of course, what good are their royal titles in the French Republic where leaders are elected, not anointed. "Ah, so Maman plots a coup. A fine group to take down the republic!" She smiles at her private joke.

Georges stands before her very still. "Do not speak of this to anyone, Mimi." His tone holds a warning.

Sudden fear grips her chest. She fingers the black pearl hanging around her neck, staring at him. Outside bells from La Madeleine toll the half hour. Laughter comes from the kitchen downstairs—Lily and the kitchen maid. "You will miss Christmas, Georges. It's only two weeks away."

Georges's expression softens. "I shall return soon, one week at most. When your show is over, I thought perhaps we could visit my villa at Antibes, on the coast."

She nods, hiding a flash of anger.

A week turns into four weeks, without any message from Georges. Christmas comes and goes. Lily and the maid hang some mistletoe for good luck, but Émilienne forbids a tree. Saint Nicholas never found her as a child—no need for him now.

One January day Charles arrives, asking to see Émilienne. Lily conveys the message, and Émilienne hurries down the stairs and into the salon. "What is it?" she asks feeling breathless.

He stands, holding up a newspaper rolled in his hand. "Sit down, Émilienne. We have something to discuss."

Charles sits, too, waiting until she is settled, then taps his hand on the newspaper. "It seems Georges d'Ange is involved in something rash. The news is not clear, at least not yet."

"What do you mean?"

He tosses the paper onto the couch and leans back. "The Duc d'Orleans was arrested here day before yesterday."

"Orleans, back here in Paris? Why was he taken?"

"Despite our revolution over a hundred years ago, it seems he plots a coup to overthrow the government. Down with the republic! The royals demand their thrones and privileges be returned. This is treason." After a pause, he adds, "Others are involved, although they are not yet named." He looks up at her now.

Georges.

She closes her eyes as he goes on. "Monarchists! Royalists all. They would destroy our freedoms, our rights, destroy everything we have gained since the revolution."

She shakes her head, unable to speak. Georges pledged his love to her, assured her all was fine. Yet she has no real doubt that he is involved. With this he could ruin their lives—their future together.

Charles leans forward, hands on his knees. "Is Georges a part of this?"

"I don't know," she lies, turning her eyes away from his. "I know nothing of a plot." Just then, she recalls his anger when she teased him about plotting a coup.

He, too, will be arrested if he returns to Paris, she realizes. The thought jolts her. As she looks at Charles, he seems to recede—wavering, and she passes her hand over her eyes. When she looks again, there he is, now looming before her.

"Rumors are Georges's maman, the Duchess d'Ange, is the instigator of the plot." Charles watches her as he speaks. "You are certain? You know nothing of this?"

She drops her head, hiding her tears. "Of course not," she says.

"Good." With a sigh, he rises. "I hope not, for your sake, Émilienne."

Émilienne hides at home that evening and the next while the storm breaks in the press. She has had no word from Georges since the Duc d'Orleans was arrested, and she cannot pretend onstage right now. A courier from the theater calls on her each day, and each day she claims illness. Her understudy must take her part until she is well, she snaps. Let *her* dance.

She must trust. She must preserve the dream, the love she and Georges have for each other. Soon Georges will come home, and life will resume as before.

It's not long before Monsieur le Directeur sends a letter demanding her return to the show. Otherwise, she shall be replaced at once. Lily hands her this message, waiting while she reads.

Émilienne tosses the note aside, sliding down into the pillows. "I must sleep," she moans, turning her head from Lily.

"No, Émilienne!" And, before she can blink, Lily yanks the quilt from the bed and, leaning over her, in a tone Émilienne has never heard before, says, "You must show yourself to the world. You must be brave, Émmy."

Émmy?

"Now." Lily stands firm. "You'll send a reply to the theater, announcing that you will perform tonight."

At this, Émilienne sits up straight in the bed, clutching a pillow as she watches Lily bustling about, grabbing a dress—her best afternoon gown—from the armoire, and her corset, her petticoats, dropping each item on the foot of the bed, wordless.

"What are you doing?" Émilienne says at last.

"You must leave for the theater in one hour. I shall have the carriage called around."

Émilienne drops back into the pillows. "I cannot. Not without knowing if Georges is safe."

Lily stops and turns to her. Her tone is hard. Émilienne almost does not recognize this Lily. "Forget Georges d'Ange for the moment. You must be seen again in Paris or lose your place in line. Les Ambassadeurs will find someone else to take your show if not. Do you want to return to Montmartre dragging your dresses behind?"

She closes her eyes, thinking of Lily's words. Of course, she is right. At last, she pushes up. Wiping away the tears, she swings around and drops her feet on the floor.

Sitting at the dressing table, Lily hands her notepaper, a pen, and ink, and Émilienne writes the note to the theater—it was nothing but a slight illness, she is well now and on her way. Émilienne d'Alençon shall dance tonight! Lily takes the note in hand, sending it on by courier to Les Ambassadeurs.

Émilienne moves slowly as Lily helps her dress, packs for the evening, and calls the carriage round. At the theater one hour later, Monsieur le Directeur stands in her dressing room, waiting.

He inspects her with his eyes. "It is good to have you back, Mademoiselle d'Alençon." His tone and words are clear. Lily was right, she has returned just in time. And he does not leave at once. He stands in the doorway, glancing at his watch.

Émilienne smiles, she flirts, sitting at her dressing table while he waits as if fearing any minute she may flee. At last, a flat smile comes under the mustache, and he turns to leave. "Curtain in a half hour," he says. Then, bracing his hand on the door, he adds with a warning, "I shall see you backstage before the show."

She stares at the space where he just stood, worried now. She must do something fast.

At Émilienne's request, a few days later, Lily purchases two sweet white rabbits. Émilienne holds each one close, petting it, until they are no longer shy. Then Lily has them dyed pink. That afternoon, in her best dress, Émilienne parades the pink rabbits down the boulevards on golden chains.

Gil Blas immediately reports the news—"*Émilienne is back! Grander than ever!*"

Perhaps the mistletoe did bring luck. It seems her relationship to the missing plotter, Georges d'Ange, gives her a certain notoriety that sells, and now *Gil Blas*, along with all the other journals and newspapers in Paris, record her every move. *Her heart-shaped lips are roses,* journalists write, *honey to bees.* Praising her beauty, *"those thick arched brows over brown eyes flecked with gold. The adorable snub nose, rosy cheeks, a complexion like fresh cream."* Gentlemen collect her boudoir cards, photographs of the young courtesan.

Paris now knows Mademoiselle d'Alençon simply as Émilienne! One name, the sign of a star. Even workmen on the street know her, calling out when she's around. They remind her of Henri—she winks and sends them cheeky smiles. Occasionally, she meets Henri on an afternoon, and they talk about old times. Henri, married now, seems happy enough. Each time

they part he wraps her in hugs, never shy about claiming it is
he, not Charles, who made her name.

Émilienne, La Belle Otero, and Liane de Pougy—all three
are pronounced by *Gil Blas* as the most beautiful women in
Europe. Otero, the Spanish enchantress, is best known for her
fiery dancing, Charles writes. Liane, for her celebrated dancing
as well. But Émilienne is famous for her joy and spirit, as well
as her beauty.

Despite her fear and longing for Georges, at Charles's insistence, Émilienne accepts invitations from various gentlemen
after the show. She accepts their gifts too—an emerald broach,
several glittering bracelets, necklaces worth fortunes, she suspects. Lily insists on purchasing a safe, something small enough
to hide in the armoire but large enough for her ever-expanding
collection of jewels.

Each evening, she dines with someone new. Once again, she
is the girl every man desires. But after frolicking on the boulevards each evening, in the early morning hours before the sun
rises, she returns to her own bed alone, weeping and raging,
sometimes unable to sleep, prowling the rooms of her home. She
swears, when Georges returns, he shall pay the price. He shall
realize that Émilienne is no longer his little rabbit dresser—she
has put the black pearl away and no longer wears it.

CHAPTER TWELVE

One day, Lily wakes her as usual at one o'clock. She opens the shutters to cold sunlight streaming into the room and places a letter on the table by her bed. The envelope bears the crest of the Duc d'Ange.

Sitting up, Émilienne takes the envelope from Lily, staring at the crest for a moment. She tears it open. "My dear Mimi," Georges begins. She skims to the bottom of the page, then reads the letter again. At last, dropping the note onto the bed, she looks up at Lily, her eyes filling with tears.

"He writes that he loves me, misses me, Lily. He is safe with the family, he says. He will write again, as soon as he is able. But . . . no news on his return."

Day after day, disappointed, frightened, she paces the floor in the entrance hall waiting for another letter. Gone for so long now, Georges has only sent one love note to his Mimi. Even that was short and to the point. *Has she lost him now?* A listless feeling pulls Émilienne down. She comforts herself, tells herself

Georges will choose her over his maman if she disapproves of their love. Why, he is head of the family.

In February of the new year, to Émilienne 's relief, Les Ambassadeurs extends her contract, offering a wonderful new show—dancing the role of a caged nightingale longing for freedom, promising a secret treasure in exchange. It is an old tale, altered a bit for the show. The trusting captor, at last believing the bird, opens the cage. But as the nightingale flies away, she taunts her captor for believing a promise.

The show is an instant hit. Every night, while the audience cheers as the curtain falls and rises and falls again and flowers flood the stage, Émilienne thinks of the lesson in her dance—*never trust a promise, even Georges's*.

Beware. The first time this warning flashed through her head, for some reason she thought of the strong Eiffel Tower Henri built, so tall and yet as beautiful as delicate lace—perhaps Alençon lace. And all that iron held together by so many small, hot rivets, Henri had said.

In that same moment on the stage, smiling, winking at the men in the audience up front, she told herself that she is also too strong to fall, she is as strong as that steel. She told herself that in times like this, when trust fails, she requires special strength to sustain her faith—like those rivets holding the tower's iron lace steady and strong.

On most nights after the show, Émilienne returns home alone. She is a star now; she should be promenading the boulevards to be seen, as Charles would say. But alone within the walls of her own home, she feels comforted, steady. Here she can think more clearly without having to smile. Why, Georges sat in this chair before he left. Georges lay beside her in this bed.

Yet he has been gone too long. Is she a fool to trust his promises?

One afternoon in late February, Émilienne awakes to find Liane standing over her, pursing her lips, with Lily looking on from the doorway. "What do you think you are doing, Émilienne? Hiding?"

With a shrug, Émilienne reaches for her robe and slips it on as she rises.

Liane turns to Lily. "Bring some tea."

As Lily departs, closing the door behind her, Émilienne strolls to a chair near the windows and sits. She looks up. "Are you my nursemaid now?"

Liane comes to her and drops a folded journal into her lap—*Le Gaulois*. "I thought you might like to read this here, in private." She places her hand on Émilienne's shoulder. "And before someone else mentions the news."

Émilienne lifts the journal. Strange how she cannot feel the pages with her hands. They are numb. Her eyes seem to blur, then clear, as she looks down at the words and begins to read.

The story is brief and brutal. At the request of the family d'Ange, it seems, on behalf of his family and all of France, the brave young duke, Georges d'Ange, shall lead an important and dangerous mission into the Belgian Congo. The expedition, to carve a commercial passage to Egypt from the Congo, leaves immediately from Marseilles.

A list of names of other adventurous young men joining the expedition is provided. A few of the Princelings are named, she sees—this is the duchess hiding the young men until the news dies down, she is certain. Blinking back tears, she tosses the journal onto the floor while her thoughts spin.

Liane sits across from her.

"The journal is dated last week." Liane's voice turns soft, filled with pity.

She lifts her chin. Ah, how she hates such pity.

"They are probably there already."

The room is silent as Émilienne rises, walks to the bed. Lying down, she closes her eyes. When she opens them again much later, Liane is gone.

CHAPTER THIRTEEN

PARIS, 1890

A letter arrives from Georges a few days later. Lily brings it on the tray, along with her tea and British scones, which Lily appears to think she will eat. She sets it down on a table beside her favorite chair. When she is gone, Émilienne sits down, opens the letter, and reads.

> *My darling, sweet Mimi, I long for you. A family interest forces me to lead an expedition into the Congo.*

She closes her eyes for a moment. Georges is vague, and his maman, so shrewd.

> *I have no choice, my darling. The decision is made by the family council. And, of course, Maman insists I must lead as head of the family. This should not take long. We are off tomorrow, my love.*
>
> *We shall begin our work at Stanley Falls, moving*

*from there through the jungle, northeast toward Egypt.
You must not worry, Mimi. We shall be together again
in weeks. Some of my old friends came along on a lark as
well. We are stocked with every essential food known to
man, including several cases of good champagne.*

*I must go. Here! I have kissed the spot in which I
shall sign my name. The kiss and all my love is yours.*

Forever, your Georges

He had no choice, he writes.

She clucks her tongue, hitting the arm of the chair with her
fist. Does the Duc d'Ange not understand his power? He is the
one who should make decisions, not old men sitting around a
table. Not his maman!

She closes her eyes, takes a deep breath. She makes her own
decisions, why not Georges? If she had left decisions to her own
maman, she would be doomed to scrub floors and launder other
people's clothes and die an early death.

She stares at the spot, the invisible kiss on the letter, and
flings her hand around the back of her neck, squeezing the
muscles there. Suddenly she feels sick. He is truly gone. Her
Georges is really in Africa.

Setting the letter down on the tray, she looks off. Stan-
ley Falls . . . she has never heard of the place. Struggling to see
Georges and his men hacking their way through the Congo,
her imagination fails. She has only ever seen Georges and his
friends at play.

A well of sorrow, of something tender lost and utter hope-
lessness, opens inside Émilienne. This time, she understands.
Standing up, she walks to the window and opens the shutters,
letting in the faint, hard light, then looks out, realizing that this
time there is nothing she can do. There is no way to bring him

back—neither jealousy nor temptation, nor pleading will do. It is a matter of time.

Perhaps the duchess, at last, has succeeded in parting the lovers.

She has never felt so lonely.

Lying down on the bed, she longs for escape, for nothing but sleep. To sleep, to slip into dreams and forget the letter she just read. How she misses Georges. Still, she must smile, be gay tonight and tomorrow night and the next. The audience pays to see her perform, to see her smiles—that is one price of success.

Swinging her feet to the floor, she rings for Lily.

"I must leave soon for the theater." Her voice moves up a notch. "Help me dress, please." With a glance at the gloom outside, she thinks she must lift her spirits. "I want to wear something bright and cheerful," she says to Lily. "Perhaps that new dress I bought last week. The green one? Yes, that will do."

"Émmy?"

Already she has reached the dressing table, and she turns at Lily's voice. "Come. Help with my hair." False cheer, even just a smile, can turn a mood from black to . . . pink, if not a happy red.

Lily moves behind her, working the comb through the tangled curls. Suddenly, she bursts into tears. "It is just . . . oh . . . poor you. Poor Georges!"

Émilienne turns around, taking the comb from her hand. She sets it down, holding out her hands. Lily sinks into her embrace. "We shall manage, Lily. He will soon return." As Lily dries her tears, Émilienne turns back to the mirror. Once fury over the Duc d'Orleans dies down, Georges will return.

Right now she has one reason to smile. Les Ambassadeurs has something special for her, a dance created around Émilienne, choreographed just for her. Dance of the Seabird will carry her in birdlike flight to new heights. In a few days rehearsals begin. Lily says this performance is certain to carry her straight to the Folies Bergère after her next commitment with Menus-Plaisirs is complete.

Won't Georges be impressed with how far she's come. She almost laughs. Even an orchid might not look so bad right now.

She smiles into the mirror at Lily. And why not? Why shouldn't she smile?

※

At the beginning of March, another letter arrives. She finds it on the tray as she's leaving for the theater. Tonight is opening night, and she dances the Seabird dance for the first time in front of an audience. Slipping the letter into her reticule, she waits to open it in the carriage.

My darling, my only love,

How I miss you, long to hold you in my arms. Despite the heat, I feel cold here without you. Save all your warmth for my return, Mimi.

Some bad news. Julien has got dysentery. I am worried we will all catch the disease. He seems to get worse every day.

More bad news, of less importance . . . we lost the champagne last week, every bottle, broke on the rocks. Rain swells the river, and the current runs fast. The sweltering heat, mosquitoes, and snakes are bad enough. Now even worse with the champagne gone, our last connection to the real world too. Drink a bottle for me, darling.

We could all use that drink right now. Such a scramble we are all in down here. The French, Germans,

Belgians, the British, everyone claiming rights to the Congo. Sometimes I wonder why we are here.

No time to write more just now. I send this missive with all my love.

Your Georges

Dysentery. Émilienne closes her eyes, takes a deep breath, bows her head, and prays. *Please, please, keep him safe. Let him come home to me.*

She folds the letter with care, placing it in her lap. She stares through the window as Paris goes by, struggling to see Georges's face. Struggling to recall every detail of his beautiful face. Each feature comes clear on its own, but when she reaches for the whole image, his face does not appear. Perhaps, already, she is losing him. Minutes pass before she rises above the fear. But she must because what powers dark thoughts bring.

Liane is right. She must put the unending worries aside—focus on the good. Come what may. She presses the letter to her heart. *Soon Georges will come home.*

Nothing warms Émilienne more, and calms her mind, than the moment she walks into her dressing room with Lily. The two girls stop in the doorway, staring at flowers already overflowing the large space before the show even starts—her favorites, roses, gardenias, lilies. Les Ambassadeurs has spread the word about the new dance, the Seabird.

Émilienne stands, pulls off her gloves one finger at a time, and hands them to Lily. "Lovely," she says. "But too many." She lifts her nose, sniffing. "The gardenias overwhelm the room."

"When I go down, call someone to take half of these down

to Minette." She has grown fond of the girl. Minette has come to every rehearsal, studying Émilienne's every move. She will love them.

"Now, come help me with this costume." She walks behind the dressing screen. "And remove the cards from the flowers, Lily. Leave them here so I shall know who sent which bouquets."

Lily chuckles, coming around to assist Émilienne into her costume. For this dance, she wears a white, long-sleeve maillot with gray-and-silver stripes to her wrists, light gray tights, a flowing silver tutu made of silk that sits just below her calves, and ballet slippers. Downstairs, the music signals the start of an act—her performance is next. The last show this evening highlights the star.

"How do I look?" she asks Lily when the suit is on.

Lily takes two steps back. "Lovely. With the special lights reflecting the colors, especially the silver, you will work magic."

Émilienne moves to the chevet mirror, inspecting the costume. "Good," she pronounces. With a mischievous smile she turns back to Lily, thinking of the young society girls in the audience, each hiding every inch of skin before her marriage—even their ankles, even the undersides of their wrists. "This will do."

Sitting down, she holds out her foot, one and then the other, while Lily slips on the dancing slippers and ties the satin ribbons. After, Émilienne sits down at the dressing table.

Downstairs the audience cheers.

"We are late. Come help me, Lily!" Émilienne reaches for the cream she works into her skin, protection against the heavy makeup used onstage, while Lily opens the box of mineral greasepaint colors. Blotting excess oil from her skin, Émilienne searches the box, picking out her spectrum of shades, the ones she uses onstage—a stick of Leichner No. 2 for the base. This color—a light pink—she has found, is soft and easy to spread, and it is close to the color of her natural complexion. She chooses rose for her cheeks, with a dab on her chin for the bright lights. Lily lays before her a row of small sticks of paint. These, for shadows and light. Then Émilienne dusts her face with powder while the final chords of the act rise from below.

Leaning forward, Émilienne slicks Carmine No. 1 on her lips, a deep, dark rose. With quick precision she finishes, slicking white paint over her eyelids, lining her eyes and brows, and adding the wet mascara. Downstairs the music stops—the sound of applause begins.

"Quick. Your hair!" Lily stands behind her with combs and brushes. "We must hurry, Émmy."

"They can wait. Before the hair, I need my dots."

Lily steps back, watching as she adds a red dot at the corner of each eye for the dreary wash the footlights create. "Now."

Émilienne sits back with a final sigh. There will be no pompadour for this show. Her hair swings free onstage with the movements of the dance. Below, for a minute comes silence before loud applause again—curtain calls. And then the voices rise into a chant. She looks up for an instant, listening, then lifts her brows to Lily in the mirror. Already they chant her name— *Émilienne! Émilienne!*

"Oh, we must not forget the bracelets." Pulling a jewel box toward her, Émilienne lifts two diamond bracelets, each an inch thick—gifts received only a week ago from King Leopold of Belgium. She has not met him yet, though it's only a matter of time. She hesitates for an instant, wondering if this king also sends men to die in the Congo. But it was Georges's maman who sent Georges to the Congo, not this admirer.

The thought flies away as Lily locks the bracelets on, and Émilienne lifts her hands, admiring them. The diamonds will glitter as the seabird soars in her dance, sparkling as sunlight on water.

With the audience growing louder, Émilienne takes a deep breath and stands—just in time. Below the piano strikes a note, and the music begins.

With Lily close behind, she hurries down the stairs. Winding through the backstage workers and lights and fans that create the ocean's breeze, she finds her mark at center stage in the circle of light. The opening melody begins, soft, sensuous, and now she poses motionless, torso twisting toward stage front, arms high and winged behind her. Closing her eyes, she imagines . . . she feels . . . the soaring gull over the waters off Deauville beach.

This moment of peace, for Émilienne, brings a feeling of freedom as the music swells. For the first time since Georges left, she feels pure joy, preparing for flight.

The curtains part, revealing the white bird caught in light— glittering, gleaming in stillness—and the audience gasps at the beauty of the moment, this glimpse of perfection before dancing begins. In turn Émilienne breathes in their love, the adoration that feeds her, helps her heal. In this instant, Émilienne and her audience are one. The white bird smiles just before she spins into the dance.

Now she lifts, flying on the music, breathing in the salty air. She loves the wind and cold, the ocean spray as she spreads her glittering, gauzy wings.

On the other side of the footlights, the audience seems to hold its breath.

Émilienne is no student of formal ballet. Instead, she dances in slippers, unconstrained by rules. The years have shaped her muscles, toned them, turned them hard. She has taught herself to dance, creating illusions, moving on the musical flow. She spins across the stage in almost perfect pirouettes, becoming the music—it is hers. The audience breaks the silence, bursting into applause as she flies through the clouds in leaping jetés, wings spread wide, then bending as the seabird dives through the water and up again.

When at last the music slows, the seabird stops, balancing on her toes, very still, pulled up with torso tight and straight and strong, as if one long line runs straight from her toes through the top of her head. She lifts her leg into arabesque, arms behind poised for flight, her back now arched, head high, holding the pose while the audience is hushed by the sight.

The ephemeral silver bird slowly folds into herself, wings tucked as she settles on the waves below.

In silence such as she has never heard before, the people wait. She owns the stage. A triumphant thrill runs through her, and the audience feels it too—peace, sorrow, and joy, the freedom, the welcome. In this moment, not a sound breaks the spell while the silver light around her fades to dark, and the curtains swing closed.

Then it comes, just for her—the roar, the moment she most loves—calls for Émilienne as the audience stands! The wild applause, the flowers thrown, time after time the curtain calls, until flowers cover the stage and the curtain closes for the last time. Turning, she smiles at Lily waiting offstage. They walk together to her dressing room, sisters now.

The audience loves her, her people love her. Still, they call for Émilienne.

CHAPTER FOURTEEN

Not until mid-March does another letter arrive from Georges.
This one dates back to February 21.

> *Darling Mimi,*
>
> *I am sorry to write we lost Julien. It was the dys-*
> *entery. I'm uncertain if I am catching his disease, but*
> *I don't feel well. I cannot fight the climate. But do not*
> *worry, my love. They say not to worry, that I seem better*
> *than yesterday.*
>
> *Though, if I am not soon better, I shall be forced to*
> *give up and return to Europe a failure. Then we could*
> *be together.*
>
> *What should I hope for, failure while holding you in*
> *my arms? I cannot come back admitting failure, Mimi.*
> *My heart is one thing. I long to hold you. But I am the*
> *Duc d'Ange. As Maman says, my obligations are clear.*
>
> *Oh, to be able to fling my arms around you, Mimi.*

Write to me every day, your letters come slow. Tell me about the new show and everything else. You cannot imagine how lonely one feels out here, especially at night when I close my eyes, thinking of you.

If we cannot make more progress, we may turn back to the Oubangui to explore other rivers. Here the waterway is narrow. We spend all day in the bush tearing at vines that seem to suffocate every living thing. Vines, mosquitoes, snakes. I can't think which is worse. I think you might have trouble recognizing me, my darling. Even in Brazzaville they tell me I have changed.

I think of you every night, Mimi. I think of the curve of your lips, the color of your eyes, your golden hair spread across the pillows. Please send a letter soon.

This one comes with all my love.

Your Georges

❦

Émilienne sits before the mirror backstage, dressed, waiting for the music cue. Behind her, Lily works to slip on the tight maillot worn under the tutu. For the past week, since the Seabird dance, she has felt almost suffocated in the costume. Quite uncomfortable, even though it was designed and sewn just for her only a month ago. As Lily moves away to find the tutu, Émilienne spans her hands around the waist, moving them down, over her belly.

For an instant her mind turns blank, and then again she slides her hands down, turning side to side in the mirror. Lifting her eyes to her breasts—almost visible beneath the maillot as tight as skin—she cups them, feeling a new fullness there. Closing her eyes, she lets out her breath, suddenly putting it all together. What a fool she is!

This is the middle of March. Of course. Georges left a little over three months ago. A baby grows inside.

Her lips curl up at the corners, a slight smile with this thought. Georges's baby grows inside—her boy. She is certain the babe is a boy, the next Duc d'Ange. When she opens her eyes, gazing into the mirror, she spots Lily standing behind her with the rest of the costume. Their eyes meet.

Émilienne sits down, elbows on the dressing table, leaning forward, her face resting in her hands while Lily grips her shoulders. Below, the announcer's voice comes loud and clear—act one is ending now. She is number four.

"Émmy! Are you all right?"

"Yes, yes." Rising, she grips the back of her chair. "I am fine, just fine. Hand me the tutu, Lily, or I shall be forced to greet the audience half dressed."

She must gather her thoughts.

Slowly, she turns back to the mirror, stroking the spot where the babe lies. It occurs to her—surely Georges will come home when she writes the news. They shall marry before the baby shows. The future has changed in a wink. She holds Georges's child, and her own.

Lily touches her shoulder. With a start, she clears her head. Turning, she smiles now, hugging the young girl in a flood of joy.

She is now a maman.

What will he do the moment he learns? What will his first thought be?

Right away he must return, find a larger home for his family. And she must find a good *nounou* to take care of the child.

The moment she returns to the apartment that night, she clears her dressing table, places a pen, a well of ink, and her best vellum on top. Then she sits down to write the letter to Georges that she has been composing in her mind for hours. She hadn't known how to respond to his last letter to cheer him. The news of her success with the Seabird dance will bring a brief joy, but this, the coming babe, will carry him home. She smiles as she writes, picturing Georges reading the joyful news.

※

Weeks pass. Already the end of March and no correspondence arrives from Georges. Perhaps he is still ill?

No, she will not think of that.

Every day since the discovery, she has sent a letter. Surely, by now he has received at least one joyful note about the babe. It is likely his letter is on the way with news about his return.

When one arrives, Lily will tell her so. But already Émilienne feels the baby's weight. How much longer can she hide the secret?

Reaching home late one Tuesday night in April, after her show and dinner with Caroline and her gentleman friend, Émilienne finds Liane waiting, sitting alone in the bedroom. She stops in the doorway with Lily right behind, gripping the doorframe, eyes locked on her friend.

Two o'clock in the morning. *What is Liane doing here?*

But already she knows. Of course, she knows. She closes her eyes. Even as she asks the question aloud, she reads the answer on Liane's face.

Georges is gone.

Shaking, she moves into the room, then she sways, and Lily catches her just before she falls. Liane takes one arm and Lily the other, and together they steer her toward the bed. The same bed in which the babe was conceived.

Everything's gone wrong.

Lying down, head on pillows, she looks up at Liane, then

turns her eyes to Lily. She cannot speak. She rests her hands over the babe, covering his ears, willing Lily and Liane to go, to disappear.

"It was in the newspapers today, Émmy." Liane's voice speaks from far away.

She squeezes her eyes closed, waiting. "All right. Hurry. Tell me now."

Liane's voice is quiet. "He died two weeks ago, the newspaper says." She holds onto Émilienne's hand. After a beat she goes on. "It says he died at nine twenty in the morning on that day, in a place called Kabinda." Then she says, "The family is arranging transport back to France, but it could take months."

Her first thought is that Georges never answered her letters telling him of the babe.

Her second thought—what was she doing that day, at the moment he died? Was she out that evening with an adoring gentleman while Georges lay cold? She has lain with no one else since Georges left. Nothing but mere flirting. But still, her mind goes dark, her head hurts at this thought. There are no words for the pain.

Beside her Liane strokes her forehead. Lily goes off for tea. She takes a deep breath. "I am carrying his child, Liane."

Liane's hand stops for a second. "Are you certain?"

"Yes. I wrote him the news and have not heard from him since." Her voice cracks. "It has been a while since I received a letter."

Lily arrives just then, and they fall into silence. After she places the tea on a table and leaves, Liane climbs into bed with Émilienne. She rolls into Liane's soft arms, resting her head on Liane's shoulder.

"I will help," Liane whispers. "You are not alone, you know."

Émilienne swallows her tears, nodding. Did Georges even receive her letters about the babe?

Tears slip down her cheeks. The child she and Georges made together still lives. If he comes a boy—surely, he shall be a boy— she will name him Georges. But will the duchess ever hear? The thought sends chills down her spine. The woman is powerful, capable of any evil, she thinks.

"I will be all right, Liane."

Minutes pass, then Liane speaks. "Neither you nor I know anything about babies." After a beat, she adds, "There are ways, you know."

"No!" She looks up at Liane, her tone fierce. "He is mine, mine and Georges's. I will raise him. Protect him. Why, already I love him."

"And if it is a girl?"

"I will love her just the same."

"But how will you live until you are able to dance again?" Liane whispers.

"I will not stop until I must, until the babe shows." She shakes her head, as in a fog. "When I cannot work, I suppose I could sell some of the jewels Georges gave me. I imagine they are worth a fortune. And this apartment is mine, that is a comfort." She looks off. "He would surely want this for his child."

Sell some of her jewels. That will get her through the time, until she can dance again after the babe is born. The idea delights her—she has a plan. As hours pass and her tears dry, leaning against Liane, at last she falls asleep.

A few weeks later, Émilienne sits in a corner of the bedroom, reading, when a loud noise downstairs startles her. Again, it comes, and again and again, and she looks up, frowning. Someone is banging on the entrance door downstairs.

As she closes the book, she hears Lily storming up the stairs while calling for Anson, the new butler and guard. *What is going on!*

Rising, she drops the book on the chair and starts for the bedroom door just as Lily bursts into the room, gasping for breath.

"What is all the noise?"

Holding her hand over her heart, Lily sucks in a deep breath while Émilienne waits.

"There are three gentlemen downstairs who say they must see you. Immediately. I could not keep them out, they pushed their way through the doors." She pats her chest. "I tried to keep them out, Émmy."

Lily drops onto the chair before the dressing table, still breathing hard, looking at Émilienne. "They wait in the salon. They must talk to you at once—"

"Merde! Who are they?"

Lily shakes her head. "I don't know. I believe they said they've come from a bank." Standing up, she looks about. "Where is your robe, Émmy? You had best get downstairs."

With a sigh, Émilienne says, "Tell them I shall be down shortly. They must wait."

As Lily moves from the dressing table, Émilienne takes her place, waving her off. "Lily, go . . . go! I will come down soon." Without another word, Lily leaves, closing the door behind her.

Picking up her comb, Émilienne arranges her hair. A bit of lip paint, a touch of powder. Looking at her reflection, she sees fear. *It only Georges were here. He would know just what to do.*

When she appears under the high arch leading into the downstairs salon, the men look up. They do not stand. Three there are, wearing top hats, frock coats, and vests. Each one studies her as if Émilienne is the household help.

Across the room, behind them, Anson scowls. He stands with his arms crossed, feet apart, and watching the men, ready at any moment for a street fight.

With a nod to him, she strolls into the room and takes a chair across from the men, arranging her skirts. When she looks up, they face her in silence, without moving, a wall of black and gray. She lifts her eyes to their top hats—first, second, third— waiting until, one by one, each removes his hat.

She gives them a furious look. "What is the meaning of this intrusion?"

The first answers.

"We come on behalf of the Duchess d'Ange, mademoiselle, and at the behest of lawyers of the estate and interests of the Duc d'Ange, deceased. We represent Banque Paris."

Hearing these words aloud silences her at once. Her mouth turns dry, thoughts scramble, her tongue will not move. She waits for more.

The banker glances about, then back at her. "This apartment . . . being a portion of the late young duke's estate . . ."

Fury rises. She holds up her hand, and the man stops midsentence. "This is my home, gentlemen. This apartment is neither property of the Duc d'Ange nor his maman, the Duchess d'Ange." Rising now, arms at her sides, she glares down at the little group. "I demand you leave my home at once."

The other two men turn to the first.

The banker peers over his glasses. "I am afraid you are mistaken. It is you who must leave. The name of the late Duc d'Ange is on the deed of this property, now property of his estate, which the family claims."

This cannot be.

"The young duke's estate and the family council have engaged our assistance. It is of their opinion that he died a broken man, having spent his fortune on such *folies*." He settles the glasses up high on his nose. "You must prepare to leave at once, taking only your clothing and nothing more."

"How dare you!"

The banker begins to read. "Please, listen to the edict," he says, holding up a piece of paper stamped with a gold seal. "With reference to the property located at . . . acknowledged by this court as property of Georges, Duc d'Ange, and now of his estate . . . forthwith Émilienne André—known as Émilienne d'Alençon—and her retinue are hereby ordered to vacate the premises of the property immediately."

Waving the paper, he looks up. "You may take your clothes and personal items, but nothing more when you leave. You must vacate the premises before we lock the doors at five o'clock this evening."

"The duchess does not own this place."

"Mademoiselle. Did you hear the edict I just read?" With a glance at his companions, he continues. "This is an order issued by the court. Do you understand?"

"But . . ."

Pulling off the glasses, he storms toward her, shoving a thick stack of papers into her hands. "Read these, if you please, or hire your own lawyer. But meanwhile, you are ordered to vacate the premises at once." He looks down at her. "My girl, it is the edict what counts at the moment."

Stepping back, holding on to his lapels, he stares at her. "You shall find the deed to this property on top, right there." She glances down.

"As it states here," his finger touches the page, "under the law as it stands, this property belongs to the duke's estate."

Struck dumb, she stares at the deed in her hands.

Georges lied. He let her believe the apartment was hers, her own.

He clears his throat. "Now, mademoiselle! You may leave on your own, or—"

She lifts her eyes. "I shall not."

". . . Or we shall assist you and your maid in that effort, in which case you shall be called before the courts to explain your reluctance to obey the law. And, furthermore, in such case, you shall both forfeit rights to all personal belongings left on the premises." A cold smile appears on his face. "Of course, in such an event the bank will not be responsible for damages, you understand."

When she does not speak, he moves close. "Do you have an attorney, mademoiselle?"

She shakes her head.

"As I thought, they are expensive. And you have no case either way. You may take this up with the d'Ange family lawyers, of course. But only after you have gone. Representing the family and the bank, we have work to do here today."

Lily appears beside her, then. Resting her hand on Émilienne's arm, a gentle touch, she lowers her voice. "Come, Émmy. For now, let us pack and leave. Perhaps later you . . . we . . . shall settle this in the courts."

Émilienne spreads her hands over the blooming belly for comfort. The banker's eyes drop, and when he looks up, she sees he understands. The secret is no longer her own.

Lily turns her toward the archway, leading her through the entrance hall toward the stairs.

If she attempts to speak, she will weep. So, she lifts her chin instead. Never will she weep before these men.

As her foot touches the first step, she hears one of the bankers behind her moving toward the entrance. She stops and turns, staring at a mass of men waiting just outside, workmen wearing dirty shirts and pants and boots, wearing caps and bandannas on their heads. Some in wooden shoes, like the ones she used to wear. Those will scratch the floors.

Lily walks beside her up the stairs. "You must remain calm," Lily whispers. "For yourself and me. For the babe."

Hurrying now, with Lily right behind, she rushes to the armoire. Opening the doors, she puts her finger to her lips. The workmen remain downstairs, talking to the bankers.

Pushing aside the hanging dresses, she reaches back, feeling for the safe. With another glance at the door, she pulls it toward her, turns the dials, and lifts the lid, reaching for the jewels Georges left, gifts he gave to her.

The sound of footsteps comes on the stairs.

"Lily, quick!" Reaching into the box, she lifts the jewels from the safe and hands them to the girl. "Hurry. To the bed." She pulls a dress off the hanger.

Lily places the bundle of jewels on the bed, and Émilienne covers it with the dress just as someone knocks on the bedroom door.

"Mademoiselle d'Alençon?" The voice calls, and before she can answer the third banker pushes into the bedroom, stopping just inside. In his hand, one of her empty trunks. His eyes skim the bed, the room.

Seeming satisfied, he sets down the trunk. "There is another one left in the hallway. You may use both. And"—he clears his throat and coughs—"let me know if you need more."

"We shall need two more," Lily says while Émilienne stands mute.

He nods, watching Émilienne. "I will have a workman bring them in. Ah . . . this is a pity, mademoiselle. But I am told to wait here while you pack." He disappears then, calling to a workman from below. Moments later, the workman drags a second

trunk and third inside. When he has gone, the banker falls into
the chair near the windows, looking out.

Lily carries dresses from the armoire, laying them flat inside
the first trunk. With a glance at the banker gazing over the balcony, Émilienne secures the jewels under the dresses while Lily
brings more.

With a sigh, she turns to Lily. "Bring your belongings, too,
Lily. We shall pack together." Looking about, her eyes light on
the dressing table. "There, we must not forget those things. And
my hats, shoes, everything in the dressing room."

Hours later, when her stomach grumbles and the trunks are
packed and locked, Émilienne pockets the keys. "Find Anson,
Lily. He must come with us. He shall drive."

Lily nods and disappears.

Turning to the banker now watching them, she says in her
most curt tone, "We are ready. Have your workmen bring down
the trunks. My carriage shall wait across the street."

"Taking the carriage, are you?"

Émilienne glares. "The carriage is mine."

For an instant he hesitates, then, nodding, he follows her
down the stairs.

Émilienne moves toward the entrance door. But suddenly,
she stops and turns. "What of the cook and the kitchen girls!"

"Already gone," the banker says from behind.

She swallows the tears.

Georges betrayed her. *Did he ever love her at all?*

Just then Lily comes through the front door. Moving to
Émilienne's side, she whispers, "We are ready. But where shall
we go?"

"To Liane." Moving toward the door, she stumbles. Lily
takes her arm. "Already three o'clock," she murmurs. "Let us
hope Liane is home. We have nowhere else to stay." Turning,

she gazes around for one last look. This is the only place she has ever felt at home. She blinks back tears. Now it is gone, along with Georges.

She takes Lily's hand in hers and squeezes it. "We will start again. We will survive. I have had plenty of practice surviving, after all."

CHAPTER FIFTEEN

PARIS, 1891

Liane's apartment, given to her by a titled lover years ago, is small but elegant. Marble floors and lovely woven carpets on the ground floor, with silk-covered walls and high ceilings. Émilienne especially loves the comfortable salon, with a fireplace and windows lining the street.

On this February morning, she sits by the fire in Liane's salon holding Elisa, her daughter, almost six months since birth last September. Émilienne's eyes are fixed on the beautiful child—the shape of her delicate skull covered with the light blond baby fuzz. Some of her features mirror Georges's, but she has her maman's long lashes and heart-shaped lips and a pale pink complexion with blushed cheeks.

She had thought she was carrying a son. How could she not have known that Elisa waited inside! She loves the musical name she heard one night, standing outside the Folies Bergère, dreaming—even before the time of the rabbits. Smiling at the memory of that night, she wraps a corner of the pink blanket around the babe, cradling the child in her arms. Outside, wind whips the rain while the fire keeps them warm.

"There you are!" Liane saunters into the room and sinks into a chair across from her. "Madam Serruier has come. The other wet nurse has just left." She smiles across at Elisa, snuggling against her maman. "She's upstairs, says she shall come down for the child in a moment."

A warm feeling flows through Émilienne when she holds her babe. "I hate giving her up ever, even for an hour."

"But you must," Liane says with a little laugh. "She is hungry. And we must find someone to care for her when you start dancing again as well."

"Yes, it's time."

At the sound of footsteps, the two women look up. "I have come for her," the woman says, crossing the room to Émilienne. She lifts Elisa from her maman's arms, and a smile crosses her face.

"Such a lovely girl." With a glance at Émilienne, she adds, "She will be beautiful, like her maman."

Émilienne watches her leave, then turns to Liane. "Yes, I think it's past time I return to the dance, my friend. I have sold some of the jewels Georges gave me, but . . ."

"The tiara?"

"No, not that." Liane gives a wry smile, and Émilienne looks off. "I shall sell it soon enough though. You are kind, Liane. But we need a spot of our own, Elisa and me."

Liane shrugs. "You are welcome here as long as you care to stay, you know."

A bell rings from the entrance as she speaks. Liane looks around, then pulls a cigarette from a silver box nearby. "Lucette will answer the door." She holds up the cigarette. "Would you like a puff?"

Émilienne shakes her head, thinking of Charles Desteuque and his rules. "Thanks, but no. I need *Gil Blas* more than ever now. Don't want to get in the habit."

"How is Charles? I haven't seen him in over a year."

Émilienne shrugs. "He's found another girl to turn into a star, I suppose."

With a laugh, Liane closes the box. "True. He won't stop until he is in the grave."

A maid appears at the door. Liane turns her head. "What is it, Lucette?"

"A visitor for mademoiselle," she says.

"Gentleman or lady?"

"A lady," she says, with a glance at Émilienne. "She waits in the carriage. Her man presented the card."

Liane turns to Émilienne. "Are you expecting someone?"

"No." The maid walks to her, not Liane, handing Émilienne the card. As the girl departs, Émilienne looks down and blanches.

"Who is it, Émmy?" Liane's voice sings out.

"How did she find me?"

"Who?" Liane's eyes grow wide.

Émilienne looks up. "The Duchess d'Ange has arrived."

Georges's maman. Before thinking, she rises, and Liane stands, too, holding up her hand. "No!" Liane's voice is stern.

Émilienne stops.

"Do not go to the door. I shall send Lucette." She glares at Émilienne. "Sit down. Make her come to you." As she speaks, she rings the maid's bell.

A few minutes later, a tall, haughty woman leaning on a cane appears under the arched door from the hallway, with Lucette trailing behind.

Impulse moves Émilienne to stand, but instead she leans

back, staring at the woman who sent her son to death in Africa, the woman who took her lover and her home. As the duchess enters the room, she understands—Georges's maman has nothing left to take, except Elisa.

The duchess has come for the child.

Barely breathing, Émilienne waits in silence, watching the duchess move to the chair across from her. "Mademoiselle d'Alençon?" As she speaks, she removes her gloves.

Émilienne nods.

"I have come for my granddaughter," she says, as if asking for a cup of tea. When she gazes at Émilienne now, her eyes are hard and cold. "I shall get right to the point. What is your price?"

"My price?" She lifts her hands, cupping her face as if to steady her thoughts.

The duchess taps her cane on the floor. "Don't act the fool."

"How did you know?"

The royal smile is thin, cruel. "I already knew from your letters, you simple girl."

She stares, shocked. "My letters . . . to Georges?"

"Of course, I read them all." Dropping the gloves on her lap and sitting back, she seems to study Émilienne. "After you mentioned the news of a baby, I stopped sending them on to my son."

Émilienne lets out a cry. "Georges was mine too. He loved me. Elisa is borne of him."

"Nonsense." She leans slightly forward, meeting Émilienne's eyes. "Listen to me, girl. I have come to take my grandchild home." Each word from her mouth comes crisp and sharp, cutting through to Emlienne, as loud as the sounding of bells from Sacré-Cœur on the summit of Montmartre.

She looks off. Georges never even knew!

"Mademoiselle?"

Émilienne gathers her thoughts, her courage. Turning her eyes to the duchess, she thinks she has never hated anyone before as she hates this woman. "Never!" Her voice lifts a key. "Elisa is *my* child."

"Then," in a different tone, a softer tone, the duchess says, "if you love the child, mademoiselle, you must think first of her. Think who she is, think of the life her father's family will provide."

Émilienne grips her hands in her lap, silent. Still stunned.

"You may think you can manage with a child in the moment. But how many years have you left on the stage?" She flutters her hand. "Beauty, youth, those are fleeting times in a woman's life. In a few more years, when those gifts are gone, who shall care for Elisa then?"

Émilienne's throat closes so she cannot speak. Oh, how she despises this woman. And how she loves Elisa. She cannot think with windstorms crossing her mind.

"With her royal family, the girl shall hold her place in the world. We shall provide everything she needs to rise in life, to succeed. With us, she shall be safe. Secure. Loved. Happy. She will have the best education, good health, tutors. She shall have anything she desires, and she will make a good marriage. With me, with the family, Elisa is d'Ange."

Émilienne's heart races as she gathers her thoughts. "You took my home. You tore us apart, Georges and me. You stole away Elisa's father." Slowly, she rises, looking down at the woman. "But you shall never have my girl. Leave! Get out! Leave me, now."

"Selfish!" The duchess pushes up, leaning on her cane. "Would you have your child living your own life, no better than a prostitute?" She takes a step closer. "Give the babe a chance in life. Name your price."

"Get out!" Émilienne screams. "Get out!"

Lily appears in the doorway, then Liane.

The duchess holds Émilienne's eyes. "Think of what is best for the child rather than yourself. We, her family, can provide any want, any need. Think of the babe . . . if you truly love her."

Before Émilienne can speak again, the woman turns, striding toward the door, cane tapping as she moves along. Émilienne follows. Lily comes toward her, taking her arm. Ahead, the duchess gives Liane a nod as she passes. At the entrance hall, her valet awaits. There, she stops, turning back, peering again at Émilienne.

"I shall return tomorrow for your answer. But if you do not come to your senses soon, my lawyer shall begin the proceedings. Then we shall let the courts decide." With a cruel smile, she adds, "If we go to court, all Paris will talk of this. The story will brand the child forever as the daughter of a woman who sells herself to the high bidder."

Émilienne feels the angry flush as she lifts her chin, glaring at the duchess. Before she can say a word, Georges's maman turns about and, with her valet, disappears.

Standing beside Liane and Lily, Émilienne's head spins, hearing the threat over and over in her mind. Elisa could be branded a prostitute if the duchess takes her to court. Worse, she understands—the duchess speaks the truth. Émilienne sinks to the floor.

The duchess comes again on the next afternoon, at the same time, with the same offer of money, enough to soften most blows in a dancer's life.

Émilienne fought with herself all night. She no longer weeps for Georges—he betrayed her. But she cannot give up her babe, the child of her heart.

After the duchess leaves, she falls into a chair, staring into the darkness. Again she refused to give up Elisa. But her heart knows something more. As much as she fights against it, she must think of Elisa, not of her own desires. Who can know what the future holds for a girl like her, depending on youth and beauty to survive—the duchess is not wrong. Her own life moves forward one day at a time. Why, she has been absent from the stage for months and months, and already she worries her starlight fades as other girls take her place onstage.

It was only luck that Elisa was not born on the streets—heavy with child as Émilienne was, with no place to live after losing her home. She shall return to the stage soon enough, and she shall win her place in the stars again. But a few years from now? What will happen then?

These are thoughts she has never allowed to darken her dreams.

Elisa deserves the best in life. Still, the worst question remains.

Prostitute or princess? Maman must choose.

On the next day, again the duchess returns. Again Émilienne says no.

But this time, when the old woman leaves, Émilienne knows. She knows what is right. She must set aside her own feelings, all the hatred, and do what she must for the babe.

That night, she holds on to Elisa, holding her close, dreading the morning light. She memorizes Elisa's sweet face, her rosebud lips—yes, like Maman's!—and her father's eyes. She listens to the babe's soft breathing. She weeps with Elisa's small head tucked under her chin.

The next morning when the duchess arrives, Émilienne

carries Elisa down the stairs in a soft blanket, holding her tears. In the entry hall, she hands her to Liane with not one look toward the Duchess d'Ange. Then she turns and makes her way upstairs without a backward glance. In the bedroom, hearing her child's cries, she turns her face into the pillow and sobs. Life is over. She will never last this day. She shall die from a broken heart.

In her mind she follows the sounds downstairs—the duchess's voice and then Liane's. She almost hears her babe breathing. When the door closes at last, and the carriage pulls away with her child, she stares at the ceiling for hours, imagining where her babe is at the moment. She tells herself that Elisa shall have the best life as a girl of d'Ange. No *Grande Horizontale* for her girl.

She is no longer the daughter of a girl from the butte Montmartre, a dancer named for a fragile piece of lace.

On this day, something hardens inside Émilienne's heart.

Part Two

CHAPTER SIXTEEN

This September evening is a special night—Elisa's birthday. Thirteen years have passed since Elisa was taken. Tonight, Émilienne dances the Seabird for her girl, the child she will never know. Gas lamps shine through fog at the entrance to the Folies Bergère on this fall evening as she arrives, spreading her golden glow over the streets.

The Folies Bergère! How long she dreamed of dancing here before that first offer years ago. She and Liane have both taken turns as lead dancers on this stage since then, until now.

Liane no longer dances. Matrimony has finally changed the order of things for her. As Princess Ghica of Romania, she sets her sights on things she believes are more important than dancing, like writing poems and stories. She has plenty of inspiration after all. And she still has her gentlemen in Paris too.

Monsieur le Directeur insisted on an encore of the Seabird dance in Émilienne's last contract—one of her most famous performances. She would have had it otherwise, as this dance is special. She thinks of it as her girl's dance, Elisa's dance. She has refused to dance it since Elisa was taken away by the duchess.

But the coincidence of the opening of the show on her girl's birthday changed her mind. Although each movement in this dance takes on grief greater than despair, for Émilienne, it now also celebrates Elisa's other life, a better life. Perhaps it will bring her closer to her child while she's dancing. This is a dance of truth as well as of longing and sorrow.

But even this dance does not banish the pain. She will never be more to Elisa than, perhaps, at most, a ghost from the past. Still, dancing the Seabird for the second time, and for the Folies no less, will create a legacy of sorts for her daughter, even if never understood.

Émilienne closes her eyes for a moment as the carriage rolls through the streets toward the Folies theater. She was so young back then, so fragile after the babe's birth. Coming back from a long absence was hard, so hard. Slowly, slowly, after Elisa was taken, she fought her way back as Émilienne. Menus-Plaisirs, Les Ambassadeurs, Moulin Rouge, the new Olympia, and dancing throughout all Europe.

Until at last the Folies called. At last, and she was quick to rise. But it was Émilienne au Bal des Quat'z'Arts that made her the Folies star. For the first time ever, a courtesan's name graced the name of the ball. At the first performance, together, the press seemed to speak as one, announcing her "brilliant success," such success that she filled the Folies theater after that for months.

But tonight is different. Performing the Seabird dance tonight will make her name once and for all, she is certain. And she is determined that no one will ever forget. She pushes back the tears and the memory of all that has occurred. As the carriage slows before the theater, she takes a long, deep breath.

She must always look ahead.

"Anson!" Leaning forward, Émilienne calls to him as they reach the front entrance. "I shall get out here rather than at the stage door."

Lily helps her off with her fur, another gift from Wilhelm—Kaiser Wilhelm II of Germany. The man is difficult, possibly mad. But his gifts are some of the finest.

As the doorman comes to help her out of the carriage, she looks back up at Lily. "I shall come to the dressing room within the hour, Lily. See that my costume is ready, please." She turns a bright smile on the girl. "And if any orchids should arrive . . ."

"Yes, I know." Lily lets out a little laugh. "I shall send them on to the new girls."

"I won't have much time, a half hour at most for costume and the makeup. We shall have to hurry." As she turns, she spots her new posters at the entrance doors. She stops as the thought strikes—Émilienne André stands here gazing at pictures of herself hanging at the entrance to the Folies Bergère! Memories come, long ago nights when she wandered down the rue Richer just to see the posters at the Folies door, the new acts, the famous dancers. She was a young girl dreaming one day she would see her own posters here.

And now she owns the Folies stage. A thrill runs through her. She would throw back her head and laugh with joy if she were alone.

Instead, she lifts her chin, flattens her shoulders, pulls up her torso, nodding to the doorman as she walks inside. As she vowed years ago after Georges died and Elisa was gone, she has survived.

Now, all of Europe calls for Émilienne.

On this evening, Étienne Balsan awaits her in the theater's grand foyer for a glass of champagne before her show. After tonight's performance, she shall meet him for dinner at Maxim's.

This wealthy gentleman has followed her performances of late, sending flowers and small gifts each time. He is a kind man, Liane says, and one of the richest in all of Europe.

As she enters the large hall, two stories high and filled with friends and admirers, Émilienne feels the stir, the change of cadence as she appears. Pausing for an instant just inside the door, she adjusts the fingers of her long gloves while heads turn. Her pale gold dress shimmers in the lights, she knows, enhancing her curves. And, for a change, Lily wove her curls into silken braids wrapped at the nape of her neck—a new style for Paris to contemplate. Now she glides through the parting crowd, feeling the whispers, the surprise.

Suddenly a familiar voice rings out, calling her name. She hesitates, then turns, recognizing Leo's voice. Leopold II, King of the Belgians, former lover, walks toward her, sweeping her with his eyes head to foot. Behind, he leaves two lovely girls.

She grows cold at his approach. She ruined him in their short liaison, the gossips say. But, years after Georges died in that part of the Congo that Belgium now claims, she learned the full extent of evil in the man. Stories of natives harvesting rubber trees deep in the bush, with no protection from the deadly, sticky mess. Brutal tales of slavery. Such suffering she cannot forgive.

She prays Elisa shall never know of her father's time out there.

Reaching Émilienne, he takes her hand, lifting it to his lips, murmuring her name as if she is a piece of fruit for his dessert tonight. "Good evening, my darling." His voice is strained. "It's been too long, naughty girl."

With a soft laugh, a protective trick she has learned, she whispers, "Much too long, Leo, but"—glancing at the two young women waiting, she adds with a wink—"I must say you don't look lonely." With a quick move she lifts her skirts, moving again through the crowd, feeling his eyes on her.

She is not a hard woman, not immune to the wound she left deep inside this man, this king, who just will not let go. But she thinks of Georges, and all that suffering at Leo's hands, and walks on.

"*La belle, ma belle.*" Étienne's voice rises over others as he comes toward her now, holding two glasses of champagne. When she takes one, his smiling eyes run over her. More than once he has suggested the possibility of an arrangement, a long engagement as his mistress. He will capture her, he says, sweeping her away to his château, Royallieu, in Compiègne.

She agreed to visit his château soon, but nothing more—she loves Paris. She loves the stage and footlights, the audiences and flowers, and her wealthy gentlemen. She gave up on love. Now it is strictly business, and her lovers pay. Her heart stays out of these liaisons.

But as Étienne tips his glass to her, she sees the spark of victory in his eyes. Étienne Balsan is a man used to having what he desires, she knows, in his polite and mannered way. Liane says she is a fool not to accept his offer. It is a gentle reminder that every day she's getting older, and as his mistress, she would have security for life, even if in the future they should part.

Placing his hand on her shoulder now, he turns her toward his waiting group of friends, most of whom she knows. Émilienne smiles at their jokes, feeling beautiful, comfortable, desired. Tossing her head back in laughter, she gathers them under her spell. She's learned all the tricks from Liane and Caroline and also from experience. Émilienne has come a long way from that young girl in wooden shoes who so easily wore her heart on her sleeve.

As always, her Seabird thrills. Ten curtain calls tonight, with Étienne and his friends seated in the center box before the stage.
In the dressing room, she winds her way through the forest of
flowers, heading for the makeup table and mirror. A small box
wrapped in silver paper and ribbons waits there. Smiling, she
picks up the card, scanning the note inside—Étienne.

As she opens the box, she starts, then stares at the perfect
matched pair of blue diamonds inside. Blue diamond earrings,
the most expensive stones in the world, she has heard. She lifts
one from the box, holding it, turning it to catch the light, admiring the round cut, the blue depth of the diamonds. *Look
how the stone catches fire.*

Lily leans over her shoulder, silent, admiring the gift.

"Blue diamonds," Émilienne says with a sigh.

Lily steps back. "Someone loves you, Émmy."

She ignores that word, *love.* In a blink she calculates the stones'
worth—many thousands perhaps, or more. Of course, Étienne's
wealth is unlimited, as is his playful soul. She stares at the mirror
before her now, thinking again of his offer. He desires she take up
residence at Royallieu with him, for so long as they both agree.

There is a better word than love, she thinks. *Security.*

She pulls her monocle from the drawer, fixes it to her eye,
and examines one of the earrings. The color—an intense blue,
with no noticeable secondary hue—is quite unusual.

High clarity, she sees. She will have her jeweler confirm.
Holding the gem up to the light again, the sparkle she seeks
appears. Magnificent.

Carefully, she places the diamonds back in the box for now.
Then she leans back, still musing.

"I shall wear the light blue satin this evening," she says at
last, looking up at Lily. "The simple one. It will be lovely with
the new earrings."

"Yes." Lily pulls the dress from the line behind the screen. "Where are you off to tonight?"

"Maxim's." The perfect place to show off her gift. "Bring the long pearls, too, Lily. And the petite filigree bracelet, the gold one."

Those were the duchess's jewels. Émilienne sold most of the d'Ange jewels left to her by Georges while waiting for Elisa to arrive—the pearls, a ruby broach, the gold bracelet, and a few others. She sold the tiara for enough to purchase an apartment in a hotel on avenue de Friedland in the 8th arrondissement. She smiles at the thought. Quid pro quo for the Duchess d'Ange— one apartment for another.

But the most important jewel in her mind is the black pearl. She shall save the pearl for her girl. One day, when Elisa is married and the old duchess is gone, she will find a way to get the black pearl into Elisa's hands.

"Émmy? Are you all right?"

Lily interrupts her thoughts. She looks up. "Yes. Yes, of course." Reaching for the jar of cream to remove the stage makeup, she gives Lily a smile. Now, looking at the time, she sees that already she is late—but Étienne will wait. He likely holds court in the grand hall downstairs, as usual entertaining friends. Étienne Balsan desires her, she knows, as he proves with the blue diamonds.

Slipping on the dress and turning around for Lily's help with the buttons, she wonders what will come from this night. Then she turns, observing her reflection. Moving closer to the mirror, she frowns. There are those lines again at the corners of her eyes. She steps back quickly, glaring at the new electric lights framing the mirror, exposing flaws.

A half hour later, they pull up to Maxim's doors. Hugo strides out to greet them. The maître d' takes her hand, greeting

her as she emerges from the carriage. Étienne bounds out behind.
Through the windows and doors of Maxim's place, soft light
glows, casting its spell.

They drift first into the bar, on passage through the crowd,
where the two lovers, Émilienne and Étienne, are handed glasses
of champagne for a toast. But after, Étienne calls for his usual
whiskey and soda, the new drink, and Maxim's is the only place
thus far to serve it.

Everyone talks at once in the bar, ebullient voices rising
and falling amid kisses and laughter and music coming from
the dining room. Why, Monsieur Cornuché himself comes out
to greet them—he, the new owner of Maxim's.

Émilienne throws back her head, laughing as two dancers from the Moulin Rouge climb onto the bar and dance the
cancan, then everyone starts to sing. Mirrors abound, reflecting
light, dazzling, doubling and tripling the scene, multiplying the
magical effect. Oh, the joie de vivre! As if the whole of Paris is
captured forever in this one scene.

Hugo shows them into the dining room, and every head
turns, greeting them as they move through the packed rows of
tables to their own in the center of the room. Each table holds a
shaded lamp, glowing pink light to enhance the women's beauty.
From across the room Nellie Melba, the great soprano, greets
her with a wave. Nearby sits Mata Hari.

On this glorious night Émilienne thinks neither of the
past nor the future. In this moment, beauty is hers, and always
she shines.

She sits, and Étienne settles back, lifting his glass. Just then
someone calls her name, and before she turns, Liane leans over
her shoulder, kissing her cheek. Étienne rises, greeting her.

Liane takes a chair across from the two lovers, resting her
chin on her hand with a wide smile. At once Émilienne spots

the brilliant diamonds dangling from her wrist. Leaning across the table, she touches the bracelet.

"Lovely," she says. "Someone new?"

The waiter appears just then, setting a silver bucket with iced champagne and three glasses on the table. "Compliments of the house, Monsieur Balsan," he says.

Étienne nods, and the waiter uncorks and pours.

"I thought you might notice." Liane gives her a look. "Given to me by a new friend. My husband does not mind." Liane's new husband, the prince three times her age, lives in the South of France. They seldom seem to meet.

With a glance at Étienne engaged in another conversation, she whispers, "Have you read my latest book?"

"I have." Émilienne smiles. "*Grandes Horizontales*, as they say, have a tale to tell."

Two lines appear between Liane's brows, but then she nods and smiles.

"You did that well, my friend." Liane did not write of Émilienne in her story, nor of herself, she is convinced. Although the book did bring Émilienne down, describing in detail the realities of a girl's life as a demimondaine—the rough, cold ways of some gentlemen and society. The two of them have lived as they must to survive. *And look, just look around—there is no suffering here at Maxim's.*

Émilienne picks up the champagne and sips.

With another glance at Étienne, now turned away, Liane gives her a hard look. "Is it true you are thinking of leaving the stage after your contract with the Folies ends, for Étienne?"

Étienne has asked. Émilienne thinks of those little lines at the corners of her eyes and looks off. *Why not accept?* Across the room, the artist, Sem, captures the scene. She wonders if years from now Maxim's shall still be the same. She nods in the artist's direction. "Georges Goursat has got us now."

Liane laughs. "You avoid my question, silly girl."

She leans toward her closest friend. "No," she whispers, making the decision on the spot. "I will agree to visit Royallieu after the show closes, but nothing more. Not now. Besides, he has not made a formal offer yet."

Truth is, she has not been offered another contract to dance when the Folies contract is up. She tells herself that perhaps things will change after reviews of her encore Seabird performance this evening. She is thirty-four years, but the mirror tells her she still holds on to her beauty. When the offers arrive, she shall choose. And really, until she has a contract, leaving Paris for residence in a country château will be a good excuse.

CHAPTER SEVENTEEN

ROYALLIEU, 1904

As the carriage pulls up to the entrance in the courtyard, Émilienne takes it all in. Royallieu is situated in a lovely setting of forests and fields, much like all the other châteaus she has visited over the years. Fall and winter are busy times of year for theaters in Paris. But, for her—why, at mid-November already, the theaters are all packed, yet she's not dancing. Despite her performance, she's had no offers. It's good she's visiting Royallieu, her excuse for the season's absence from the stage. Better than admitting she has no contract.

Although she has not yet decided how long she will stay.

Anson hands the reins to a waiting boy, climbs down from the driving seat, and comes around. She feels irritable from the tiresome ride as he opens the door, helping her down from the carriage along with Lily. Perhaps she should consider purchasing one of those new motorcars. Forty miles from Paris, and in a carriage the roads are never smooth.

But now, standing and breathing deep the brisk, cold

country air, her spirit revives. The sun shines; she shall have luck. This is a beautiful day. Brushing a curl back from her forehead she greets Étienne's head butler as he approaches. Two young boys in livery follow him.

His name is Yuri, he informs her, bowing, welcoming her to Royallieu. Étienne is out riding, though he should return shortly.

With a nod, she leans against the carriage. "I shall wait for him out here."

Yuri's accent is Russian, she realizes, and his manner slightly abrupt. With a small gesture he orders the boys to carry her luggage upstairs. She's brought three large bags along, a selection of clothing for fall and winter weather, just in case. And then there is another trunk for Lily. Lily follows, warning the boys to handle the bags with care.

Pulling a small flint lighter from the carriage, she leans back again, crossing one foot over the other, lighting a cigarette while taking in the scene. The cigarette seems to startle Yuri. She smiles. This is his bad luck because she has learned to count on a good smoke now and then. She laughs inside as Yuri returns in a fast trot to the château. Besides, she has seen other women smoking cigarettes in Paris. It should not come as such a shock.

She inhales and looks around. No flowers here, just hedges and benches and cobblestones. Royallieu is decidedly a male home. She looks beyond the hedges, over pastures, and further on to a forest in the distance. In the other direction, two foals romp in one of many fenced-in fields. Étienne is known for his fine racing stable. Blowing smoke, she smiles at the foals' antics, their youth and energy.

Suddenly, a shout comes from afar. Turning, she spots two horses racing full out toward the château. Étienne is in the lead—but who is the other rider? A young boy, perhaps, and now he is closing the distance between the two. They fly through an opening in the hedge together. Émilienne laughs at the expression on Étienne's face as they rein in their mounts close, too close to her carriage.

With a salute, Étienne dismounts. "Pardon, *ma belle*. I meant to greet you in a more leisurely manner."

She tosses the cigarette onto the stones. "You forgot to instruct your mount."

Throwing the reins to a boy, Étienne pulls her into his arms. "Welcome to Royallieu!" And he plants a kiss on her nose. She senses, rather than sees, him smelling her fragrance, a gift from him not long ago.

Over his shoulder, she watches the other rider dismount. When he pulls off his hat, long dark hair tumbles out. This is no young boy. The girl wears a man's jodhpurs and shirt and a loose wool jacket. Émilienne recalls a bit of gossip about this young woman, Étienne's *petite amie*. Youthful and pretty, she arrived at Royallieu with Étienne one day several years ago and still resides at the château.

So, how interesting—the gossip is true. Étienne releases her now as the girl strides toward them. Given Étienne's proposition, this is a curious situation. Close now, she thinks the girl pretty enough, with dark hair, dark eyes, and—strangely—skin darkened from the sun.

The girl rests her hand on Étienne's arm, seeming to study Émilienne as she speaks. "Étienne has told me all about you, mademoiselle." She has no easy smile. "I am pleased to make your acquaintance."

Émilienne tilts her head.

But Étienne interrupts, teasing, grinning down at his *petite amie*, no taller than Émilienne. "Ah, you have arrived at last," he says. "You are too slow, my girl. I thought I lost you back there."

Lifting her hand from his arm, he turns to Émilienne with

a slight bow. "Mademoiselle d'Alençon, may I present to you, Mademoiselle Gabrielle Chanel."

Émilienne nods. Her smile is real as she looks at this young girl, a grand rider, a decade younger than Émilienne.

"I prefer Coco, mademoiselle."

"Coco, then. Pretty, and such an unusual name."

Coco adds, "Come with me, please. I shall show you to your rooms."

With a glance back at Étienne, turning to speak with a groom, together they walk toward the château entrance, chatting. But the girl seems somewhat reserved; conversation does not come easy at first. As usual, Émilienne's good nature at last pulls a smile from her, and now she seems more relaxed.

The idea of Étienne handling two mistresses intrigues Émilienne, even though she is a woman used to complicated situations. How will he juggle two lovers at the château at once?

As they enter the foyer, the grand hall, Émilienne loops her arm through Coco's arm. "I watched you ride in. Where did you learn? You are quite skilled, I think."

"Étienne taught me."

"Such freedom you must feel riding astride with no bothersome skirts. And in men's jodhpurs! Where did you ever find them?"

The girl laughs for the first time, a pleasant sound. "In Étienne's drawers."

"Ah, excellent choice," she says. "But it seems to me they're a bit small for him. Why, they fit as if they were made for you." She glances at Coco, eyes sparkling. "You must introduce me to your designer and seamstress at once."

"You are looking at her."

Émilienne slides her a look. "My, you are a talented girl."

In the high entrance hall, she looks about. To the right, sun floods a large salon through open windows. To her left, several arched entrances from the hallway lead to a ballroom. It was on this side of the château she'd spotted a long terrace winding around to the back of the château.

"Your room is on the first floor, mademoiselle, right up these stairs."

"Call me Émilienne, *chéri*."

As they reach a door, she adds, "Such a lovely day, even with the cold." She ties her coat closed. "I believe I shall take a bit of sun on the terrace. Would you like to join me while my maid unpacks?"

She is curious about this girl. And, if Étienne persists, before she even considers an agreement to reside out here, she must clarify the girl's status. She never takes second place.

"Yes, let's." Coco's tone perks up. "That's a lovely spot. I shall call for tea." Her dark eyes peer at Émilienne. "Do you like English tea?"

"Of course. Give me a few minutes with Lily here, and I shall meet you on the terrace."

When Émilienne arrives, Coco stands at a stone parapet on the terrace, looking out over the fields and pastures. She sweeps her arm from north to south, from Étienne's stables to the forest. "I believe Étienne has the finest racing stable in all Europe."

Étienne is known for his racing horses not just on the Continent and Britain but also in Brazil, she has heard.

Sitting at a small table, Émilienne pours tea. "It is impressive. You are an excellent rider too. How lovely you can enjoy it." With a smile, she adds, handing a cup to Coco, "And, judging from your riding clothes, you have an eye for style. Tell me, how did you develop a talent for sewing?"

"I learned from an elderly aunt in the South of France, not far from Lyon." She shrugs. "That is what old ladies do. They sew." Setting down the cup, she leans back, resting her arms on the chair. "As for design . . . well, I sew for myself for comfort."

"Wonderful idea." Émilienne watches her. "I also prefer comfort over style, but in my profession, this seldom works." She laughs, and once again, Coco gives up a smile. *Ah, a small success.*

"I knew some seamstresses once." Émilienne looks off. "When I was a girl, I lived in a lodge with my maman, and the seamstresses worked over our rooms. They always had beautiful things to see and touch—lace, ribbons, velvet, and silks." She smiles, turning back to Coco. "When they had lace, they always called me up to see."

Even as she speaks of the joyful memories, the dark ones rise.

Émilienne holds her expression still, unmoving, almost hearing the crack of the thick leather strap, almost feeling the cuts in her skin. And Maman's hard, sharp eyes, never forgiving, not her girl. From the past comes Maman's voice, calling her, and fear rushes through, and at once she is that little girl again, racing for home, only to be locked out again for the night—she wasn't fast enough. She clears her throat, blinks tears away, surprised. She has not thought of those days in quite some time.

Setting down the teacup, she pulls a cigarette from her pocket, a Muratti, machine rolled.

Coco rises. "Étienne keeps a lighter in the library. I shall be quick."

After Coco returns with the flint, Émilienne tips it to the cigarette and takes a long, deep breath. The warmth is relaxing. She looks up at Coco. "Forgive me. Would you like one?"

"I think I might. I've never tried." She sits up straight. "Will you show me how?"

"Well, of course." Émilienne pulls another from her pocket, recalling her first time. She lights the cigarette and hands it over to Coco. "Look here, now. Watch me first."

As she inhales again, Coco plants the cigarette between her lips, watching. Then she inhales.

"Almost right . . . like this," she says, pulling smoke in and letting it stream out slowly.

Five minutes later, Coco sits back in her chair, smoking, imitating Émilienne's way of holding the thing between her fingers, of tilting back her head for the streaming smoke. Coco catches her eye and lets out a laugh. "You might be a bad influence, Émilienne."

"I have been told that before."

Coco looks off. "Why do you think men don't like to see women smoke?"

Émilienne shrugs. "They have their rules. We learn to break them." She leans back, tilting her hat for shade from the sun.

"I'm glad you're visiting Royallieu. Most of our lady guests are so dull."

Émilienne looks up. "While you are here with Étienne, it's best to swim in the same stream."

"Pardon if I sounded rude."

She shakes her head.

After a pause, Coco adds, "Étienne and I are no longer lovers, you know, although we remain great friends."

Émilienne works to hide surprise at this blunt revelation. After a moment, she waves off the words. "That is between you and Étienne, *chéri*. None of my concern." Still, she cannot hold in the laughter. "You are quite a girl. I see why Étienne is fond of you."

A blush rises in Coco's face.

"I think we shall be friends."

Coco nods. A smile hovers.

The girl is not so bad. Coco will not be a hindrance after all.

Twilight. Clouds of pink and lavender, streaked with silver blue, sink toward the horizon. Reluctant to leave the fresh country air for her room, Émilienne has exchanged her coat for a fur jacket and a small blanket for her legs, and she now lies on a long chair on the terrace, half asleep. Coco disappeared an hour ago. Suddenly, voices catch her attention. Startled, she sits up, smoothing her skirt over her knees just as the door opens for a group of gentlemen, who stop to gape. Étienne follows, making introductions—some she already knows.

"The ladies are upstairs resting," Étienne says.

Of course. And none of them are wives.

"Dinner is served at ten," he adds as the men spread out around a table for cards, pulling up empty chairs. Count Léon de LaBorde, an old acquaintance, calls out, "Émilienne! Come, join us!"

She is good at the game. But politely, she declines. Rising, she moves to the parapet, bracing her hands on the cool stone ledge of the low wall, breathing in the crisp, fresh air. The scents of hay, turned soil, and smoke from the kitchen drift to her—all so different from the city streets of Paris. In the distance, a black horse and rider appear, a sleek thoroughbred with his trainer. She watches as they circle the track.

Shouts from the card players break the spell. Turning, she lifts her brows as Coco pushes through the door, still wearing those jodhpurs and that shirt and jacket. Her long dark hair still hangs loose. A gentleman motions, and she walks to him, leaning down. He whispers something in her ear, and she throws her head back, laughing now.

This is a different girl. Émilienne smiles—she likes Coco Chanel. An almost protective feeling rises in the moment. Gossip has it that she's a girl with no home, and that is why she now lives here.

And she does not appear threatened by Émilienne's appearance and fame.

The girl saunters over to Émilienne, followed by whistles from the players.

"We are off to Longchamp tomorrow," Coco says. She nods toward the horse, and they both turn. "He runs tomorrow. Sunloch, he's young, but Étienne favors him."

The beautiful animal stops for a moment, his graceful neck stretching as if catching a scent, then takes off toward the stables. Émilienne watches until he is gone. "I'd put my money on that one."

"You like to gamble on horses?"

"Yes . . . once in a while."

Over the years with her gentlemen, she has learned a thing or two about the races. With money, gambling is an easy thrill. Risks have never frightened her. Sometimes, she thinks perhaps she prefers gambling to watching the horses run.

Feeling Coco's eyes on her, she gives the girl a smile, turns on her light. Coco jingles coins in her pocket. "Perhaps I shall give that a try tomorrow afternoon." With a sideways glance at Émilienne, she adds, "You will come with us?"

"I never miss a race when presented with the opportunity."

"Coco, we need help over here!" Leon again. "Étienne refuses to stay. We need a fourth."

Coco looks up, mugs a face, then strolls toward the table.

Émilienne turns back to the sunset and pastures and horse—Sunloch and the trainer have disappeared. Suddenly warm hands brush her shoulders, and Étienne, standing behind her, kisses her neck.

"Your Sunloch, he is a beauty, Étienne."

"Yes. Sixteen hands, all muscle. You've seen him run?"

She nods.

"He's in the money."

"Fine lines." After a beat, she adds, "Like his owner."

"We are off for Longchamp tomorrow." He strokes her bare neck. "How about taking a ride in the morning before we leave?"

Her voice turns soft. "I always enjoy a good ride."

He slips his arm around her. "Let's go someplace quiet and explore that thought."

She turns about, letting him steer her toward the doors. Three hours to dress for dinner at ten. Plenty of time for love.

After an early breakfast in bed, Émilienne emerges from her room the following morning dressed for a ride. She wears a fitted white blouse pinned with a gold broach just under her chin, a split skirt, black stockings, and long leather boots. Her riding jacket, an uncomfortable thing with eight stays, nevertheless molds her waistline to a handspan. Lily braided her long hair and put it up for the ride.

Laughter from the small dining room comes as she walks down the steps. Following the noise to the breakfast room, she finds only Coco, Étienne, and Leon already awake. Everyone else still sleeps. Royallieu hosted a late night.

Étienne looks up, then Leon, both greeting her as she enters. Everyone is hunched over newspapers, legs stretched under the table, relaxed.

Coco glances up over the top of the rag and gives her a sleepy look. "Hello! Come sit beside me, Émilienne."

A maid offers coffee, and Émilienne nods. While she pours, Coco shakes the paper and folds it once. "Listen to this! Have you heard of that Indian woman invading Paris? Though she's not of Indian origin as she claims—Dutch!"

Leon glances up and frowns.

"Yes, you know the one. She calls herself Mata Hari. According to this story, she is a hit at the Musée Guimet." With a glance at Émilienne, Coco asks, "Have you seen her dance?"

Émilienne sips the coffee and, grimacing, sets it down. Too hot. "I have not yet had the pleasure." She stirs the drink, cooling it. "But I've heard she's quite fierce."

Coco lets out a laugh and begins to read. "*She moves like a cat, her entire body trembles when she dances.*" She glances at Leon over the top of the paper. "She trembles, they say! And strips off her costume piece by piece in time with the music."

Leon leers. "Piece by piece? Everything?"

Étienne chuckles.

Coco peers at the newspaper. "I suppose so. They don't say."

"I would guess not. If the gentlemen are paying for the dance, why show everything for nothing more in return?" Émilienne grins, lifting a brow.

Leon's voice turns dry. "Well, the news is worthless if they don't tell the finish. Here, then. In the name of friendship, I shall force myself to view the show to the finish. If she bares it all at the end, I shall tell."

Émilienne reaches for a cigarette, picking one from a case in the center of the table. "Étienne's expensive American tobacco, Lorillard," Leon says, leaning for the lighter.

As it flares, Émilienne lights the cigarette, and, sitting back, lets it dangle from the corner of her mouth. "So, perhaps she gives the men a full look for free?" She curls her lips. "Surely, Mata Hari must know that nothing worthwhile in life is free."

"My guess is that girl is far from free." Coco tosses the paper down onto the table.

Émilienne studies her. *Do you come free, Coco?* Has she ever negotiated an arrangement with Étienne—protection of sorts, if he ever asks her to leave?

Reaching for the monocle she carries in her pockets, Émilienne picks up Coco's newspaper. She fits the glass over her eye, reading of Mata Hari, feeling a touch of irritation. She met the woman once, an arrogant young dancer. From what she's heard, Mata Hari is just a step above the prostitutes in Montmartre.

Leon pushes back his chair and stands, sticking his pipe in his mouth as he looks over the group. "I look forward to giving you all a full report next week on Madame Hari. Now, if you will excuse me?"

Coco looks up. "Don't bother. I hear she's a tart."

"Don't be so quick to judge, little Coco. A woman's nude beauty should never be judged by her character. Art is oblivious to morals," Leon says. "You must think of the thing from a man's point of view."

Émilienne studies Coco.

"No need," Coco says. "A woman knows a fake when she sees one."

Leon grins. Chewing on his pipe, he leaves.

It occurs to Émilienne that she has never come across Coco in Paris. Coco is no courtesan, at least not yet. But neither is she an independent woman. If she's got no other plan for survival than Étienne's generosity, she'd better get started on one. She is a strange young girl, serious yet easy with gentlemen, almost more so than with the ladies.

Does she not grow bored out here in the country?

Étienne made it clear last night that he seldom calls Coco to his bed these days. Glancing over the top of the paper at the girl, she wonders if Coco's days at Royallieu are numbered. For some reason, she hopes not. Coco just needs time, time to grow, to learn to face the future with clear, wide eyes.

Tilting back her head, Émilienne blows smoke at the ceiling. She should be dancing in Paris tonight and dining at Maxim's. Are her own days dancing numbered? She's certain a contract offer is on the way, and she will soon return to Paris. Her audiences will miss her. They will *demand* her.

Still, the sudden heat in her face burns. She ducks her head, telling herself that life at Royallieu is a nice change. Perhaps, even, she might be content out here if she accepts an arrangement with Étienne. And, of course, she would enjoy traveling with him, following the horses from Europe to Brazil.

One thing is certain. With Émilienne d'Alençon or without her, the time will come when things at Royallieu shall change. She wonders what will happen then to Coco.

CHAPTER EIGHTEEN

Longchamp racecourse on this fall afternoon is alive with flags and banners flying against a clear blue sky, a parade of carriages and occasional automobiles, and everyone bustling, crowds on parade. Already carriages are packed on grass along the race-track, claiming spots for picnics and celebrations.

Sunshine washes the scene in fall's golden glow. Émilienne catches every eye as she saunters along the pathway toward the entrance, with Étienne on one side and Coco on the other, greeting acquaintances. Ladies glitter in their jewels and color-ful dresses and large hats.

Today Émilienne wears her favorite afternoon dress, a slim blue linen gown, fit snug around her curves. Blue is her color. She looks her best this afternoon, she knows. Folds of the collar fall soft at her cleavage, pinned just in the right spot with a mauve-colored flower. A short blue jacket trimmed with black lace pulls all eyes. And like most other ladies this afternoon, Émilienne wears a wide-brimmed hat for shade from the sun.

Ribbons, a few flowers, and white plumes of ostrich feathers frame her face.

Coco chose a lovely new dress in beige trimmed in black, flattering her complexion. Étienne had this made, she said, as a surprise. She has a limited wardrobe, she shared with a laugh. "He purchases my clothes. This is Étienne's way of assuring I never appear in public wearing his jodhpurs."

Coco has few jewels, though, given Étienne's great wealth. He seems not to have supplied his *petite amie* with even the minimal requirement of jewels. But then he is a practical man. If jewels are not necessary for a relationship, why should he spend his money? Jewels are investments, good as money in the bank, and necessary for a demimondaine when she grows old, past her time. It seems Coco has overlooked this basic means of survival.

On this afternoon she wears a three-strand necklace of pearls borrowed from Émilienne, at Émilienne's suggestion. The pearls look lovely against her sunbrowned skin.

As they approach the entrance to the racing grounds, Émilienne pulls from a box at the gate the morning line and program on the horses, jockeys, and latest odds. Étienne takes her arm and Coco's, steering them both through the gates. As always, Émilienne feels the excitement of the races the moment they enter. She loves the color and sparkle here, the smiles and laughter before the horses run. Before bets are won and lost, everyone is gay.

Lifting her nose as they enter, she seeks the scent of the place—the musk, hay, raw wood, smell of oil, and hard-earned sweat. They pass the beginning of the enclosure, where on the private backside horses are stabled and tack rooms serve as living quarters for the grooms and their assistants. Ahead near the stands, trainers promenade horses in the paddock while gamblers watch.

At the entrance to the backside, Étienne stops. He will meet them back in this spot in ten minutes' time, before the first race starts, he says. Sunloch runs in the first. Just then a jockey wearing his colors walks up, and Étienne disappears with him. Émilienne lifts her parasol and takes Coco's arm as they stroll along.

"I owned a horse several years ago," Émilienne says, watching Coco tilt her face to the sun, walking as she does without a parasol. "He was a good one. A beautiful stallion named Bienveillant,"

Coco snaps her head around. "How exciting. Did you race him?"

She laughs. "That was a fight, but I got him on the track once. Women are not favored in the game, you know, but a friend helped me, and I managed to sign him up for Les Aigles at Chantilly."

"They allow a woman to do this?"

"Only women with the very best smiles." Émilienne winks, waits a beat, then adds, "I invented the name of an owner when I entered him—the Duc d'Lençon. Of course, everyone realized at once. It created a furor at first. The journalists loved it, called me the lady who makes both men and horses run."

Coco stops, frowning. "Outrageous to treat you that way, Émilienne."

She shrugs, taking Coco's arm, walking on. "I was amused. I even invented a stable with all the details." She laughs at the memory. "I gave them so much information—all false. The club gave in, allowed him to run."

"I don't believe you!"

"Yes. He even wore my colors, blue and bright yellow." With a sideways glance, she smiles. "I am a wicked girl." As she speaks, she remembers Jules Chéret's popular poster for one of her shows, showing a gentleman mocking prudence while he hides from temptation behind a big yellow umbrella.

Of course, Émilienne was the temptation.

"In the end, the auditor admitted he saw no problem. And damned if Bienveillant didn't win. The jockey was Lassance." A former lover. She tilts her hat against the sun. "It was just play, a joyful fête. *La Presse* said that horse's win brought nothing but happiness to the world."

Ahead, the bookmakers come into sight, milling about under the branches of a wild, old oak. "Come. Place a bet?"

Coco shakes her head. "I don't wish to gamble, but I shall see how this is done."

Nearby, voices catch Émilienne's attention. "*There she is! Émilienne d'Alençon, I tell you it is her!*"

Coco hears, too, and glances over. Émilienne smiles and waves, and a man blushes, bowing as they walk by. Picking up their pace, they pass the stands, private for aristocrats. Although, with Étienne attending, she and Coco shall be allowed.

"I love racing," she says. "I love the horses. The thrill of the race, not knowing if you will win or lose. I love it better than Maxim's, I think."

"I'm happy riding them at home, at Royallieu. Étienne's stable does the work. I prefer looking at fashions here." Just then a breeze kicks up. Two young women walking toward them grip the brims of their hats, as do Coco and Émilienne.

"Look at those two old boats," Coco says. "Not the girls. I mean the hats." She turns to Émilienne. "Why do we wear heavy hats like these, loaded with fruits and flowers, anything one can find, it seems. So uncomfortable." Coco shakes her head. For the first time, Émilienne really looks at the young woman's small hat. Although bearing ribbons and flowers, it is smaller than most, with the brim rolled at the sides.

"Sometimes I wonder who convinces us to wear such impractical things."

"Forget such things." Émilienne picks up her pace. "It's getting late, and I must place my bets."

As they reach the bookmakers, Émilienne pulls the morning

line selections from her sleeve. In the soft breeze, red, yellow, and gold leaves flutter down around them from branches of the tree. She runs her eyes down the line, studying the horses, the records, the odds, confirming her earlier choices.

She looks about—given the crowd she cannot see Brevard.

"Too many people," Coco says, backing away under a shady tree. "I'll wait here." As she speaks, Émilienne nods and begins working her way through the ever-moving mass of men until she spots his hat—a black bowler with a pink flower stuck into the band.

"Good morning, Brevard."

He turns and smiles, with a slight bow. "Mademoiselle."

She moves beside him. "Tool Box, in the fifth. How does he look?"

Not a muscle moves as he speaks, looking down at his writing pad. "Fauchon is the chalk."

For a moment, she hesitates. Glancing at the morning line, the odds are four to one. She planned on putting her money down on three races, but Brevard rarely gives a tip.

Seconds pass, then she leans close, whispering. "Fauchon, in the fifth then. To win."

He writes in his book. She hands over the notes, thirty thousand, every franc she brought along, and takes the ticket.

Within a minute, the transaction is complete.

Fauchon is the chalk, sure to win. Turning back toward Coco, it is all she can do to hold back her dance. What a wonderful, beautiful day this is, and she is bound to win.

And this time there is no risk.

꧁

They meet Étienne near the enclosure where the stands are almost full. Steering them toward the entrance, he vouches

for the ladies to a gentleman at the gate, and the three enter
together.

Coco lifts her chin as she walks in, Émilienne notices, a bit
amused. The grandstand has the best seats, of course, but she
has spent many days at gay parties in carriages near the turf.
She does enjoy watching Étienne, who seems oblivious to the
long looks from several ladies sent in his direction as he escorts
Émilienne and Coco into the private space. A good mark for
Étienne. She glides along on one side of him, floating and thinking of the win she will have.

Settling into the comfortable seat, Coco sits on one side of
Étienne, and Émilienne, on the other. For an instant, she gazes
with longing down the racecourse at the mass of carriages parked
on the grass and the carefree, rowdy crowds. The picnics were
much more fun. But that was when she was young and care-
less. That was before she was known as the most beautiful girl
in Paris. Now, she attends the races with gentlemen privileged
to the private seats.

When the first race is called, the familiar thrill shoots
through Émilienne. She sits up straight. And here they come,
the thoroughbreds and the jockeys in their silks and colors, with
the escorts, moving toward the starting gates—there, moving
easily into the third chute is Étienne's thoroughbred, Sunloch.
Some horses enter the chutes more willingly than others. But,
once inside the gates, the animals sense the excitement, too,
snorting, pawing the ground, impatient to go.

She glances at Étienne, but his eyes are riveted to the horse.

At last, the gates burst open, and the announcer shouts,
"And . . . they are off!"

As the horses break, her blood races. She would stand now,
cheering with the gentlemen, but society would talk. Pushing
ahead the announcer begins his work as the horses race for the

turn, two in the lead seeming in a dead heat. This is the first race, Étienne's big race—but she waits for the fifth, Fauchon. In her mind, she calculates her winnings. One hundred twenty thousand francs, if she has luck.

Now the field nears the turn, and she leans forward to see, and then—Étienne, grinning, turns and slips his hands around her waist and lifts her up so that she's standing on the seat while he holds her. Now she can see as the field heads toward the finish . . . and here—Sunloch moves up, he's fighting for the lead! But no, now he's behind by a hand, and the jockey in the lead stretches, urging with his whip . . . while, yes . . . yes . . . here he comes, Sunloch again . . . and the two thoroughbreds hit the finish line . . . first . . . aah, no! . . . with Sunloch second.

She feels Étienne's excitement fading as he helps her down, settling her back into the seat. Coco pats Étienne's arm as he sits between them again. When he turns to Émilienne, he shrugs and smiles. "He's young, coming along."

When the winner is announced, heading for the circle, she grips her program. Four more races to go. A sharp, high voice rises in seats nearby. Turning in that direction, her eyes meet those of an older woman staring at her. In the instant the woman yanks her husband's sleeve, and he glances at Émilienne. Quickly, he looks away, as does Émilienne.

Just then, Étienne slips his arm around her shoulder, pulling her close. He must have seen. Such a gentleman, Étienne Balsan.

When the fifth race is called, Émilienne sits up straight as the horses appear, heading for the chutes. She keeps her eyes on Fauchon, on number three and his colors, red and gold. He looks frisky enough for a good run.

As the horses break, charging down the track with Fauchon third before the turn, she almost feels let down, a strange sense of ennui, knowing ahead of time which horse will win.

The risk is gone, and with it the thrill—the fun of the game. Although, she shall win one hundred twenty thousand francs, she tells herself again.

Étienne hugs her when Fauchon hits the finish line, and she pretends the surprise, of course. Well, with such winnings, that thrill is real. Just then, Coco leans across Étienne, beaming at her new friend. Years of acting, of pretending onstage and off with certain lovers, come to her aid with wild congratulations all around.

But really, when you cheat, things are different. The story is only about money. The fun is gone.

Never again, she swears.

Later, that night, Étienne mentions the arrangement again, living with him at Royallieu perhaps. She wavers—he is such a kind man, a gentleman, lifting her up in the enclosure this afternoon, even though she is not of his class—all for the better to see. What a fine man he is. A thoughtful man, never afraid to break social rules. She wishes she could love him.

If she agrees, they could take a lazy voyage to Brazil, traveling after the races, he says. He keeps a stable there. And, as her protector, he would secure her future—it would be assured.

She decides that she shall give his offer to leave the stage some serious thought. After all, a girl could do much worse than Étienne Balsan.

CHAPTER NINETEEN

Late on the following evening, a damp, cold Sunday night, rain comes in gusts, driving against the stone walls of the château. Rain has spoiled the day. Some of the gentlemen, including Étienne, are situated in the library, playing cards again, while their ladies watch and gossip. Émilienne supposes Coco is with them. Just then two lovers wander past the open door, heading in the direction of the stairs.

Émilienne is comfortable lounging alone in the salon, stretched out on a long, soft couch before the fireplace with a small crystal glass of absinthe and a good book in her lap. She has discovered Étienne's library and *The Moonstone* by Wilkie Collins. So far, it's almost as engrossing as *The Woman in White*. Still, she looks up, thinking again of Étienne's proposition.

Her choices loom.

Étienne's offer is generous, and all worries about her future, if any, would be over if she accepts. But she loves every moment onstage—*how can she give that up*? Every muscle in her body tightens at the sound of the first note of her music. Thinking of that moment waiting for the curtain to rise, posing, the lights working magic, always she feels such a connection with the audience. Not to mention the flowers, the gifts, the applause, and the excitement when later she enters Maxim's.

Most of all, she misses the audience's love.

If she gives up the stage for Étienne, people will soon forget.

But she realizes the prime of a courtesan's life is brief, depending on youth and beauty and wealthy men. What will happen when she has more than two faint lines near her eyes, and Étienne, as all rich men, grows bored? A wealthy man's mistress is always young and beautiful, and always gay, helping him forget his own inevitable march through the years.

Although, with an arrangement, he would be bound to keep her secure, even in old age.

She lights a cigarette, staring at the flickering fire. If she agrees, what would she do all day, every day, having given up the stage? Follow Étienne and his horses?

Exhaling, she watches cigarette smoke curl toward the ceiling. Liane seems happy enough after giving up her dancing for her prince. She would think Émilienne a fool to turn down Étienne's offer at her age.

And Étienne is an excellent lover.

No! She shakes her head. She is still young, still holds her good health and beauty. Why should she give up now? Why submit to the whims and dictates of one man and society's rules just because she has found a few annoying little lines in her complexion?

She smiles to herself, having reached the decision. Here she shall stay with Étienne through early spring. She was right to pack winter clothes, just in case. Spending the winter at Royallieu with her lover, an interlude, is an easy explanation for missing a season of shows.

On the other hand, she misses Paris.

Setting the glass down on a table a bit too hard, with a sigh, she leans back, closing her eyes and smoking. If Elisa were here with her, her path in life would be different. She would have hired the best, gentlest, and smartest *nounou* to care for her girl.

She juts out her lip, smiling, imagining the child's room. She would have had Elisa's bedroom walls in white, with a garden of flowers painted on them—reds and yellows and different shades of green. And she would have had white lace curtains on the windows instead of shutters, essential for little girls. She'd have bought a house in the country, and her girl would have had a pony and learned to ride.

Elisa would have gone to the best schools. Her maman is rich now—she smiles at this thought too. If Elisa were with her now, she could have anything she wanted. Anything her heart desired.

But she'd have found out about her maman—the Grande Horizontale—*soon enough.*

And again, as the duchess said, what then?

Émilienne blinks back tears.

"Ah, here you are!"

Coco's voice startles Émilienne. She wipes her eyes and sits up straight as Coco takes a seat across from her. "Well, hello. I thought you were playing cards."

With a glance at the door, the girl picks up a cigarette from the table and lights it. "I grew bored. And I've had too much champagne." Inhaling, she looks about.

"You don't need permission to smoke, you know."

Coco smiles, caught. "It's quite nice to have you around." She swings her feet up onto the couch, tucking them under her. "I suppose men did make this rule, that ladies shouldn't smoke. But I find tobacco quite pleasant."

Then, turning to Émilienne, she says, "You give me courage, Émmy. You are so free! Gambling, smoking, saying whatever you please. I admire your independent spirit."

"It's sometimes a dangerous way to live."

Coco nods. "Can you teach me your tricks of gambling on horses? It looks easy enough."

The girl does not own a sou. Émilienne lifts her glass toward Coco. "Here's my tip: stay away from bookmakers. Stick to what you know, or sure enough, you will lose."

Coco lifts her brows. "I never think of losing."

Émilienne smiles. Coco has all the confidence of youth, with such choices before her. "What do you plan for your future?"

"Who knows? Étienne says I may live here as long as I like." After a moment, she adds, "This is my home."

Émilienne looks off—poor girl. Does Coco understand she lives on Étienne's mercy? Things could go one way or the other at any moment. What will happen to her if Émilienne accepts Étienne's offer of residence at Royallieu?

In that case, she would assure Coco's welcome, she supposes.

But Coco's precarious position here does not depend upon Émilienne. If not her, then soon enough, another woman will catch Étienne's eye, and it is likely Coco would soon be forced to leave. How would she live without Étienne? Why, if not married, she would have to choose between the fate of all poor girls—hard labor or the life of the demimondaine. She can think of no other way in between.

"Perhaps I will sing onstage." Her tone is vague as she waves away smoke. "I met Étienne while singing onstage and gave it up. Did you know?" She smiles. "He was quite persuasive."

"What did he have to lose? You were free."

Coco looks up. "What do you mean?"

"Make yourself comfortable and listen." Émilienne smiles

as she removes the cigarette dangling from the corner of her mouth. "At your age, a girl not born into society, with no family to support you—father, brother, husband—you must prepare to face life as it comes."

"But—"

She holds up her hand. "Allow me to finish."

Coco remains silent, watching her.

"You are young and pretty. Men, like Étienne, fall in love with girls like us but never marry them. Yet, still, you're old enough to understand the value of finding a protector."

"A protector?" After a beat, she says, "Ah, you mean a lover who agrees to care for me?"

"Yes. A man, to secure your future, even should you part."

Coco's voice turns cool. "Oh, that. Well, I will never allow myself to depend on any man."

"You are already dependent on one man—Étienne Balsan." Émilienne lets out a laugh. "A girl cannot afford to give away her only asset. You must always negotiate with a lover, receive something of value in exchange. Bank notes or jewels or, as I said, a promise of protection, before you give yourself to any man . . . even Étienne."

"Étienne and I are only friends now." Coco glares at her.

"Listen, child." Émilienne twirls her hand in the air as she goes on, gentling her voice. "I meant no harm. It is not my business, but I care."

She takes a deep breath, steps out on the edge of a cliff. "Have you ever thought what you would do in the event Étienne asked you to leave this place?"

Still wearing an angry expression, Coco looks away.

"This is important. You must give your future some thought."

When Coco shrugs, Émilienne says, "You have a talent for sewing. Look how you fit Étienne's riding clothes."

"I have no desire to stitch ladies' clothes." Coco looks back at her. "Although sometimes I do look at the things we wear and wonder why we don't demand changes, comfortable dresses instead of wearing corsets and heavy skirts and huge baskets on our heads."

Émilienne claps her hands together. "There is an idea! Fashion."

Coco grins. "Perhaps I shall try my hand at designing something new instead of wearing Étienne's old clothes." Then, with a sly look, she says, "You would have me work, earn my way?"

"One way or the other, Coco, you need a plan. At first, I danced for coins. Now I dance in theaters. For me, dancing is play." She tilts back her head and blows smoke. "I have lovers too. But for the most part, excluding Étienne, lovers are work."

Coco's face closes. "I shall never leave Royallieu. This is my home."

"Still, you must have a plan in mind . . . just in case."

Coco's face softens, but she says nothing more.

Weeks have passed, and Émilienne remains perfectly happy at Royallieu with Étienne—and without Paris. Turning her eyes toward the windows this morning, she feels comfortable, almost loved. Étienne spoke the words last night when they made love, but of course, he must tell every mistress the same.

Lily has set a fire blazing, though the room stays cold. Rising, throwing on a warm robe, she combs her hair, paints her lips, and hurries down the stairs—breakfast calls. Coco calls out as Émilienne reaches the entrance hall, and she stops and waits, looking up. The child still wears those jodhpurs and Étienne's old shirt. The jacket appears to have come from his wardrobe too.

"Come riding with me," she says. "Even bare of leaves the forest trees are beautiful."

"Not today . . . I'm off for breakfast now." Besides, this is November. Too cold for a long ride.

Just then an unfamiliar carriage rolls into the courtyard. Neither the colors nor the crest is familiar. Coco moves toward the courtyard, and Émilienne turns, continuing on down the hallway, hunting food. Behind her, Étienne's voice echoes from upstairs, and another deep voice calls from outside, and the chorus is joined by Coco.

Entering the small breakfast room, Émilienne smiles, greeting Gabrielle Dorziat and Leon. They both look up from newspapers. The news and journals are delivered to Royallieu from Paris every third day. Breakfast here is always casual. She is glad to see Leon still wears his robe, as does she.

"Good morning, Gabrielle. You must have arrived last night?"

The pretty actress smiles. She, too, is a girl made by Charles.

"Yes, around midnight."

"I've heard rave reviews of your performance in *Antoinette Sabrier* in London. Congratulations." Émilienne takes her seat at the round table as a maid arrives.

The maid sets before her a hot, buttered baguette, a smudge of blueberry jam, and a cup of Étienne's special coffee from Brazil.

Leon folds his newspaper, tossing it on the table as he looks up. "Everywhere in Europe, people are beginning to panic, predicting war. One just does not know what to think!" He taps the newspaper, looking across at Émilienne, shaking his head. "Unrest in Britain . . . most of the stories come from the Brits. Because of the old queen."

Gabrielle laughs. "Leon, she is dead. Have a little respect."

"Queen Victoria?" Émilienne asks, chewing the delicious baguette, crunchy on the outside, still soft in the center. "Why bother her? With nine children spread all over Europe and Russia now, I think she has done her work."

"Never mind the sop, Émmy. The royals thrive on intrigue . . . and power." Gabrielle lifts a cup of chocolate. "If you doubt, take a look at Kaiser Wilhelm II and his spreading empire."

"I have." Émilienne knows him well. She drops her eyes at the thought, spreading jam on the bread. Memories of the kaiser are unpleasant. Wilhelm is a rough, eccentric man, and often she has wondered if he is truly mad.

Leon glances from Émilienne to Gabrielle. "I seem to recall you are both familiar with Victoria's brats."

"Prince George, her grandson, is not a bad fellow. In England he likes to be known as the Peacemaker." Gabrielle sips hot chocolate. "I agree regarding Wilhelm. He is an aggressive man, always thinking of war."

"Breakfast!" Coco's voice floats into the room as if drifting on a cloud, followed by Étienne. "I am starved!"

Leon rises. "Take my chair, Coco. I shall leave you all to war and madness."

Gabrielle looks up. "I'll come upstairs soon."

Coco orders her usual breakfast when the kitchen maid arrives. One soft-boiled egg, plain toast, and tea. When the girl is gone, with a glance at Étienne already engrossed in the news, Coco leans toward her, whispering. "I met Boy Capel. He only just arrived."

Émilienne lifts a brow. "Boy Capel is here?"

Her eyes shine as she nods. "Do you know him?"

"Of course. Everyone knows him, darling."

Every eligible woman in Paris is acquainted with Arthur

Capel, known generally as Boy. And quite a few married ones as well. All women fall in love with him, in vain. It's a rite of passage, she supposes.

Her heart sinks. Coco seems younger than her years, not worldly enough for Boy. He is fast and rich, with a woman waiting in every city.

"We've been friends for many years," Émilienne says in a low voice. "British, his family hold interests in coal and transport, so he's often in Paris. Though he travels through all Europe on business."

Coco leans toward her. "Is he married?"

"No." There is more to this answer, but she ventures nothing. Boy Capel is a man who will agree to marriage only if it comes with steps to the top of the ladder in society—and a title, perhaps. He is a confirmed bachelor, at least until he finds a woman with the right qualifications. Beauty. Wealth. And most important, the right social connections.

Coco straightens, spoons into the egg, tastes a bite of toast, and looks up. "Étienne says we leave for the racecourse today around two o'clock."

"Yes. Will you come?"

The kid's cheeks turn pink. "Not this time. Boy invited me to ride with him this afternoon."

While Coco finishes breakfast, Émilienne studies her. With Boy Capel, she may need some help. Again, she lowers her voice. "Would you like to wear my split skirt for riding today? It's very sleek, and I have a lovely blouse with a black velvet ribbon . . ."

Coco's response is quick. "Oh, no. I prefer comfort, Émmy."

Émilienne draws back and nods. Coco, such a strange young girl.

CHAPTER TWENTY

Christmas and celebrations of the new year have come and gone, and months have passed. April flowers are just beginning to bloom, and Émilienne remains at Royallieu, taking things day by day. Although Étienne and she remain lovers, they have also become good friends. Royallieu is so pleasant, and she feels at home here. But Étienne no longer speaks of a formal arrangement, and neither does she.

Truth is, she's begun to miss Paris again. Perhaps if she returns to the city now, theater directors will take note. She has been away for too long, Émilienne knows, gazing through the windows of the breakfast room out over the fields. If she waits much longer, she will seem like yesterday's dream.

Across from her, Leon hides behind his newspaper, as usual this time of day. Beside him sits another woman she does not care to know. Leon sometimes brings along different lovers. She wonders if Gabrielle is aware. But then she is not his mistress, has not yet agreed to a formal arrangement with Leon.

Coco walks in with Boy Capel. He has become a regular week-end guest at Royallieu now. Boy is dressed for riding, but Coco still wears an old robe, her hair long and loose, as if she just rose from her bed. "Tea, and a croissant and jam," she instructs the maid.

Then, turning to Émilienne, she says, "Boy mentioned last night he saw you dancing with a snake once, at Menus-Plaisirs a few years ago!" She shakes her head. "I don't believe him. Is it true?"

"I, for one, shall never forget her performance." Boy signals the maid for coffee.

Émilienne shrugs. "Yes, when I was younger. It seems long ago. You do what you must to eat." She laughs. "But the snake was nothing poisonous."

"*Le Gaulois* loved you—I had never read such an . . . interesting . . . review." As he speaks, Boy rests his hand over Coco's, and Coco smiles.

Ah, little girl.

"I shall never forget the way the snake curled around you." With a glance at Coco, he adds, "She was a swan in the story. You should have seen her dancing in fog. They did tricks with the lights."

Émilienne smiles, remembering. "It was fun. We had two real swans onstage. But I had to sing a little, as the swan, and *Gil Blas* wrote that while *I might be graceful as a swan, I also have its screeching voice.*"

Boy grins, leaning toward Émilienne. "I forgot to look for the swans."

Coco glances from one to the other, as if annoyed. If already the child is jealous, she has a lot to learn.

Just then Étienne leans in the open door, greeting the breakfast group. Catching Émilienne's eyes, he lifts a brow and nods toward the hallway behind him.

Setting down her coffee cup, Émilienne pushes back her chair and rises. "I shall see you later," she says to the room. Leon looks up, thumping the paper. "The news is bad today. Perhaps we should all crawl back into our beds."

"Sounds like a good idea to me," Émilienne interjects. She winks and disappears, joining Étienne in the hall.

Before she can say a word, he takes her arm, steering her away from the door. "Please come with me," he says under his breath. "Let's go up to my room. We have a problem."

In his room, Étienne closes the door behind her, then, clasping his hands behind his back, marches to a window and turns around. His eyes are fierce, his brows lie flat and low.

"Émilienne, the woman is impossible! She thinks only of herself."

"Who, Coco?" Étienne rarely shows anger.

"No, no, my wife." Pulling an envelope from his vest, he drops into a nearby chair, slapping it against the arm of the chair again and again.

Raising an eyebrow, she looks at the envelope. "Is this a letter from her?"

"Yes. Here." Half rising, he shoves it into her hand. "Read for yourself, or you will never believe what she demands." Sitting back, he leans on an elbow, chin in hand, looking off. "Damned woman."

The wax seal on the envelope, embossed with the Balsan crest, is broken. The note inside has been crumpled—in his fist, perhaps—then smoothed flat again. The message is short, signed by Étienne's dull wife. Madame Balsan's sister's daughter, a plain girl, as Émilienne recalls, is engaged to be married. For personal reasons, the ball announcing the engagement must take place soon, right away.

Next Saturday night, at Royallieu.

Startled, she looks up. Étienne's face is stone.

The niece lives in Paris, he explains, the suitor in Lyon,

and since Royallieu is situated, by Madame Balsan's account, between the two, the château is the obvious choice for the ball. Workmen shall arrive on Thursday next. The wife shall arrive on Friday evening, around six or seven o'clock.

Émilienne lifts her eyes. "I shall return to Paris at once."

"No." His voice is hard, his cheeks flush with anger. "There is no need to rush. I will not have you inconvenienced."

"We have no choice."

He lowers his eyes, his lips pressed together. "Stay until Thursday, then. We have plans for this week."

She hesitates. The thought of rushing to leave on account of his wife annoys her. "All right," she finally says. "But what about Coco? Boy usually arrives on Thursday. I suppose he may want to handle her. If not, I shall take her with me when I leave."

"I'll discuss the matter with him." Étienne comes to her, and, sliding his hand behind her neck, bends for a long, deep kiss.

At last, Émilienne pulls away. "I must dress now. I must call Lily to help with the arrangements."

He nods, and she heads for the door. Then she stops and turns back to him. "Your wife is in some hurry to announce this engagement."

"She has been trying to marry off the girl for years."

Émilienne closes the door behind her and leans against it. Such a sudden change in plans. But perhaps this is for the best. Envisioning Paris—the lights, the busy streets, the cafés, suddenly she feels relieved. She has stayed too long.

She misses the bustle of Paris. The shops and cafés, the lights on the boulevards at night, the music and dancing.

And it has been too long between theater engagements.

Émilienne lounges on the terrace a few days later, soaking in the sunshine. The air is cool, but the sun warms her. With her eyes closed, she smiles. The pungent scents of pine, new-cut grass, and jasmine drift around her.

This afternoon she wears a long-sleeve linen dress trimmed in lace, in honor of the blooming spring season. A large straw hat covers her face from the sun. From a distance comes the hum of busy stables, soothing sounds, like busy bees.

She sighs with pleasure in the moment, wishing life was always delicious like this.

"Émilienne?"

The voice is a disrupting jolt. Turning her head, she peers at Coco, who sits down beside her, hands clasped, face glowing.

"I have looked everywhere for you, Émilienne. Have you time to talk?"

Lifting her brows, Émilienne looks to her right, her left, and back to Coco. "Given I am merely wasting time, I suppose so." Sitting up, she hugs her knees. "What's on your mind, *chéri*?"

"Boy."

"Ah." That was blunt.

"He says he loves me, Émmy." Coco frowns as she speaks.

"But that's wonderful!"

Still, she does not smile. "I want to keep this a secret for now . . . but I need advice."

"I won't tell."

She nods, hesitates, then says, "We rode in the forest yesterday afternoon, and he told me so . . . then . . . he said nothing of marriage."

Émilienne snorts. She sits back, fixing her eyes on Coco. "It's too soon to speak of marriage, if ever, little one. If Boy says he loves you . . ."

"If ever?" Coco looks at her, askance. "If he loves me, why not want to marry?"

She almost laughs but does not wish to hurt the girl—though better truth than lie. Love and marriage are two different things in wealthy families. Their young men are treasures, investments, expected to marry well. More than an expectation, this is a command. A poor girl like Coco has no chance. Boy will choose a real lady, a woman who can lift him high in social circles. Best of all, one with a title.

Émilienne struggles for the right words. "Listen now. For a man in Boy's position . . ." But already Coco frowns again. The girl is so young, so naive. She hesitates, begins again, careful with her words. "You must try to understand. For a man like Boy, marriage is an important business proposition."

"Business!"

"Come. Sit here beside me." She pats a space beside her on the long chair. "This has nothing to do with you, not really."

Coco shakes her head.

"If Boy Capel vows his love, just enjoy it. Love is wonderful." Even as she speaks, Coco's eyes fill with tears. "I'm sorry, Coco. Dreams and life often conflict." She reaches for the girl's hand, but Coco withdraws, sitting back.

Coco's smile turns bleak. Her voice hits a high note. "I don't accept what you say, Émmy." Her eyes are clear as she adds, "He'll be back Thursday. We'll talk. Perhaps . . ." and her voice drifts off.

Coco is tougher than Émilienne thought. One never knows; she may find a way to breach the family barricades. An unwanted thought rises—her own inability to breach the d'Ange family barricades when Georges fell in love with her.

If he ever loved her at all.

But she shakes off the memories.

As Coco looks off, and the silence grows, Émilienne slides back down into the chair again, lounging, tilting the hat so it shades her eyes. Speaking of barricades, Coco will find out soon enough the power a family holds in matters of love and marriage. Thursday—wait until Coco hears they must leave in favor of the wife. Will Boy even arrive after Étienne tells him the news?

Now she pretends to sleep. None of this is her business. It is not her business to teach Coco the ways of the world.

Thursday comes all too soon. Preparing to leave, Émilienne stands before the long mirror regarding her image. She has chosen one of her favorite gowns for travel back to Paris, the green-and-burgundy-striped satin, which, even with the full skirt, highlights her curves.

She picks up her hat and gloves. Étienne must have handled the news with his usual savoir faire, as Coco has not complained so far. In one half hour she and Coco shall leave for Paris in Étienne's carriage. Her bags are packed, waiting near the bedroom door for a footman to carry them down. Tomorrow, Étienne's wife and entourage will descend on the château.

A shout from outside turns her toward the window. Crossing the room, she watches Coco and Boy racing their horses across the fields—Boy has come after all. She cannot believe her eyes. The carriage taking them to Paris waits in the courtyard. Workers arrived early this morning, already preparing the ballroom for the festivities.

She frowns, irritated. Perhaps Coco's bags are ready, and she plans to travel dressed to ride. Émilienne turns away from the window, scanning the room for forgotten things. Picking up her skirts, she leaves. This is a lovely day. She will wait for Coco on the terrace.

Standing at the balustrade, she watches the stable boys exercising the horses. Minutes pass, and then behind her, from the hallway, she hears voices. *At last, Coco arrives.* As Émilienne turns about, she's surprised to see Coco standing there with Boy Capel.

She sees it in his eyes before he even says a word.

I should have known. As always, a woman must solve the problem.

Boy is roping her into telling Coco the worst of the news. She glares at him. The poor girl is his responsibility now, his or Étienne's. Not hers. Perhaps in this situation Boy should trouble himself to exercise the management skills for which he is known in the business world.

He gives her a pleading look. "I have tried, Émmy. Only a woman can explain this situation to another. A woman like you, one who understands."

A sharp pain shoots through her chest. But Boy is right. Only a woman like her understands. Only a woman like her can explain.

Before she can blink, Boy disappears. And, of course, when she begins, Coco refuses to understand at all—not at first, at least. Émilienne recognizes at once the look in her eyes—fear, humiliation. She is wounded. All Coco thinks of right now is Boy and the threat of losing her only home.

In the end Coco is forced to accept the inevitable. A mistress almost never wins over the wife. They must both leave for Paris. Boy's offer to let Coco stay in his Paris apartment was a bit of salve on the wound. But the long wait while Coco packs her clothes strains Émilienne's patience. If Étienne's wife sends her maids ahead to prepare the rooms in advance, rumors will spread like lightning. The story of Étienne's mistresses fleeing from his wife would amuse all of Europe.

As the carriage rolls out of the courtyard, Émilienne sees Boy Capel riding across the field. He never even looks their way. *The bastard.*

Beside her in the carriage, Coco sniffs, pulling out a handkerchief. Feeling irritable, considering the drama of the afternoon, Émilienne glances at her. Coco, still madly in love with Boy, suffers. Émilienne pats her knee. But her voice is firm. "Listen! You have no choice, so you must look ahead, not back. Try to enjoy this weekend in Paris. Forget Royallieu and Étienne and Boy, just for these few days. On Tuesday you shall return and find everything the same."

Coco sniffs again.

"Things could have been worse," she says. "The wife could have decided to stay on for a while."

Coco emits a bitter laugh.

Émilienne has had enough. "Get used to this, kid. Family always wins." She lifts a finger. "Never attempt to come between a man and his family."

"But—"

"Don't be stupid." Her tone is sharp, she knows, but she has other worries to ponder. "You must learn to be tough."

After a pause, Coco leans close. "I have a secret to tell." She dabs her eyes with a handkerchief. "I am with child."

Émilienne turns to her. "Boy?"

Coco seems to hesitate. Then she lifts a shoulder. "Perhaps. Although the father could be Étienne." She looks off. "Time goes either way. I really don't know."

"How many months?"

"About four months. I am not certain."

"How are you hiding this!"

Coco shakes her head, looking off. "With a corset."

Émilienne leans her head back against the seat. Either Coco lies now or Étienne lied to her earlier saying he no longer takes Coco to his bed, but it makes no difference to Émilienne. This is not her concern; the problem is Coco's. Still, she almost smiles, envisioning Étienne's face when he hears this news, and then Boy's.

As Coco falls into silence, Émilienne gazes at the countryside, once again thinking of her own babe, Elisa. At least Coco claims two fathers for her child. She, Émilienne, had none to look out for her child after Georges died. She struggles to remember, to envision Georges's face, imagining how he would have looked if he'd received her letter telling him he was a father—and the other letters the duchess read and withheld.

Georges would have flown to her in the instant if he'd received that letter, no matter his maman's concerns. A storm of hatred for the duchess washes over her at this thought. And sorrow. How different life would have been if Georges's maman had never interfered.

But even so, that small voice reminds, sooner or later her secrets would have surfaced. Her years as a courtesan would have branded Elisa too.

She blinks back tears. Sometimes life plays tricks on a girl. Oh, what she would give to see Elisa again, just one more time, to look at her from afar, to find out how she grows, if she seems happy.

A thought stuns Émilienne. Perhaps she *could* see Elisa. Perhaps she should travel to the ducal village to see her girl from a distance. That should not be too difficult. It is a small village, Georges once said. Surely a girl Elisa's age leaves the castle from time to time. Would she recognize her babe?

Of course. A mother knows her child.

The thought simmers, warms her—excites her.

Besides, Elisa would not know who she was even if they stood face-to-face.

What has she to lose? Pressing her lips together, she closes her eyes and decides.

Yes. She will take a trip to the d'Ange village. This may be her last chance. Elisa is thirteen now, almost a young woman of marriage age. Soon she shall be wed and will disappear into another family, in another place. For this one time, she must see her child.

CHAPTER TWENTY-ONE

In Paris on the following afternoon, Émilienne sits alone on a bench on a platform at the Gare du Nord, with a small valise at her side. The d'Ange village is south of Lyon. She wears a dark, fitted day dress, a simple dress for the warm weather; long, white gloves; and a large, stylish hat.

For this quick trip, Lily pulled her hair back and twisted it into a woven bun. She is off to see Elisa for one last time.

Lily waits at the Paris apartment with instructions to tell no one where she has gone. She knows the secret, of course. Long ago Lily learned to keep her tongue. She smiles, thinking of Lily and how long they have been together. Why, she and Lily have grown up almost as sisters would.

Now, the train is late. Staring down the track, she fingers the black pearl she wears around her neck, the one Georges gave to her so long ago. She wore it today because it has come to remind her of Elisa. Surprising herself, she realizes that despite all the valuable jewels she has been given over the years, this little pearl is the most special.

With a sigh, she settles back. Delay is common on this line, she has heard. Just then a steam whistle blows in the distance, and she starts. A few passengers amble up to the spot where she sits. The whistle comes the second time, and the train appears in sight. Porters rush up the platform steps. One comes to her, offering help, but she shakes her head. She has only the small valise.

As the train slows to a stop and passengers disembark—businessmen in suits and workmen alike, women and children, and an occasional dog or cat, followed by porters and bags—suddenly many reasons why she should not get on this train rise, turning in her mind.

At last, when everyone is aboard and the first whistle blows for departure, Émilienne picks up her bag and climbs the steps into her carriage, heart pounding. She touches the black pearl. What will she see in the village? Will she have the strength to stay hidden and silent?

A few minutes later, the locomotive whistle blows, steam rises, and the train begins to move. Settling down, she places the valise beside her and takes a breath. At least now the decision is made, and she is alone. She leans her head back against the wall and closes her eyes, already feeling tired. As the train picks up speed, the rhythm of the wheels lulls her into a long, deep sleep.

The train arrives at Lyon by way of Orleans at five fifteen the next afternoon. She smiles at a porter, flirting as she leaves the train, wondering which way to go. He advises her on a guest house in the center of the village and locates a driver with a motorcar to convey her there.

The drive is short, but the road is rough. The sun moves toward the horizon as they arrive at the village walls. Here she is at last, in d'Ange. Entering through the gates, the narrow, cobbled streets are busy, almost blocked by lorries and farmers returning home from the town market.

She looks about, studying the place in which Elisa lives. It is much as Georges described, much as she imagined. The duchy includes a small village behind the walls, with a castle perched in the center. Past the castle, through a still-crowded market, and a short distance from the gates, the motorcar stops before a nondescript two-story brick house squeezed between rows of shops, now closed.

On the train, it occurred to Émilienne that the place to start her search for Elisa would be her school. Of course, with bad luck, Elisa has her own tutors, or perhaps a school located within the castle walls.

If so, she shall find another way.

Inside the guest house, as Émilienne requests a room for two nights, she looks up at the elderly man behind the counter. "Where is the town school for young ladies, monsieur?"

He squints at her over his glasses, handing her a key.

"I have promised to visit the child of a friend on my way to Lyon."

He asks the child's name. He knows most of the children in town, he says.

"Françoise." A common name these days.

He shakes his head.

"Just ask the mistress—she will find the girl." His expression softens. "I will give you directions. One moment, please." Reaching under the counter, he retrieves a blank piece of paper. "Here," he says, placing the page before her, now drawing lines for streets and boxes for buildings and houses. "It is not far. Nothing is far from everything else in our village. Now . . . as you can see, this is the way . . ."

Her room up a flight of stairs is small, with one window looking out over red rooftops to the high castle looming over the town. Dropping her bag on the floor, Émilienne moves to the window, watching the clouds changing colors as the sun sets behind the castle. Mountains in the distance take on a lavender glow. Perhaps, if she is lucky, tomorrow she will see her girl.

The thought lifts her spirits. Excited, she turns away and looks around. The bed is narrow, just for one. A wooden table holding a black telephone sits near the bed. These, a small wrought iron chair near the window and a table with a bowl for washing, are the only other objects in the room.

Tomorrow she shall rise early. Picking up the telephone, after several long rings, the old man answers at the desk. "Please ask someone to wake me in the morning. At seven o'clock."

"Seven o'clock," he repeats. "Yes, madame. Someone will knock on your door."

Hanging up the telephone, Émilienne looks at the bed, suddenly exhausted. Turning off the electric light, she falls onto the bed fully dressed. She plumps the pillow, rolls over, and closes her eyes.

※

Church bells wake her. By the bells, already it is eight, although she heard no knock on the door. She gazes at the bare wall before her, the wood door, and then, sitting up, she scans the room, stopping at the window. From here the high castle battlement in the center of town checks her view of anything beyond. Oh, how she hates this place.

Quickly, she washes, using water in the bowl and a folded cloth on the table. With no mirror, she smooths her hair, tucking in loose strands. She will dress like the village women—a plain cotton skirt to her ankles, a white cotton blouse with off-shoulder sleeves, and a short, loose vest. She smooths her waist with both hands, unaccustomed to feeling extra flesh. Perhaps she should have brought a corset after all.

Downstairs the innkeeper proffers his excuses for forgetting the call, offering hot chocolate, fruit, and a baguette to make up for his mistake. But already her stomach churns at the thought of seeing Elisa. Instead, she lifts an apple from the tray, thanking him. Slipping the apple into a pocket, she hurries out to the bustling street. She shall eat the apple later, once her twisting inner parts are calm again.

Hurrying through the winding alleys and streets, following the old man's map, she turns into a narrow passage between two buildings, a cut-through to another street, as the map shows. There, as she emerges from the dark passage, entering a wider road, she pauses. Straight ahead, within sight of the castle, is a small but imposing building built of glistening white stone. Elisa's schoolhouse, again, according to the map. The street before her ends at the d'Ange castle to her right, just a short walk to the school.

A green lawn, surrounded by a low iron fence, protects the schoolhouse. Long rows of windows across the front of the building on upper and lower floors face the street. The shutters are open now. Laughter to her left catches Émilienne's attention. She turns to see two small groups of young girls strolling in her direction—all wear identical uniforms, long red pinafores with thick straps and high waistlines, worn over high-necked, long-sleeve white blouses. Most are accompanied by an older woman, a governess or maman, perhaps.

Please . . . please . . . don't let me have already missed her.

She stares at the castle entrance at the end of the street. There, the gates stand open. Perhaps the open gates are a sign.

Perhaps Elisa will still come this way—if she is to come at all. Her heart beats like a hammer in her chest. Uniformed guards mill about, while two stand at attention at the gate.

Émilienne settles on a low step of a deserted building behind her, facing the schoolyard across the street. Here, overgrown bushes on either side of the steps and low-hanging branches shield her from view. As she waits, she looks across the street, straight ahead where a nun in black habit has come to the school fence, lifting her hand to some girls, beckoning them on, then herding the girls inside.

Now, she waits, pressing back into the branches, making herself small each time the schoolgirls pass. When Elisa arrives, she must not catch even a glimpse of her maman. Sitting back, she rubs the apple against her skirt, then takes a bite.

Émilienne is merely a ghost of the past as she nibbles the apple, waiting in shadows.

At last, the church bells toll again, and this time the count is nine. A stir comes from the direction of the castle entrance. Her heart quickens again—if she is still to come, this is the time. For a moment Émilienne trembles, and all of a sudden she cannot catch her breath.

She is Émilienne d'Alençon, she tells herself, breathing in— slowly, slowly—and then breathing out, never lifting her eyes from the castle gate. Suddenly all four of the guards at the entrance stand at attention.

There she is. Immediately she is certain this is Elisa, coming her way.

Her heart pounds as she leans forward, dropping the apple and peeking through the branches, eyes riveted on the girl. Her girl—a mother knows. She is tall for her age, already a bit taller than her maman. And look, how she holds herself so straight and proud as she passes through the guards. Why, already she is beautiful, lovely. Just look at the shining hair, silver in the sun, like her father's.

But she also has a certain way about her, reminding Émilienne of herself at that age—the way she holds herself, pulled up through her torso, shoulders flat, swinging along. As she passes the guards at the gate, smiling, Elisa takes a little skip.

One of the guards behind her smiles as Émilienne's girl strolls out into the sunshine with a little sway to her hips, just as Émilienne used to do when she was that age in Montmartre. Clasping her hands, she almost laughs aloud. Elisa is a girl who loves life!

Peering through the leaves, Émilienne feels the satisfaction of an empty vessel filled. She crosses her arms, hugging herself, struggling to hold back a wild desire to race out onto the street and touch her daughter. The yearning comes so strong that she forces herself back, farther back against the higher step, hiding even deeper into the branches. Elisa must remain innocent; she is a girl who shall never be touched by her maman's reputation—a girl who shall be admired by everyone she meets. Who shall fall in love, make a good marriage, and have many children.

A friend joins Elisa now, a girl about her age it seems. Elisa smiles, and the two link arms as they walk along.

Elisa is happy here.

Not a muscle in Émilienne's body moves as the two come close, strolling in the direction of the schoolyard, heads together, laughing as girls will do. Her eyes fix only on Elisa. She bites her lips, careful that she doesn't call out. There—the girls walk now across from her on the narrow street; they push through the schoolyard gate.

What if . . . a small voice whispers.

But she dare not, no matter what! She . . . will . . . not . . . move . . . from this hidden spot. She remains still even as the old ache crawls through her again, pain from head to toe, limb to limb. She does not move while tears slip down her cheeks, blurring her eyes. She prepared herself for these feelings, this yearning for the child to whom she shall never speak.

She would give her life for one minute with Elisa, she thinks, watching the nun come out to greet the two. But no. It is Elisa who matters most—it is Elisa she must protect.

When Elisa disappears inside the school, Émilienne slumps, quietly sobbing, wilting as violets wilt in the sun. This is the last time she will see Elisa, she knows. Soon her babe will marry and disappear into a stranger's home.

For a long time Émilienne sits on the step behind the branches, staring at the schoolhouse door, remembering the day the Duchess d'Ange took her babe away. She sits on the step, holding on to the black pearl, rolling it between a finger and her thumb.

CHAPTER TWENTY-TWO

Lily greets her with a surprise upon her return from seeing Elisa. Monsieur le Directeur at the Folies Bergère has sent a note—would mademoiselle be interested in a new show he has in mind?

The Folies has called!

She was right not to give up. After fleeing Paris for Royallieu in the fall when she had received no contract offers, after hiding for almost six months in the countryside, she has not been forgotten in Paris after all. Émilienne reaches out to Lily and the girl comes into her arms. "At last," Émilienne whispers.

"He asked if tomorrow morning is convenient, and I told him, yes," Lily says. Her smile is wide, her eyes shine with excitement. "Rehearsals must start tomorrow to meet the schedule."

Stunned, filling with joy as she hears the words, Émilienne feels a wave of relief. This is a sign she was right not to agree to Étienne's proposal. Despite her time away, audiences still love her! She is not too old to be sought out to dance after all.

The following morning, sunshine slants through the open

shutters, waking her early. She smiles at Lily's old trick, making certain that she arrives on time for morning rehearsals. Yesterday, everything changed with the summons to the Folies stage. Strange how luck sometimes turns things about. Stretching, feeling well and strong, she gazes about the room. Then she kicks back the quilt and swings her feet to the floor.

How wonderful, rehearsal for a new show!

Reaching for her robe at the end of the bed, she slips it on, then rings the bell for breakfast—something light. Tea, and toast with jam while she dresses. Later, at the dressing table, she looks up as Lily enters, crossing the room to place the tray on a nearby table. With a nod, Émilienne continues brushing her hair. "I shall need my rehearsal costume today, Lily—the white blouse, red-striped skirt." Worn, loose clothing, something comfortable for practice. Retrieving the clothes, Lily places them on the bed along with Émilienne's ballet slippers.

In the carriage she leans back, feeling the thrill of building a new show. As the Folies theater comes in sight, Émilienne orders Anson to drop her right in front. Entering through the grand hall, she winds her way toward the stage. Already she hears the tap-tap of the ballet mistress's cane marking time with four young dancers.

Halting beneath the stalls, she watches for a moment. The ballet mistress, the great Mariquita, is known for her high standards. The four dancers onstage with her are clearly trained in ballet, unlike Émilienne. Her stomach tightens at this thought. Madame—as the dancers call her—was once premier dancer for the Paris Opera Ballet. She will not be an easy mistress.

Entering the promenade, Émilienne turns—out of habit—seeking Toulouse-Lautrec. There, he's off to the side, already sketching, wearing his uniform this morning, a frock coat and top hat. When he glances up, she waves. The surly artist merely nods and returns to his work. She has been gone too long when even Toulouse is a welcome sight.

Now, the dancers pause onstage. Mariquita peers down at Émilienne. "Come along, Émilienne, you are late." Madame stands with feet apart in second position, with her hands on her hips, skirt pulled up at one side and hitched at her waist. Lights over the stage turn her henna hair to orange. "I was beginning to think we would have to replace you with Otero."

Émilienne's laugh sounds false, even to her. Already one count against her, untrained as she is. "I have come, as agreed, madame." Onstage, turning back to the ballet girls, Madame releases them, motioning them offstage.

"We shall start down there," Madame calls, coming down the side steps from the stage—swanlike, her long neck and straight back give her dignity, although she walks with splayed feet as a duck.

"One moment." Émilienne sits down beside Toulouse. Removing her shoes, she changes into ballet slippers. Now, musicians begin arriving, pulling their chairs near the foot of the stage. Madame stops, speaking with them as she motions toward Émilienne. The pianist nods, runs his fingers up and down the scale.

Standing, Émilienne hitches her skirt up and, walking to a square box on the floor near the stage, rubs her slippers in the rosin to keep from slipping. When she looks up, Madame waits in the center of the promenade, while a stagehand drags a ballet barre over.

"Anytime, Émilienne," Madame says in a singsong voice. She taps her cane with the words. At this, the pianist stops the scales and hits a few single notes. "We do not have all day."

Émilienne grips the barre, determined to give her best. Madame begins her count for the warm-up, and Émilienne thinks of nothing but the timing of the music and the tapping of the stick—one, two, three, four—back straight, shoulders down, chin high, neck long, bending, straightening, tightening.

This is not the Opera Ballet, but still she feels the stretch of her muscles, the control when she slowly lifts a leg, centering herself as she imagines the same magical line she felt in the Seabird dance, a line from her toes through her head, pulling her torso up.

Still the muscles pull. It has been too long.

Three-quarters of an hour later, they move onto the stage where Madame marks the steps in the routine and Émilienne follows, counting the beats for the movements of the dance. The choreography is difficult, although the other four dancers, trained in ballet, unlike Émilienne, will take on the most difficult combinations.

But Émilienne is the *étoile,* the star, and the show should center on her. Madame has given her simple steps as the story unfolds—five village girls competing for the same young man. In the end, Émilienne wins his love. Her performance—and, more important, her beauty—will leave the audiences wanting more. Over and over again they practice on this first afternoon—always one more time, with Madame—and dancing fills her with new strength and joy.

When the great Mariquita at last calls a break, Émilienne sinks into a chair beside Toulouse. "Well?" Émilienne turns to him.

Toulouse looks up. "Not bad for a beginner," he says. Before she can snap a reply, he returns to his sketch. Émilienne leans close for a peek. At least he has made her look pretty this time. Toulouse, who claims to love the demimondaines, with one stroke of a paintbrush, like Émile Zola with his pen, can sometimes destroy a girl.

Toulouse, noticing her scrutiny of his sketch, glances up, looking annoyed. But Émilienne is enthralled. "You have caught something here, Toulouse. The connection between a ballet mistress and the dancer."

His hand continues moving across the page. "This one has the look of war."

His words silence her at once. Then he adds, "But any moment in time between two women is likely war." Closing the sketchbook, he rises. Lifting his cane from the back of the chair, he heads for the bar, close to the musicians' stand. The barman nods and, reaching underneath, comes up with a bottle, handing it over to Toulouse-Lautrec.

The artist lives in his own world. The man was born with legs that appear slightly bowed and twisted, making it difficult for him to walk at a casual gait, but no one should ever consider Toulouse an easy mark. Just then Madame calls. Émilienne rises as the ballet mistress motions her up to the stage again.

Suddenly, looking up at the stage and Madame, she pauses, uncertain, thinking of that extra layer of flesh she noticed at her waistline. And those thin lines spraying from the corners of her eyes, and now, two vertical ones between her brows. Youth and beauty have always carried her before this, and a few dance steps she learned over the years.

Always, dancing was play. Today she must work.

The thought flicks across her mind that dancing becomes more difficult with the passing of each year.

✸

Two weeks later, opening night for her new Folies show is a success, according to the newspapers—with three curtain calls, although she used to garner more. Charles at *Gil Blas* remains quiet. Distracted by his newest girl, she supposes. A flood of flowers cover the stage, and more arrive in her dressing room.

She was surprised, however—more than surprised—when Monsieur le Directeur, who was standing in the wings, motioned the four other dancers, younger girls, to take the second and third curtain calls along with her, at her side. The first few curtain calls should belong to the star.

She should have known this would come, of course. In rehearsals, Madame's choreography placed the four young dancers onstage with her throughout the performance. Émilienne's only moment alone in the spotlight comes when she wins the young prince's love over the other dancers at last.

Never has Émilienne d'Alençon shared the spotlight onstage like this. It is because she is not trained formally for ballet, she's certain.

This show has been different from her usual routine. Rehearsals were long, every day including Sundays, working from ten in the morning until ten at night. Each night Lily welcomed her home with heated clothes for her tight, aching muscles, unused to the demanding work after her leisurely sojourn at Royallieu. In the past, Émilienne—as the star—placed limits on her time in rehearsals.

On the second night of the show, she spots an empty box in the theater at stage right. And each night thereafter, the audience seems to shrink. This is the fault of the choreography, she thinks. The performance deserves one star alone. Not one with four smaller stars circling her throughout the dances.

In the past things were clear. The audience came to see Émilienne.

Sitting in her dressing room, thoughts come, alarming her. The truth is, she moves slower now, her muscles are still tight, despite the exercises and stretching. Spending half a year lounging at Royallieu was a mistake. Her hands no longer span her waist without a corset, and the dance is difficult while wearing one. She insisted on gaslights in her dressing room, although le Directeur complained—gaslights are softer than bright electric. Gentlemen still call, though not as often as before. And on some evenings, while lifting champagne at boulevard cafés, she longs to sink into her bed at home, to close her eyes and fall asleep.

One evening, Étienne surprises her when he is in town. Onstage, she spots him in his box, and after, he sends a note inviting her to dine. Except for a quick visit to Royallieu to assist Coco's baby's birth—a difficult reminder of Elisa, she stayed as briefly as she could—she has not seen him since her departure. She does not want to miss him while he is in Paris. She has come to think of Étienne as one of her closest friends. And, from his letters since she left Royallieu, she senses he also feels the same. He no longer mentions an arrangement.

She turns to Lily, smiling. "This one is from Étienne. Please cancel my dinner engagement tonight, Lily. I will dine with him instead." Étienne always lights up an evening.

Lily nods, turning toward the door. There she pauses, looking back. "What excuse shall I give to the gentleman who waits, Émmy?"

She looks up. Her tone is vague. "Have I canceled him before?"

With a wry smile, Lily nods.

Émilienne turns back to the mirror, throwing up her hands. "Well, just tell him anything . . ." She flicks her hand in Lily's direction. "Anything you can think of—I don't care."

"All right." She hears the hint of disapproval in Lily's voice. But what can she do? Étienne comes first, even though now they are only friends.

Picking up the cloth for removing the greasepaint, she

hesitates for a moment, staring into the mirror. Her stomach flutters. She has insulted a gentleman with whom she agreed to have dinner. Will she regret this snub one day when her beauty fades?

Setting down the cloth, she lights a cigarette, fanning smoke. Then she shrugs.

She is wealthy now and shall take care of herself when she is old, when the time comes. She shall worry about old age when the time comes. Dismissing these thoughts, she leans toward the mirror, cleaning off the makeup. Besides, she is a girl who never gives a damn, she likes to say.

✿

Within a week of the show opening, clouds turn dark as *Gil Blas* writes only a dutiful review on the Folies show, with brief compliments to Émilienne as well as the other four dancers. A few nights later, with Gabrielle, Émilienne spots Charles at Café Anglais with Simone, one of the four dancers in her show. Charles does not yet spot them—too busy ordering glasses of red wine, delivered in a small mechanical train to his table.

Gabrielle leans toward her, whispering, "Charles escorts the girl all over Paris, almost every night. Just as he did for us."

Émilienne nods, sipping champagne. "He's empty without a grateful girl on his arm. Have you noticed? He fills himself with us."

"Still, he made us, Émmy. We love him. No?" She turns to look.

Émilienne lets out a laugh, thinking of all his rules. "Of course!"

They both quietly laugh and stop to greet him when they leave.

But as days pass, as her show closes, Émilienne waits for good news, for a note, a theater asking her to perform—solo. More days pass, then weeks without even a tick of interest from the Folies or any other theater.

Now, she spends her days sleeping—much too late, as Lily says. And she spends her nights parading down the Grands Boulevards of Paris, sometimes on the arms of one of her gentlemen friends. Sometimes with Liane or Gabrielle or Caroline. As Charles used to say, the important thing is to be noticed.

Lily approaches her one day as she sits on the balcony in the twilight, holding a book in her lap, looking off.

"Perhaps you should visit a few of the theaters, Émmy."

Startled, Émilienne looks up. Lily's cheeks are rosy, flushed. But still, she continues. "You know most of the directors in Paris. They would welcome you!"

"Make the rounds of the theaters, did you say?"

She nods, still blushing.

Émilienne looks down and opens the book. "That's not necessary, Lily. A lull between shows is not unusual. Theaters do not coordinate their schedules, *chéri*. One show may close while another goes on for extended weeks." Leaning back in the comfortable chair, she begins flipping pages. "Now where was I in this story!"

But when Lily is gone, she stares at the pages before her, unseeing. She will never beg for parts. She is Émilienne! Besides, everyone feels this same malaise when a show closes. Every girl worries about what comes next.

All she must do is wait. The theaters shall come to her.

She shall not worry about theater calls. She shall enjoy the beautiful spring weather. She shall unloose the corset, have some fun. Carrying the book into the bedroom, she tosses it on the bed and rings for Lily. This afternoon she shall join Liane and

Gabrielle at Café de la Paix, their usual spot now that Liane is married and Gabrielle is in between rehearsals.

❧

The moon is full later that night, shining over Paris. Stars twinkle, a clarinet calls from a nearby corner, and Émilienne's mood lifts right away. Liane and Gabrielle and Émilienne leave the Café de la Paix at midnight, parading from cafés to cabarets, reminding her of Georges's marauding band of Princelings in the old days. So long ago, that seems.

Feeling joyful, Émilienne flashes her eyes, dancing, singing, drinking champagne.

But as the night wanes, her thoughts slow. And it seems each time she lifts her glass, someone pours another. She leans on her elbows, chin in her hands, listening as the music turns to songs from years ago, bringing memories of her lost girl and of Georges's betrayal. Tears blur her eyes, thinking of the sweet times she has missed with Elisa. Too soon Elisa will turn sixteen, an age to marry, and as a child of d'Ange, she shall marry well. But Émilienne shall never see her girl in a wedding gown. Nor will she know when the time comes and Elisa carries her own babe. Her stomach churns.

Turning, longing to flee, she looks about for Liane or Gabrielle, but through the crowd and smoke, they have disappeared. As Émilienne moves from the table, she stumbles, falling, but for a strong arm swooping her up, encircling her waist just in time. A man's voice whispers, he shall help.

They dance, moving too slow for the music. When he caresses her, his hands are warm, comforting. When she sighs, he pulls her close. She rests her head upon his shoulder, feeling light, floating now while they dance, moving together to the slow, seductive beat.

Later, the carriage shifts from side to side, and someone shouts rudeness to Anson, a tone that she does not like. Still, her stomach churns. But then he laughs, and suddenly everything amuses; she loves to laugh. As he holds her in his arms, she gazes over his shoulder at a blur of silver stars in the night. He whispers in her ear how beautiful she is, how he loves her so.

The carriage stops before her apartment, and he holds her as they emerge, steering her toward the door. Lily is nowhere around. Together they drift up the stairs, into the bedroom, and he guides her now to the bed. There, they make love—sometimes tender, sometimes not, but she holds tight, laughing, weeping, until at last, she falls asleep.

In the morning, when she is woken by church bells, the shutters are closed. Pale light filters in from the outside, striping the floor. She turns her head and blinks. A stranger lies beside her, a man she does not know. Émilienne lies very still, straining to recall, afraid to look again. When images of the night, in that last café, slither up from the grime, she does not remember returning home.

She lifts the quilt and slides from the bed.

Now, the stranger coughs. He groans.

Crossing the room, she opens the shutters, letting in more light. Turning, hands behind her back, she studies the stranger as he moans and slides up, leaning against the headboard. He runs his fingers through his hair, then he looks about. His eyes stop on her.

The man is just a boy.

He grins. "Well, hi ho, pretty madame." His voice comes rough. He pats a spot beside him on her bed. "Why are you way over there? Come. Jump back in here, girlie!"

She presses back against the window. "Get out," she says.

He frowns, squints, looks her up and down.

Her fury rises at this inspection.

"Did I not give you a good time?"

"Leave, or I shall call the guards."

But already he is out of the bed, and she scrambles for the bell, calling Lily, shouting for Anson, just before he captures her. Gripping her waist, he turns her around, pulls her tight against him.

"A tiger, eh?"

She lifts her knee, slamming a blow, and he lets out a yell, releasing her as he doubles, then falls to his knees. Backing up, she screams again while he looks up, his face bright red now. His eyes fixed on hers.

The door bursts open as Anson races into the room, running flat out for the boy, followed by Lily, just behind. He staggers back as big Anson comes, gripping his arms, forcing him toward the door amid the boy's curses on the world.

As Anson pushes him through the door, forcing him down the stairs, Lily embraces her, whispering soothing words, smoothing her hair with calming sounds while Émilienne sobs. Lily steers her to a chair.

What happened last night? Who was that boy?

She drops her face in her hands, the evening a blur.

Lily bustles about, picking up clothes, pulling sheets from the bed for the wash, avoiding her eyes. Below more voices come from downstairs, shouting, cursing, and then the door slams, and silence descends.

Émilienne takes a deep breath and asks Lily to prepare a bath.

Soap will wash away the night. Although she is certain memories of this morning will never disappear.

CHAPTER TWENTY-THREE

PARIS, 1905

Fall again. Almost a year ago she was away from Paris, visiting Royallieu.

On this clear, bright morning, it comes to Émilienne that she has waited long enough for a theater call. Her show ended months ago, and the time has come to take charge—Lily was right. Life is dull without dancing, without the excitement of an audience. Why, she even misses rehearsals, misses having other dancers around who, like her, love the stage, love the work of putting a show together, watching it unfold like magic day by day.

By noon Émilienne is up and dressed. Lily orders the carriage while she applies a little makeup. A bit heavier than she usually prefers, but this is business, and it's best to leave an impression. She sits back, studying the job. Her strawberry blond hair still has the same tint of gold. Her lashes remain thick and dark, her skin like cream. She still has her heart-shaped lips, her turned-up nose, and a cheeky pout when she desires.

With Lily's help she slips on a fashionable dark red skirt fitted tight over her hips, with only a few petticoats, according to changing styles. She adds her favorite lace blouse and a corseted jacket of red-and-cream stripes. Émilienne stands before the mirror. She may have aged a bit, but the change is slight. And the corset hides the extra weight.

As she opens the door to the grand hall of the Folies Bergère, she breathes in the familiar scents—powder, lingering perfume, tobacco. Walking through the wide hall under the high arched ceilings, she listens to the musicians tuning their instruments inside. Excited, her pulse racing, Émilienne tightens her muscles and pulls up. Even at five feet one, she feels she stands tall and straight. With a last touch to her hat, she lifts her chin and swings into the theater through the promenade entrance under the box seats.

Walking under the stalls, she watches the dancer onstage—Loie Fuller, the new sensation. She stands there watching the ballet mistress directing the other dancers, while they listen. Only three musicians compose the orchestra area now, practicing. The pianist runs his fingers up and down the high scales as he waits, while the clarinet blows smooth, low notes. A trumpet rests on a table, where its player leans against the foot of the stage.

Toulouse-Lautrec, of course, sits at one of the small round tables on the promenade, scratching on his drawing pad. They all ignore her. A surprising little flutter of fear holds her back for an instant. Here, she has come on a whim, with no appointment. Perhaps she should have waited.

But already she has waited too long. Tapping her parasol on the floor as she walks, she proceeds toward the artist.

"Good afternoon," she says, pulling out a chair beside him.

"I do not know if the day is good or bad," he says without

looking up. "But I suppose I wish for you the best of what remains."

She smiles even as the corners of her mouth turn down. One would expect a fonder greeting, even from Toulouse. He continues sketching as before, his brush fluttering across the sketch pad like falling leaves.

"Where is Monsieur le Directeur? I don't have all day." Placing her parasol against the chair, she stands, wandering over to the deserted bar. Stepping behind the bar, she inspects the bottles, arms akimbo, until she spots the cognac. Hennessy will do.

James Hennessy. She smiles, remembering. James was quite the lover, and—thinking of her horse, Bienveillant—a man who loved a good joke. Picking up the bottle and two glasses, she returns to Toulouse. With a glance he nods, and she sits down beside him again. She pours two glasses, handing him one, and she sips the other, enjoying the warmth as the cognac goes down. She needs the lift.

"Mademoiselle d'Alençon."

She starts, turning as le Directeur emerges from the shadows. Strolling toward her, he holds out his arms. "Ah, I heard that you had come. To what do I owe this pleasure?"

She lifts her cheeks for his kisses, one then the other. Taking a few steps back, he pulls two cigarettes from his vest, offering her one.

She shall remain on her best behavior. "No thank you. I am training for my next performance."

He nods, striking a match. "Wonderful to see you, Émilienne." He rocks back on his heels, thumbs in his lapels, looking her up and down. He smiles. Pulling a handkerchief from his vest, he wipes his forehead.

"Our last show together was a delight, which is what brings me . . ." she says. She lowers her lashes.

"Oh!" He interrupts, sliding a hand toward his vest pocket. "May I offer some advance tickets for the new show?"

She shakes her head, glancing about. "Have you a place where we can talk?" With a glance at Toulouse, she adds, "Alone?"

"Ah, if only I had the time." He smiles, turning his eyes to the stage, then back to her. "But as you see, already we are rehearsing, and I also have business to attend. We've a fine young group of dancers. Do you agree? As good as I have seen in a long time." He leans toward her, with a conspiratorial smile. "Not that they could match our Émilienne, of course."

With a glance at Toulouse, he adds, "Am I correct, monsieur?"

The artist shrugs. "As you say. But there is always hope for tomorrow."

As Monsieur le Directeur turns back to her, the corners of his mouth draw down. "Unfortunate, my Émilienne, but I must leave you now. Of course, on the first night I shall have tickets waiting. How many would you like?"

She reaches across and covers his hand with her own.

"As you must have heard, I have been undecided about arrangements of late. Now, however, I have returned for good . . . to dance." She pauses, smiling her special smile. "And of course, you were first in my thoughts."

He stares at her for an instant too long. In the moment, she understands the mute rejection. The Folies has no place for her, at least not now.

With a stiff smile, she rises, and he stands as well. On his face, a look of relief. He holds out his hands, taking hers. "Soon, we shall talk." But a flush rises to his cheeks as he speaks the lie. Caught—he sees it in her eyes, she knows—his voice turns gentle. "Paris shall thrill at your return to the Folies soon, Émilienne. We must talk. Perhaps next week?"

"Of course. If I am not already booked."

He waves toward the stage. "These young girls have neither your sparkle nor your instinctive talent." He shifts his eyes to her. "But they do have contracts. You must come to see our new soloists, darling."

She looks up at the now lone dancer onstage, working with the ballet mistress. "Now this one!" He nods in that direction.

"Loie Fuller?"

"Yes, come from America. Have you read *Gil Blas* of late? She is all the talk in Paris."

The girl looks young. As young, perhaps, as when Émilienne danced with rabbits.

"Oh yes, I have. Of course."

He nods, pulling out the handkerchief again, wiping his neck. "I shall introduce you next time. How many tickets did you say you shall need?"

Émilienne is too old. This is what she hears.

"I shall let you know. And . . ." turning to watch the American onstage, she adds, "I shall make a point of watching Mademoiselle Fuller dance."

Rising, she picks up her parasol, managing a gay smile. "Now, if you will excuse me, monsieur, I must hurry off." With a tap on Toulouse-Lautrec's shoulder, she gestures toward his sketch. "The right leg is wrong. It must turn out from her hip."

"I paint what I see," he mutters. But when he looks up, she sees pity in his eyes. He knows, and he wants no part of this, dropping his eyes back to the sketch pad.

Her cheeks burn as she turns to leave, listening to the ballet mistress's familiar count for Loie Fuller's dance. Hurrying through the grand entrance hall to her waiting carriage, she leans back against the cushions, taking a long, deep breath.

"Where to, mademoiselle?" Anson calls.

"Home."

She sees nothing as she gazes through the windows on the way. The Folies Bergère has been her second home for years. What has happened that Monsieur le Directeur should offer her tickets to a show rather than a contract?

Tomorrow will be different. Yes, tomorrow she will call on Les Ambassadeurs. For years they have attempted to pull her away from the Folies. With her fingers entwined on her lap, she looks forward now. Of course, that is the answer. Once her crowds move from the Folies to Ambassadeurs, things will change.

Paris shall soon find that no one replaces Émilienne. Monsieur le Directeur of the Folies shall rue the day he let her slip away. This thought gives her strength, forces her to sit up straight. She has never been one to quit.

Still, she gazes out at the streets as the carriage rolls along, unseeing, thinking of the new thickness in her waist, the lines marring her complexion. The dancers she watched onstage this afternoon looked half her age. Panic cuts through her at this thought.

Why, at dinner the other night, even Étienne was not sorry when she put into words what they both already knew—no longer lovers, they are now just friends. She is welcome to Royallieu at any time, he said, taking her hands. But unspoken was—arriving as a mere visitor, she shall be given smaller rooms.

She lets out a short, bitter laugh. Of course, he would welcome Émilienne at any time—Émilienne, the glittering star of the Folies. The girl sought by every theater in Paris to dance, the most beautiful woman in Paris, and, as someone once wrote, the most expensive. Everyone loves Émilienne—or did.

And now?

Everything changes.

Part Three

CHAPTER TWENTY-FOUR

Her smile lights any room. Always she is aware of this and uses it to prove she is still the best, the liveliest girl around, even though she has left off dancing now—although she still has her gentlemen friends. With jewels to sell, some good luck at the racecourse, and money in the bank, Émilienne is safe without an arrangement with a protector, so far.

And she remains the most beautiful courtesan in Paris, many say—along with Liane and Caroline, of course. *The Three Graces*, Charles named them years ago. Liane lives a life of leisure, now she is married. Caroline still dances. But, instead of entertaining others, Émilienne's happy state is entertaining herself at the races, enthralled in the new challenge of horses. Or, to be more precise, betting on the horses. Racing. Studying the odds and putting her money down where it counts.

At the races, Émilienne feels a greater thrill watching her chosen horse pounding the flat, rounding the turn, and heading down the homestretch than ever she felt when audiences went wild, tearing at the curtains after a show, covering her with flowers.

At least this is what she tells herself.

She has become an expert at the racing game. This is a business, after all, with plenty of money involved. She has come to know the horses, the jockeys, the trainers, the fields, the tracks. She has learned the trick of studying the sheets, and overall, she comes out ahead. She is certain she is good at calculating risk—sometimes, far ahead of time.

Besides, why should she worry over any one loss at the racecourse? She has made a fortune in life. Although she never really stops to count—that is what banks are for. She knows the risk betting brings. She has never done things the easy way. The thrill, the suspense and waiting, all of that is just part of the reward when it comes to the horses.

And why not! Just the thought of the races at Longchamp this coming weekend lifts her spirits.

Étienne's Dark Magic runs this Sunday. She looks forward to the race and seeing Étienne and Coco, catching up on the news. She still visits Royallieu on occasion. And how things have changed there! Coco is now in the business of making ladies' hats, over Étienne's objections—at first. But Coco's little hats are all the rage in Paris. Smaller and lighter than what she'd used to call the old boats, they are much more stylish.

She lets out a little laugh at the thought of Coco's revolution. What she would not give to have heard the conversation between Étienne and Coco on that subject! Coco won. Now, Étienne even allows her to make the hats and sell them from his garçonnière on boulevard Malesherbes. And Émilienne has made certain that every fashionable demimondaine in Paris wears Coco's hats—Gabrielle, Liane, Misia, all of them. Society ladies have begun to notice as well.

This weekend she shall wear one of Coco's hats to the races. As always, Émilienne takes great care of her effect before the racing crowd. Always on display, she feels a special need to look her best at the racecourse. With Lily's help, she tends to her beauty with care. She still sets the fashion, Liane always says. Yes, she is older now, although good at hiding this. She does well hiding secrets.

On the day of the races, while she sits before the mirror and Lily styles her hair, she muses over the bets she intends to place this afternoon. She is certain to win in the fourth, with Dark Magic, and she is considering a run in the third. Caution is for those with limits, those who are afraid to make decisions, to trust the mind over the heart.

When Lily finishes, she looks up. "I shall wear the white dress today," she says. "It seems everyone in Paris wears white this summer."

Lily sets down the brush. "White suits you, Émmy. I'll get the dress."

Émilienne lifts her hand. "No, go along. This is your afternoon with your maman." She smiles. "I am not really helpless, you know."

With a kiss on each cheek for the girl, sending her off, Émilienne strides toward the armoire. She must find just the right jewels to go with the dress. She feels lucky today; everything must be perfect.

❦

As always at Longchamp, colorful flags line the fences and the entrance to the racecourse. Gentlemen wearing frock coats and top hats and smoking their cigars, and ladies strutting their best in the latest styles, bustle by, some looking back when they recognize her. Ahead, on the crowded walkway, Émilienne spots Coco, Boy, and Étienne. She hurries, catching up with them at the gate, lifting the morning line from the box as she enters.

Étienne, delighted, bids her join them at the backside where the horses are stalled. As they walk on, carriages enter the grounds, although motorcars are not allowed. She shall sit in the enclosure with Étienne, Coco, and Boy today, but she almost envies those in the carriages on the way to picnics near the course. There are no polite rules with those carefree working men and ladies of the demimonde, and a few grisettes, all restricted from the stands. Instead, they picnic and party merrily in their carriages and on blankets laid on the grass.

She turns to Coco as they stroll along. Émilienne's distress during Coco's birthing is long gone, especially since she learned the child is not welcome at Royallieu by Étienne. Coco admitted once that Boy is the true father. But Boy Capel has not yet offered to marry her, nor does he even formally acknowledge the babe, a little boy.

She fills with sympathy for Coco, wondering whether Georges would have done the same with Elisa if he had lived and—betrayer that he was—they'd never married.

"How is little André?" she whispers as Étienne and Boy stop to speak with a friend. It is difficult to believe four years have passed since the child's birth.

"He is well," Coco says, sounding morose. "He lives with a fine priest, a friend of Boy's." She looks off. "I miss him so."

Changing the subject—she cannot bear to discuss children—Émilienne looks at Coco's hat. "I see your hats all over Paris. They are adorable. I wear mine all the time."

Coco smiles. "I am officially a milliner now." With a glance from the corners of her eyes, she adds, "As you might say, I am a woman in the trade."

"Yes, and doing well. What got into you, Coco?"

"You once said I needed a plan for the future." She lifts a shoulder. "Well, this is my plan. Designing and selling hats."

Émilienne turns, shining her best smile on Coco. The girl listened after all. "I shall never wear a hat but yours. Gabrielle says she will wear one of your hats onstage soon. By the way, have you seen her in *La Maîtresse de Piano* at the Sarah Bernhardt theater?"

Coco shakes her head.

"She is quite an actress."

"Leon says it was wonderful. He hasn't brought her out to us in some time. Though I shall talk to him about that."

Just then, Boy excuses himself, striding off, and Étienne steers the two women through the enclosure gate to the backside. Émilienne has bets to place but plenty of time. Étienne stops first at Black Magic's stall. She and Coco wait outside, watching as he confers with his trainer and grooms.

After a few minutes Coco strolls off, looking at the horses. With the sunshine and heat, Émilienne stifles a yawn.

"He is fast as the wind, that one." The voice from behind startles, and she turns, looking now into the eyes of a young man, a jockey wearing the Hennessy stable colors. "Good afternoon, Mademoiselle d'Alençon."

He removes his cap, tucking it under his arm, then takes her hand and bows. When he brushes her knuckles with his lips, she feels a chill. Then he looks up, and his eyes seem to lock onto hers, as if already, she is his.

How strange, that thought.

"You see, I know your name, even if you don't know mine."

She recognizes the man, of course. Anyone living in Europe would know this man, the finest jockey to come along in many years, they say. All of Paris is enchanted with Alec Carter. He is handsome as well, though younger than she would have expected. Much younger than her. But then she has only ever seen him riding, never up close.

"Alec Carter, at your service," he says.

She smiles. "Good day, Monsieur Carter."

"Alec . . . please."

She dips her chin. "I am flattered by Europe's fastest rider. What should I think!" As she speaks, she takes his measure—the jockey is small, her height, with close to one hundred fifty wins in Europe and Britain so far, as she recalls. He is known as the Artist, the Lion. His straw-colored hair ruffles in the breeze, and every woman passing gives him a second glance. His skin is bronzed by the sun, his body built of hard muscle and bone, his laughter infectious, pulling her in.

But so young, perhaps ten or more years younger than her thirty-nine.

"You could think about having dinner with me after the races."

He is elegant, this young man.

"Perhaps." She smiles. "I watched you win the Grand Steeple-Chase last year."

"With my good horse, Dandolo." He smiles, still holding her eyes.

His eyes are bright and clear, so blue against his sun-darkened skin. He has kind eyes. His chin is strong, his lips, inviting. He describes the race in detail, as if her opinion is important. His eyes do not wander while they talk, as with so many other men. Standing there, listening, she feels something new, a connection between them. Already, she feels as if they are old friends.

Coco wanders back and she introduces them. Surprising Émilienne, her greeting is cool. "I have seen you ride," she says with a nod. "Good luck today." And then she turns away, wandering off. One jockey is much like another, to her. The girl has no understanding of this man's talent, other than his wins.

Étienne walks up with a hearty greeting for Alec. "I have been tempting him to visit us at Royallieu," he says to Émilienne. "But so far, the man resists."

"Only because of my schedule." Alec smiles. "If you would have me in a month or so, I shall be delighted." With a quick glance at Émilienne, he adds. "I have heard everything there is, beautiful. And I would love to see your stable."

Étienne swings his arm over Émilienne's shoulders, looking down at her. "Bid him come, Émmy." But before she can reply, he jumps back to Alec again. "I would like to steal you away from Hennessy."

Alec laughs, and with a slight bow, he says, "I've been with the Hennessy stable since I was a boy. But I shall look forward to visiting Royallieu."

After Étienne takes his leave to tend to his Dark Magic, Alec turns to her. "I will not wait to visit Royallieu to see you again. Will you dine with me tomorrow evening, after the races conclude?"

Her calendar is free, although this she cannot let him know. She cocks her head, as if thinking of her heavy schedule. Then suggests the following Wednesday.

He takes her hand, bows, and straightens, his eyes holding hers again. "Until Wednesday then, Mademoiselle d'Alençon."

"Émilienne."

"Nine o'clock?"

She nods. Slipping a calling card from her pocket, she hands it over.

"I ride in the third today. Wish me luck."

"You do not need my luck. They say no one can defeat you."

He smiles. "That depends on the challenge, Émilienne."

She looks at him from underneath her lashes, surprised. "I am splendid at games." With a quick smile, she turns away. She must be the one to leave first. Besides, she has bets to place. Something inside, some motor of excitement drives her now. She feels his eyes on her until she rounds a corner of the stalls. The most famous jockey in Europe is young in years, but he is brave and strong and fine. Strange, she feels as if she has known Alec Carter all her life.

Nearing the crowd around the bookmakers, Émilienne stops to study the morning line. Already she knows the horses running and her picks. But she checks the odds and makes some changes. She shall not bet on the third, Alec's race—that could bring bad luck.

Satisfied, she searches the crowd for Brevard, trusting only him to take her bets. Not many ladies in Paris are seen in this crowd, and he's always treated her with respect. When she finds him, he looks up, touching the brim of his hat. She places her bets, slipping the tickets into the small reticule hanging from her wrist. She put her money on every race but the third, and—a thrill shoots through her—she put down more than she had planned on one race, changing her mind right on the spot. Strolling back to the enclosure gate where she must meet Étienne, Boy, and Coco, she worries perhaps the lingering pleasure of meeting Alec Carter affected her good judgment.

CHAPTER TWENTY-FIVE

PARIS, 1909

She cannot stop thinking of Alec Carter. He has sent flowers every day since they met at Longchamp. They dined together last Wednesday evening, remaining until they were the only people left in the place. Tonight is something special. This evening they are off to Maxim's, where Émilienne is queen. Tonight, she gets to make an entrance with him. With his cherubic looks and his powerful young body, Alec is the newest golden boy in Paris. The city stands before him with open arms, enthralled.

In a flurry of powder and paint before her mirror, Émilienne concentrates all her skills on erasing the years. This is their first appearance together at her favorite place in Paris, and Émilienne has chosen just the dress and jewels to dazzle. When her makeup is ready, Lily arrives with the frothy pink dress in her arms. The low bodice and long skirt made of silk, satin, and tulle fit—almost, but not quite—like skin, and appear to be dusted with gold. But, in fact, the fairy dust is made with chips of tiny golden beads sewn to the fabric one by one, beads of pure gold.

Memories of Suzette and the other seamstresses in Montmartre rise as she touches the delicate fabric, admiring the beading. How many hands were required to make the dress she wears tonight? How many hours were spent late into the night to make this dress? Suzette was the one who hid her from Maman when things went wrong—she never pried or asked for explanations, always welcoming her with a warm embrace. She wonders whether the seamstress is still alive and, if so, how she fares. Working women in Montmartre have short lives.

But she will never go back until she hears that Maman is gone to her grave.

With Lily's help, she slips on the dress, and Lily buttons it in back while she stands before the mirror. The ribbons strapped over her shoulders set off her rosy, golden skin. The ribbons cross and tie in back at her waistline, under a large satin bow—her back bare. This alone will cause a lovely scandal.

Two boxes of jewels rest on the dressing table before her. She lifts the covers of each, running her eyes over the gold and diamonds and pearls. Here are the exquisite blue diamond earrings Étienne gave to her years ago. These are priceless.

Alec does not have money to purchase jewels like these. Best not wear those tonight.

She lifts a choker of diamonds, not as flamboyant as the earrings, and Lily clasps it around her neck. This was a gift from Leo years ago, before she understood the King of the Belgians' true self—the mortifying old king. Back then, she had not known the depths of his madness.

As she hands the necklace to Lily, she thinks it is hard to believe that, after all the years since Georges's death, France, England, and Germany still skirmish in the Congo, fighting over each foot of shrub. There are stories every week in the newspapers, and she reads each one, weighing everything against the unspeakable value of Georges's lost life—*all* the lost lives.

Georges used to say hacking through the jungles was necessary to create commercial routes to Cairo. One would think by now those routes would be completed. But with the three countries always in the mix, it seems not much progress is ever made. Étienne has said more than once that France and Britain should stand together out there, that Germany survives only through aggression. If war comes in Europe, he says, it will begin with Prussia and the other German states.

Lily steps back, regarding Émilienne in the mirror. "How pretty you look in that dress and the jewels, Émmy. *Gil Blas* will talk of nothing else for weeks." Moving close, she flattens the ribbons over Émilienne's back. "Neither will your young man . . . Monsieur Carter."

She hears the hesitation in Lily's voice, and looking into the mirror at the little maid, her tone turns sharp. "Alec Carter is a gentleman, Lily—please do not refer to him as a young man, as if he is a boy. He is the greatest jockey in Europe. You must give him the respect that he deserves."

Lily lowers her eyes, turning away. "Yes, Émmy."

In a huff, Émilienne gives her reflection one more quick look. But as Lily carefully arranges the pink feather boa over her shoulders, Émilienne turns around, spreading her arms. Lily steps in, and Émilienne holds her old friend close.

"I'm sorry, Lily. You did not deserve my wrath."

Lily nods. "I understand."

Oh, how she loves the girl.

Émilienne turns, picking up her hat. This just purchased from Coco, a small confection of flowers and ribbons and bows, and she places it atop her head between the gleaming twists and golden curls, securing it with pins.

Stepping back, Lily claps her hands together and says with a little laugh, "You are a dream tonight, Émilienne. No one compares with you."

❋

Her carriage pulls up to the entrance of Maxim's on the rue Royale and the coachman jumps down. Alec is faster, opening the door. Reaching in, he takes her hand, assisting her from the carriage. His hands are rough from years of handling horses.

Hugo greets them at the door. But Alec eludes the man, pulling Émilienne with him right into the bar. As they enter, the place erupts. Looking about, Émilienne laughs, tilting her head and lifting her hand, until—she realizes the calls are not for her.

They call for Alec. "*The Lion! The Lion is here! The unde-featable!*"

Blushing, she drops her hand to her side, hiding her face by turning toward him with her special smile.

The applause is not for her. She cannot think at the moment.

They're all staring at Alec, the ladies covered in jewels whispering, the gentlemen rising to shake his hand. Her days of being on top, can they truly be over?

The finality of this thought shakes her.

For an instant she freezes, uncertain. Then Alec takes her arm, and her step is sure again as he steers her through to the main room, greeting friends along the way. Hugo steps up again, leading them toward the table. As always, she looks about in wonder—the bawdy but beautiful diners, tapestries and works of art, the soft golden glow of small lanterns, all reflected in the mirrors on the walls.

Always this is a room filled with friends and admirers, the ladies, covered in sparkling jewels, wearing their finest silks and satins, the latest designs. Gentlemen in black tuxedos smoking their pipes and cigars, rising from the tables now. Laughing and applauding, calling, calling Alec's name, and the dancers on the floor stop and turn, then join the rout, and as every familiar face turns in her direction, Émilienne smiles her lovely smile, lifting her chin and lifting one gloved hand high. *It's simply wonderful!*

There is Misia, with her red hair and porcelain skin, calling to her now, as she has never done before—because Émilienne is with Alec Carter. And there is Gabrielle looking as graceful and sophisticated as ever. Better, there is Liane—oh, Liane, introducing her husband at last, Prince Georges Ghika of the Kingdom of Romania, and Émilienne stops now, bending to kiss her friend, while Alec waits. "Darling girl! So much to tell, let's get together soon."

Even Liane seems hypnotized by the presence of Alec. "Yes, yes, of course," Liane says in a vague tone, gazing at Alec behind Émilienne. "This is the Lion! You must introduce us, please."

Émilienne does, standing aside while Liane flirts and her prince panders and Alec, poor boy, must talk and talk, answering questions until he squeezes her hand, and they move on.

Just as the waiter pulls out her chair and she is placed at the table, Alec turns about, waving to someone across the room. Glancing over her shoulder, she watches a tall, beefy man with red cheeks and a wide smile coming in their direction. Alec greets him with delight—James Hennessy, Émilienne's old flame.

She feels the blush. She's known Alec rides under Hennessy colors, but she had given this no thought—to meet her old lover with her new one. Already James is upon them, and she spots whisperings between the ladies, admirers at other tables old enough to know the story of her liaison.

Gripping his hand, Alec turns to her. "My darling—someone I want to introduce . . . Baron James Hennessy, this is . . ."

"Of course," he says, interrupting, bending, and kissing her cheeks. "We are old friends." But she sees the question in his eyes as he greets her.

Far too old for Alec?

She smiles, accepting his kisses. When he has gone, at last, she heaves a hidden sigh. What did she expect—a lover's quarrel? James Hennessy always was a gentleman.

The meal is served slowly. Alec feeds her tasty bits from his plate, followed by kisses and more champagne, and soon she's laughing, forgetting everyone around her. Forgetting that she is not the center of attention.

It's not long before another tap on her shoulder brings a surprise, and Caroline, La Belle Otero, embraces her. She's not seen Caroline in several months. She's still just as intense, still the same smoldering girl who once jumped onto a tabletop at Maxim's to dance a fiery dance, and Émilienne laughing, clapping her hands, had waited for the girl to burst right into flames.

While they gossip, an easy chore, she wonders how is it that the Folies and the newspapers and reporters and all Paris still rave over Caroline, still dancing, and yet the girl is no younger than Émilienne.

Caroline has real talent, that small voice whispers inside, talent not diminished by her age. Not yet. *All you've ever had to sell is beauty, Émmy.*

And of course, beauty fades.

"When are you returning to the Folies?" Caroline asks, but Émilienne is saved from having to answer as someone a few tables away calls Caroline's name. Caroline looks up, waves, and bids Émilienne farewell before drifting off.

Memories rise, unbidden, of the evenings when she was young, and she and Georges and the Princelings and Liane brought down the house when Georges ordered champagne for all in Maxim's and only the best, and Liane, with champagne flowing and having drunk too much, rose and danced alone among the tables, shedding clothing with each step until at last Hugo took her arm, steering her back to her friends. That night Émilienne had reigned as Georges's duchess over the mayhem.

"Are you well, Émilienne?" Alec leans close, taking her hands. "You're cold!" He rubs them between his own warm hands. "Are you not feeling well?"

"No matter." She smiles, pulling back, glancing about. She must not be seen as a fragile kitten here, the greatest stage in Paris. The waiter approaches, and she looks up, glad for the respite. Her voice turns gay as she spots what he holds up.

"Look! Someone has sent champagne." Lifting her chin, she turns, her eyes sweeping the room. And there James Hennessy catches her eye and lifts his glass. She lifts her own with her brightest smile, wishing him gone.

"My money is on you, young man." She startles as a gentleman slips up on them, a stranger from Alec's look.

Without a glance at Émilienne, he grasps Alec's shoulder as if they are the oldest friends. "Well, here you are in person. Young man, I watched you claim the trophy in 1904, and, on my mother's grave, I shall see you through it again."

A waiter fills her glass while Alec and the stranger discuss the course at Auteuil and various horses, and Émilienne realizes that she is all but invisible. Setting her glass down, she sits back and, not wanting to seem like a lump of coal, pretends interest in the conversation.

Two years ago, when she was still dancing, she, too, would have had visitors to the table all night long. After all, this is Maxim's. She looks up—Misia catches her eye. On her face a look of sympathy. Misia, another of the great courtesans, the light to which all artists flutter. As old or older than Émilienne, but still always seen around and about. Each year with another wealthy lover on her arm.

Émilienne nods and, composing herself, looks away. Beside her, Alec goes on and on with his admirer, while beneath the table she makes a fist, tight, so the nails press into her skin, stinging.

Just then the gentleman leaves, and Alec turns back to her, and, as if sensing her low mood, lifts his glass high, saying loud enough for everyone in Maxim's to hear, "To you, Émilienne, the most beautiful girl in Paris."

As the music strikes up again, those words, his smile—dare she say, his love—embrace her, pulling her into the stream of Alec's lovely light. She rests her hand on his arm, looking into his eyes. He smiles, leaning close. "If only you knew the words I hold inside."

And, tipping up her chin, he adds, with a kiss that the whole world watches, she is certain, "I have much more to say about this, *cheri* Later."

She glows, sitting back. Alec Carter, the newest toast of Paris.

"Alec? Émilienne? Good, here you are!"

She looks up as Étienne stands before them. Alec rises, smiling, greeting him, and Étienne bends, kissing her cheeks. As he and Alec talk, she glances at the young girl on his arm, a kid who used to dance in the chorus at the Folies when Émilienne starred. Judging from her expression, already she has fallen in love with Étienne.

"We shall certainly visit, as soon as my schedule allows," Alec says. "I look forward to seeing your stable."

Émilienne just stops herself from frowning. Étienne should include her in this conversation. But she knows well how to interrupt men's thoughts. Slowly, she lifts her hands, smoothing her pompadour, exposing her plump and rosy breasts nesting in the plunging bodice of her dress.

Étienne's eyes turn to her at once. "We all miss you at Royallieu, Émilienne. Coco's got some hats ready." He grins—perhaps he does miss her after all, this old friend. "And breakfasts are not the same, not without you," he goes on. "Even Leon groans over his newspapers, with no one to argue his opinions."

She turns her face up as if to the sun for those fine words. "Of course, we shall come, and very soon. We shall look forward to a visit, Étienne." With a slight glance at the girl, she adds, "Why, I feel Royallieu is almost home."

He rests his hand on her shoulder, squeezing. "I shall always love you, Émmy."

When he moves on, Alec takes her hand, kissing her knuckles. Good—he is just a bit jealous.

"Do you love me, Émilienne?"

She bubbles with laughter at the small triumph, feeling younger than ever. She is still the most beautiful woman in Paris—why, did not *Gil Blas* say so in the column just the other day? Good old Charles, still at work making his girls. He hasn't forgotten her yet.

❦

Émilienne lies awake as Alec falls asleep, thinking of the twists and turns in her life before he came along. Thinking of Maman, how cruel she was. And of Georges's betrayal, assuring her that the apartment they lived in belonged to her. And the Duchess d'Ange for taking away her daughter and her home. But the fury and pain are gone, she realizes. The past, that part of her life, is dead to her now. Perhaps, because of Alec.

Turning, resting on her side, she looks at Alec. He's so

different from other men she knows. Most of her past gentle-men lovers lived in two worlds, presiding over their families, their palaces and mansions, in strict accord with society's rules. Yet also slipping into the world of the demimonde at a whim, the world of pleasure, defying those same rules for youth and beauty and sometimes love.

Alec is like none of them. Alec feels like home.

Just then Alec's eyes flutter open. He holds her eyes, then he reaches for her. "Come to sleep, my love."

His love.

His voice is low, soft, and soothing. Smiling, Émilienne nestles against him. Then, wrapped in his arms, she falls asleep with a little smile, feeling precious. Feeling safe.

When she wakes in the morning, he is gone. Jockeys begin their days early, he warned. But the room is filled with warm sunshine, and she is filled with a new glow. Love! Of course, he had been half asleep last night, but still—he called her his love.

Sitting up in bed, she leans back against the pillows, smil-ing. Lily must have opened the shutters to let the light in, her funny little way of waking Émilienne when she sleeps too late. She has left a tray on the bed beside her. On the tray—hot choc-olate, a sweet bun, and a note from Alec.

Émilienne rips the note open and reads, then folds it back again. He shall come for her at eight, he writes, and never let her go. Placing the note down on her lap, she places her hand on it and looks off. *Does she love Alec Carter?*

Alec is neither wealthy nor aristocrat. Rather, he is a plain man with a good heart.

She is his precious girl, he says, his lucky girl, and if he has anything to say about the matter, they will never part again. He is a man she can trust. Honest. Gentle. With him the word *love* means more than pleasure and contentment. She has only known him for a few weeks, but she realizes that she trusts him more than any man she has ever known.

A man like this deserves respect and truth.

Pursing her lips, she looks off.

Yes. Yes, she does love him.

She is through thinking about her past and dancing for other men. From this moment on, she will devote her time to Alec. Traveling with him. Following the races. Learning the horses—though she will keep the betting to herself.

His love has changed her life.

Within months, Émilienne asks him to move into her home. And, with grace and a smile that proves his love, Alec accepts.

CHAPTER TWENTY-SIX

ROYALLIEU, 1910

This afternoon, at Étienne's invitation, they are on the way to visit Royallieu for the weekend. It has been a year since Émilienne has visited the château—since Alec came into her life.

Alec owns a motor car now, a lovely Berliet, which he prefers to drive himself. Painted burgundy, with black leather seats and brass horns and lamps, and brass fittings on the tires, the motor car is prettier than most. And extra space in back provides room for his equipment. Still, Émilienne prefers a carriage.

On this lovely midsummer day, sunshine as clear and sharp as crystal lights the château. They stop before the entrance, and Alec turns to her. "The place is beautiful as reported," he says. "I am glad we came. I have heard many stories of weekends out here."

"They are not as wild as you might think."

He laughs, beating the butler to her door. "Allow me to judge for myself, Émmy."

Émilienne accepted the invitation with a bit of reluctance, wanting to hold on to a separation of some kind between her life before and after Alec. Their travels throughout Europe following his races had provided the necessary buffer. But now, looking up at the château, she feels that old, welcoming warmth.

"Émilienne!"

She turns to see Coco crossing the courtyard from the direction of the fields, and she waves. Ah, things have changed—a new, stylish Coco appears! She still wears jodhpurs, but even from this distance Émilienne sees they are new, as are the polished riding boots. A crisp, high-collared white shirt sets off her skin, tanned by the sun, as they say now. And the jacket, a bit longer as is the style, fits her well, emphasizing Coco's slim figure. As she comes close, Émilienne sees that her hair is wound into a new loose twist on the back of her neck.

Alec leans close. "Étienne's *petite amie?*"

She nods. "Yes, but that was over years ago. Now they are only friends."

Just then two junior butlers arrive for the bags. And Coco strides up.

"I am glad to see you," Émilienne says, holding out her arms. Coco permits a hug, then turns, giving Alec a cool look, which irritates Émilienne at once. "Welcome to Royallieu, Monsieur Carter. I have watched you ride many times."

He bows. "And I have heard much about you from Émilienne, Mademoiselle Chanel."

"I am sure." Coco's tone is dry.

Émilienne laughs, taking Alec's arm. Her eyes shine. "I have only ever given Alec the good bits, my girl."

"That is probably better than the truth." Coco steps ahead, moving along before them.

Alec lifts a brow, giving Émilienne a look.

She lifts a shoulder—that is just Coco's way.

As they enter the château, Boy Capel comes down the stairs, greeting Alec as an old acquaintance.

As they talk about the coming race, Coco turns to Émilienne. "Dinner at ten, but we gather in the salon earlier, at your leisure." With a glance toward Alec, she adds in a lower voice, "We still dress for dinner, Émmy."

Émilienne draws up, glaring at the girl. "Of course."

Just then, Boy turns, greeting her.

Coco interrupts. "Yuri will have someone show you to your room, Émilienne." Then, to Alec, she adds, "I hope you will enjoy the weekend, Monsieur Carter."

"I am certain that I shall. Please, call me Alec."

Coco seems to hesitate. Then, with a nod, she excuses herself, turning, striding down the hallway toward the terrace. Émilienne stares at her back, fury rising. But Alec takes her arm, gently steering her toward the stairs, following the butler.

At ten o'clock that evening, the Friday guests gather for dinner in the large dining room. The long table glows under gaslights turned low, the old lamps that Étienne refuses to replace with electric, at least in some rooms, much to Émilienne's delight. Crystal glass and delicate porcelain reflect the light of flickering candles down the length of the table.

Coco presides at one end of the table, with Étienne at the other, and guests in between, including Boy Capel. Eight in all. Émilienne, seated at Étienne's right, is introduced to his latest fancy on his other side, Simone Fournier, a new principal dancer with the Folies.

"Ah, yes. You danced with me at the Folies," Émilienne says.

Simone nods and leans toward her. "It was so exciting to take curtain calls with you, madame."

Émilienne draws back. Simone is one of Charles's girls,

she knows. Last seen with him at Café Anglais late one night. Charles has slipped a bit in his choices, she thinks.

As wine is uncorked and glasses filled, as the long dinner is served, laughter grows loud, and voices turn gay. Étienne proposes toasts, first to each woman at his table, with a wry touch for Émilienne, causing Simone to blush and Émilienne to laugh.

Leon then proposes a toast that seems to break the mood. "A toast to King Edward," he mumbles. "May he rest in peace."

"Hear, hear." Boy's voice. "He was a jolly fellow. Much too young to die. But he knew how to have a good time while he was here."

Étienne turns his eyes on Émilienne. "You were acquainted with him, as I recall. What was he like?"

"Oh, I first knew Edward when he was Prince of Wales." When she was young. "And later, when he visited Paris and he was king. He was handsome, funny, generous. The people loved their king."

Leon gazes at her for a moment, with a look that hides a smile, then nods. "Well put." Downing the last of his wine, he turns, lifting his glass to the server.

He waits until the glass is full enough to lift for another toast. "We shall leave Edward to sleep in his new grave. Here is to his successor, King George. May he have the courage and sense to blow threatening clouds away." Despite the smile, Leon's voice holds an ominous note. The room falls silent.

"Are you speaking of war again?" Coco asks, always one to slap down a subtle point.

Leon turns his eyes to her. "My guess is that war will come with our German friends, sooner rather than later."

Gabrielle Dorziat, sitting beside him, touches his arm.

With a glance at her, he shrugs. "We should not blind ourselves to the truth. This is just my guess, but Germany is an aggressor, and Britain's pudding George is too soft ever to rein in his cousin Wilhelm. Germany seems to seek out war. Europe needs a strongman now, given the kaiser's mad thinking."

Émilienne narrows her eyes. "Really, Leon. Let us not speak of war at dinner. Besides, Europe is at peace . . ."

"You are wrong, Émmy." Leon speaks up. "The brats born of Victoria are Europe's problem now. If war comes, we shall hold the three cousins to account."

Émilienne stares back, silenced.

"George and Czar Nicholas of Russia are too weak to hold back Wilhelm," Boy says, lifting his glass. "And the Reichstag prepares. Why, as we speak, German soldiers stand at France's borders."

Leon looks up at Boy. "They would stand at yours, too, if England were close."

Émilienne closes her eyes for an instant. Germany, right across the border. On the other side of the table, Alec remains quiet.

"The whole thing makes no sense," Boy goes on. "But it's no secret in Britain we are strengthening our navy."

"So I have heard," Étienne says.

"Enough of war," Émilienne interrupts, attempting a smile and failing. Turning to Étienne, she adds, "Perhaps the gentlemen would like to continue this conversation in the library?"

Étienne nods.

After the men are gone, the ladies rise. "Who is for a game of cards," Coco says. With a laughing glance at Émilienne, she adds, "Will you cheat?"

"It is always possible."

On their way to the salon, Gabrielle turns to Émilienne. "Alec was quiet."

"He has no interest in political talk. And the race is on his mind."

"Of course. Does he ride this weekend?"

"Sunday," she says and walks ahead. This talk of war frightens her. Children are now in charge—Nicholas; Wilhelm, who is still a boy despite his age; and George. She is acquainted with the latter two. Men who were never forced to grow up.

She has heard horrors of the war between France and Prussia and the German states, when Germany stole Alsace and half of Lorraine from France. Is such a thing possible in Europe again?

On Sunday morning Étienne and his guests pile into motor cars, off to the races at Longchamp. Alec left at dawn, as he races today, so Émilienne rides into town with Étienne and Simone instead. Traveling with Alec throughout Europe and listening to his knowledge of the tracks, the horses, and their riders has brought her closer to the sport.

At the racecourse entrance gate, Émilienne bids them adieu as Étienne and Simone head toward the stalls and Leon strolls to the stands with Gabrielle. She picks up the morning sheet and a program, scanning quickly for Alec's ride—he rides in the fourth. Lifting her parasol, Émilienne walks through the colorful crowd, past the stands where an elegant crowd mills about—gentlemen in their usual frock coats, top hats, and canes and ladies in dresses of fine silk, organdy, and tulle.

Hurrying on through the meadow toward the oak tree and the bookmakers, she passes the groups spreading blankets on the grass for picnics. Here working men and women hold court, all seeming to talk at once, their voices loud, their laughter louder, unrestrained on this cool, sunny day. The women wear skirts of rough cotton in bright colors, with blouses worn loose, slipping from their shoulders. Some still wear wooden shoes, as she used to do, which kick up the grass and dirt as people move from one picnic spot to another. They dance, they drink from big jars instead of glasses. She smiles—rough, yes, but they are having fun!

A thought surprises her. She would not mind watching the races on a picnic blanket, on a lovely day like this. She used to think sitting in the stands, in the enclosure, was the place to be. But, for some reason, the picnics take her fancy now. With a glance back at the enclosure, the difference between the two strikes her at once, the formality of the enclosure, the free-flowing joy of the picnics.

She pushes on, thinking of Coco's slights to Alec this weekend. Alec, a man who takes each person as he or she comes with an honest smile! Why, Coco started from the same origins. But, my, how she has shed that reminder like a skin.

Just ahead, the bookmakers mark their spots in the shade, with gentlemen moving around them in constant motion, placing their bets. As always, heads turn when a lady walks up. Ignoring them, she avoids their eyes, seeking her man.

Already she knows her picks for the day. Étienne's horse runs in the third, but she will not bet on him this day. The odds are too tight, the payoff too thin. Alec rides in the fourth. With Alec, she thinks the same. He is sure to win.

She has had bad luck in the past few weeks. Now, it's time to double down. Of course, she understands this brings more risk to the bargain—also more reward if she wins.

All comes out right, in the end. She never counts her losses, only her wins. She is wealthy enough, she's certain of it, even if she loses a little here and there.

Approaching Brevard, she takes a deep breath and smiles. They are not friends, but she has placed her bets with the man for so many years, and she trusts him. She also suspects it amuses him, this dealing with a woman. At first, Brevard attempted to discourage her from placing bets. He talked of the rough side of the transaction and not knowing the horses well. Once, he asked how she chooses her horse. Several ways, she replied—a feeling of connection with the horse and rider was at the top of her list, followed by the odds and numbers. He lifted his brows at that. And she had not attempted to explain.

"Mademoiselle." Monsieur Brevard nods, tipping the bill of his cap. "How does the weather look to you today?"

"Sun shines today, Monsieur Brevard." She pulls the velvet bag stuffed with franc notes from her wrist. He watches as she counts.

Brevard slides the bills and notes into the worn leather bag always hanging from his shoulder. They move together to the large table placed under the tree, and he pulls the notebook from his pocket. He picks a pen from a holder on the table and dips it into the inkwell.

Then he turns to her. "What have you in mind, today, Mademoiselle d'Alençon?"

She looks him in the eye. "Forty thousand francs on Vichnou, to win, in the first." The odds are three to one. Fairly safe.

He looks up as she gives the number, seems to hesitate—it is a large amount. Then, he asks, "Vichnou to win? Not to place or show? Are you certain?"

"Yes, of course. And the purse looks good."

"Mademoiselle . . ."

"Monsieur Brevard. I have watched this animal for weeks. He is ready."

Saying nothing more, he writes the ticket and hands it over. She hides a smile. Really, she does know something about the horses after all this time.

She checks her ticket before placing it in her pocket. Forty thousand is a lot to place on one horse, but she has put down as much in the past few weeks. One hundred and sixty thousand francs, if she's right. She fingers the ticket, then shaking off second thoughts, she moves away from the tree. Vichnou runs in the first, and already it seems the horses are heading for the gates. She must hurry now.

Perhaps she can still catch Étienne before he enters the stands. As she saunters along, she thinks of Alec and smiles to herself. Then she realizes that even if she were on his arm this afternoon, despite his racing fame, without someone like Étienne or Boy along, neither of them, neither she nor Alec, would be considered good enough alone for admission to the stands.

Alec seems oblivious to the divisions in society. He is so innocent, so kind.

Ahead, already the horses prance at the gates, some holding back, some steered by escorts. She gazes at the picnickers on the grass again, having such fun. Why waste time seeking Étienne for a seat when she shall be greeted with joy by any party on a blanket this afternoon? Why, everyone in Paris knows Émilienne.

Turning on her heels, she heads for a cheerful group near the finish line—certain of welcome. Then the announcer's voice startles her.

"And they are off!" he calls as the thoroughbreds crash from the gates. She lost track of time.

"And we have Nougat first, ahead by a length and a half . . . Cordon Rouge second, Vichnou third," he calls. "And Tristan on the outside . . ."

She stops, turning to watch. "Come on, *Vichnou!*" she mutters under her breath.

Time seems to fly, and already they close in on the turn. "And . . . Cordon Rouge taking the lead, Nougat two, Vichnou third, and Saint Cyr fourth . . . Tristan falls behind . . ."

Vichnou still third as they make the turn! Hugging herself, she stares at the field, willing the jockey to make his move.

The voice comes faster, louder now. "And here comes Vichnou moving up on the back stretch on the outside, passing
Nougat, ahead now by a length . . ." His voice lifts, booming,
"and Saint Cyr! Saint Cyr to challenge, flying past Nougat and
Vichnou by half, and . . ."

She places her hands over her heart. Vichnou! Why is he
holding back?

"Finish line just ahead, Saint Cyr and Cordon Rouge neck
and neck with Vichnou just behind . . . and . . . now Saint Cyr
pulling away . . ." He's shouting now, and as the crowd rises,
standing, cheering, and Émilienne holds her breath, the announcer shouts: "Saint Cyr . . . it's Saint Cyr at the finish! Saint
Cyr first, Cordon Rouge two, Vichnou three, Nougat four!"

No! She feels in her pocket for the ticket. This cannot be
right.

What has happened here?

In the roar of the crowd Émilienne stares at the finish line
in disbelief. The crowd cheers, Saint Cyr, the winner, prances
toward the circle, his jockey standing on the straps, lifting his
cap. But her mind goes blank.

How much has she just lost? She cannot think, cannot recall.

Reaching into her pocket again, she pulls out the ticket—
Vichnou to win, and he came in third! Third! Brevard tried to
warn her—bet to show or place as well!

Her throat dries, her temples pound. She gazes down at the
damned ticket one more time—forty thousand francs, gone all
at once.

As in a dream, she moves to a tree, leaning against the
trunk. Had she won . . . but never mind, people will see. She
can cry at home. Besides, this is not the first time she has lost,

nor will it be the last. She must not think of losing. Right now, she must make a smile.

She will think of Alec.

She lifts her chin, gazing again at the starting gates. No one must ever know. If word gets around, she will be the laughing-stock of Paris. Still, she closes her eyes. Gambling at the tables in Monte Carlo takes so much longer to lose.

Why does she so love the horses?

Ah well, she knew the risk. Win or lose, it is the excitement of not knowing that brings the thrill. She will study the horses closer in the next race, and the jockeys too. She paid less attention to that business with Alec home this week.

As she pushes off from the tree trunk, she spots Henri nearby, sitting amid a jolly group on a grassy spot in the shade. Henri! She has not seen him in years. She smiles, lifting her hand, waving.

As if he feels her presence, he looks up in her direction. Rising, he calls to her—"Émilienne! Here, come over here!" Shouting over the noise, then, as she moves toward him, he turns, speaking to a pretty, young girl sitting beside him, gesturing toward Émilienne.

Hurrying toward Henri, she forces away thoughts of her bad luck today, even as he jumps up, smiling, coming her way, flinging his arms around her when they meet.

"Émilienne." He pulls back, staring at her. "Such a long time, and you, as beautiful as ever!" Taking her arm, he leads her to his friends. The girl he'd left looks up at her, eyes shining.

"Look here, fellows, look who I have found. Émilienne!"

Her heart fills with a friendly kind of love for Henri. It was Henri who introduced her to Charles Desteuque, the same *Gil Blas* who wrote valentines to her in his reviews, who made her a star. And it was because of Henri she danced with the Exposition troop, her first contract. Her first success.

Turning to her amid the voices, Henri insists she stay to watch the races. Without waiting for her answer, he calls out, "Luca! Hand the lady a cup." Then, leaning down, he pulls up the girl sitting beside him. "At last . . . Maddie here is my Émilienne." Turning to her, he says, "This here is Madeleine, my wife."

So, this is Henri's girl. The last time she saw him, several years ago, he had set his eyes on marriage, he said. And now, here she is, his wife!

"Good afternoon," she says, taking the girl's hand in hers, pleased. "Henri has told me of you, and you are as pretty as he said." She smiles, with a glance at Henri. "You are a lucky man."

How the years do fly!

On the blanket, friendly faces look up—here, smiles, gay voices, pulling her from the earlier gloom. At Henri's insistence that she stay, he and his friends shuffle about, making room for Émilienne on the blanket. Tucking under her skirts, she manages to find a spot near Madeleine. As she sits, she swings her legs to one side for the fit of her dress. Madeleine sits down, too, and Henri lands between them. Someone passes a chicken leg around. She shakes her head, but Henri takes it right away.

Madeleine turns to her. "What an honor to meet you at last, mademoiselle."

"Émilienne."

"Yes, Émilienne. My husband has told me all about you. He says the Lion, the great jockey, is a friend of yours."

"Alec Carter."

"His race is soon, Maddie," Henri interjects.

Madeleine blushes. "Sitting here so close to the finish line, you shall bring your man good luck."

The announcer calls the horses for the next race. Émilienne leans back on her elbows, stretching out, lifting her face, gazing up into the spreading branches of the tree. A breeze carries scents of fresh cut grass and hay and horses, and a mixture of perfumes. Never mind how this looks to the gentlemen and ladies in the stands peering through their glasses. Such a lively group, these friends, and such a lovely day for the races, sitting here in the shade.

She shall worry no more. Forty thousand francs will be recouped within the next few weeks. She turns to Henri. "Have you a cigarette?"

"Of course, someone must." He calls to the group, and she feels so free, so happy here on the grass with Henri and Madeleine. When the cigarette arrives, already lit with a smudge of lipstick on the end, she takes a smooth drag, sticking it into the corner of her mouth. Already she has put the loss behind her.

CHAPTER TWENTY-SEVEN

Émilienne strolls down rue Cambon, heading home from a visit with Liane. Liane, lecturing her again about the horses, though she has won many times landing on the right bet. Liane and Lily, her only confidants. But all in all, Émilienne thinks—although she has not visited the bank to check her account—she is almost certain that, counting her wins and losses, she is probably ahead.

Glancing up just then, coming in her direction on the other side of the street, she spots Coco.

Émilienne stops.

Coco, hanging on to her reticule and a large bag, is engaged in searching for something in her pockets and fails to see Émilienne.

"Coco!" Émilienne calls.

The girl turns around, and a smile breaks out as she spots Émilienne. "Émmy, come over here!"

Already on her way, Émilienne is surprised at how happy she is to see the girl. She plants her hands on Coco's shoulders, kissing her cheeks. Then she steps back, studying her. Something has changed since last they met—Coco seems right sunny today.

"You look wonderful," she exclaims. "What's going on?"

Coco holds up a key. "This!" Turning, she points to a sign over the door.

Émilienne lifts her eyes. *Chanel Modes*, the sign says.

She places her hands over her heart, looking at Coco. "Is this yours?"

Still smiling, Coco nods. "Come in. You must see what we . . . I have done." She lifts her eyes. "I love the hat; it suits you."

"Of course. Since you made it." Émilienne laughs. "Everyone loves them. I see your little hats all over Paris now. Misia says she shall never go back to the old ones."

Émilienne takes the bag, and Coco unlocks the door, and they walk inside. The shop is small, and hats and wooden hat forms fill shelves against the far wall. Ribbons hang like streamers from other shelves, along with rolls and rolls of colored fabric, boxes of feathers, lace, artificial flowers, beads. A long worktable on the far side of the room displays an assortment of finished hats.

"You have certainly moved up from working in Étienne's garçonnière. As lovely as it was for him to loan you the space."

"Yes, it was overrun with ladies and hats. He visited unexpectedly, in Paris for the day, and walked into chaos in that small place. I knew then it was time to leave."

Émilienne laughs at the thought.

Coco turns back to her, taking the bag. She sets it down on a chair, then turns back to Émilienne. "I'm in business now!"

"I must say I am astonished." And she is astonished. Never would she have put her money on a bet that Coco could accomplish all this. Étienne's naive young filly is gone. This is a different girl.

"Did Étienne find this place for you?"

"No. Boy found it. He paid the rent in the beginning, but business is good. I'm paying him back month by month—"

"Paying him back?" Émilienne interrupts, astonished.

"Yes."

"I thought you wanted to marry him."

"This isn't the same thing. I love him, but I don't want his money. This is my shop. I make my own way." Her voice lifts with pride as she says those last words. Émilienne watches her, still stunned. Is this the same girl she first met at Royallieu?

Coco walks along the shelves, trailing her fingers at the edges with a proprietary air. "Already I make more than I spend, even counting the debt to Boy."

Success for a woman in business alone. Émilienne would not put her money on that bet. Still, "I wish you well, Coco."

She turns, facing Émilienne. "I will never forget how you helped too, Émmy. You and your friends. Gabrielle, Misia, Colette . . ."

Émilienne waves off her words. "They all loved the hats. It was a delight."

"More than that. Perhaps you might recall . . . one night at Royallieu, you set me thinking." Coco sits in one of the chairs, and Émilienne sits down beside her. "You warned I could not count on Étienne forever, that I needed a plan for my future. That I must stop depending on Étienne's goodwill, as kind as he is. And, later, after I fell in love . . . well, I feel the same way. I want to do this on my own. I don't want to depend on Boy for anything but love."

She hesitates, watching Émilienne, then says, "And someday, marriage."

Émilienne recalls the conversation well. Neither Étienne nor Boy were protecting the kid at that time with an arrangement, and Coco needed to secure her future. And neither Étienne nor Boy seemed especially interested in this problem. The choices she'd thought Coco had back then were between finding a protector, dancing and pleasing gentlemen, or scrubbing floors and such—hard labor. Coco misunderstood what Émilienne was telling her—but seems to have interpreted it beyond all expectations.

It never crossed Émilienne's mind that a woman could manage a business, much less own one.

Coco, a woman in trade! Everyone knows women are no good at handling money. Just look at the money she has lost on the horses the last few months. Bad luck. The loss on Vichnou was only the start. Since then, it seems everything has gone wrong. Without dancing, and without her gentlemen's gifts—now she's with Alec—the only way out is to sell her jewels and continue placing bets until her luck finally turns.

Coco sits nearby, quiet, gazing around her domain.

Émilienne looks off, suddenly feeling low.

A flash of jealous spite comes, and she forces it back. Coco is her friend. These thoughts will not do. But how strange this is, Émilienne down on her luck with a string of losses at the racecourse, and worried for the first time since she was young over money. And Coco at the same time riding high in her own shop, making her fortune selling hats.

Pushing up from the chair, she adjusts her hat. "I wish great success for you, Coco." And inside, she means the words. She sweeps the room with her eyes. "Just look what you have done, creating something new. I think back on the days you wore Étienne's clothes, and took his hat, and really . . ." she says with a grin, "I have to laugh. You are an artist."

Coco cocks her head. "I'm no artist, Émmy."

"Oh? I think you are." Émilienne turns, looking at her. "If not, what then?"

Coco lifts a shoulder, standing up. "Oh, I don't know. A builder of hats." Then, after a slight hesitation, she adds, "You used to say dancing wasn't work for you, that it was play. Well, this business of making hats is work. But it's mine. And I am on my own. I am free."

Free. The comment burns.

Coco must have seen the cut land because, taking her arm, Coco walks with her to the door. "I don't forget friends, Émmy. I would not have this without your good advice."

Not long after, news of Coco and her hats appears in newspapers and magazines and photographs, too, and soon they are in windows all over Paris. Even Charles writes about her hats, mentioning that every beautiful girl in Paris wears them now. Gabrielle Chanel's hats are sprinkled with magic stardust, it seems to Émilienne.

✹

On this morning, Émilienne feels a tickle at her throat. Waking, still half asleep, she glances over at Alec. He smiles. Then, rising onto his knees, he straddles her, holding her eyes as he lowers himself, covering her with his warmth.

Even now, this early in the morning, still their love feels new.

His lovemaking is always gentle, comfortable, and sweet. "I love you so, Émmy," he whispers. In the end, she weeps, filled with emotions she cannot explain. Alec, holding her in his arms, asks no questions—merely holds her close. With Alec, she understands that sometimes dreams come true.

"Tell me you love me, again."

She hears the uncertainty in his youthful voice, so she tells him once again how much she loves him.

He pulls away. "Tell me what's wrong. Something is wrong."

"No, nothing. I cry because I love you so."

He pulls her closer, and they lay together in silence.

Why, Alec loves her, he is her center in life. Still, she does not tell him of her betting on horses. In every race he would worry, ask himself whether his Émmy bets for him or against. She is not that much a fool. Besides, soon her luck will turn. She will win again. One good win, and then she shall stop.

She is a strong woman, she tells herself. Once she was the star after all.

Now? Who is she, now?

A woman in love, who enjoys life. A woman who always succeeds. Yes, she misses dancing, the smell of powder and paint and raw wood, the girls moving up and down the hallways, and she and Lily surrounded by flowers in the dressing room. The gifts. The parties. The attention.

Yes, she misses it all.

But she loves this new life too. She lays her head on Alec's chest, listening to his heartbeat. He plants little kisses on her shoulder, her neck, and she smiles. Most of the time a smile brings joy, a delight she discovered over the years.

Alec's voice is deep with emotion as he says, "From this minute on, Émmy, we are one." His hand moves round in circles on her back. "Name anything you want, my love, and you shall have it. Anything."

"I only want you, Alec." She traces his chin with her finger. "Only you."

He moves aside, sitting up. "I must leave for Monte Carlo. Won't you change your mind and come along?"

"No, darling. Not this time."

She is off to Deauville this weekend, for the races. She must make up her losses. This is a smaller meet, but she feels the luck.

"Win for me, Alec. We shall celebrate when you return."

Sitting on the balcony drinking her morning coffee after he leaves, Émilienne looks out over the city stretched before her, feeling skittish as a colt. She is relieved Alec will be away for the weekend. This gives her time to think. Soon, she fears, she shall be forced to face the truth and discover what money is left in her bank account, what jewels remain unsold in the box. She should have gone weeks ago to tally up, but still, here she sits, preferring to think of pleasant things.

A few months ago, Émilienne mentioned to her banker a need for funds without reducing the balance in her account. Her only bank account, her savings from the high days, but this she did not mention. She has expenses, she explained. The bank need not know that winning at the racecourse is now her only source of funds. What is life without its pleasures?

The banker suggested a solution—she should borrow the funds from the bank. Why, she owns her home, and she is Émilienne! So long as her savings are kept in the bank at a reasonable balance, a threshold, of sorts, she may use borrowed funds for her expenses. Businessmen do this all the time.

When she had hesitated, the banker smiled. It is not often a lady is permitted to borrow from the bank without her husband's name.

Borrow the funds—such an easy solution. She merely requested the loan, filled out some papers, and on that day the borrowed funds were deposited into her account, available to Mademoiselle d'Alençon.

"This is a smart way to manage money," he had added, escorting her to the door. "Of course, interest is charged on the loan, you understand."

That was two months ago, but now the money is gone, left with Brevard at the racecourse. She must make another loan from the bank or find another way—another win.

Just then, Lily walks out onto the balcony.

"Good day, my girl." Émilienne turns around.

"I had thought, perhaps, if you don't mind . . . I would like to visit my family in Neuilly this weekend. Just on Saturday and Sunday, if that suits?"

Émilienne arches a brow and smiles. "Of course, you may go." A flush rises in Lily's face. "Someone special, my girl?"

Lily nods. "A very nice gentleman." Smiling, she ducks her head. "He understands numbers. Keeps the accounts for Monsieur Williams, an Englishman who owns the feed store in Neuilly."

Émilienne's first thought is a prayer Lily will not fall in love and leave. A second thought whips right back—how selfish, after all these years.

"I'm happy for you." Then she asks, "How long have we been together?"

Lily laughs. "I have lost count, Émmy."

A long time. Lily is her family. Lily, Alec, and Liane. The possibility of losing Lily does cloud the day ahead. Whatever will she do if Lily marries and goes away?

But Lily deserves love too.

As Lily turns to leave, Émilienne sinks down in the chair beneath the sun. Her eyes soon close. One day she shall write her story, numbering the years learning to dance, learning how to dress like a lady—white gloves and all. How best to please a man. How to pretend to love, seduce, take wild chances, trust luck, laugh sometimes when she longs to weep.

How to survive.

Coco will survive. Émilienne never would have thought, but there she is, a woman smashing through the barriers, ignoring rules. Sure, at first, with Boy's help. But look at her now, a woman who took a chance in fashion. On her own, and on her way to success, a milliner now. And so young. Coco will succeed if she just holds on, creating a path for women coming after to follow.

And Émilienne shall write of love. Even the hard sides of love have taught her lessons—Georges, his loss, his betrayal. But then came Elisa, a gift. She will never write about Elisa. Still, for her, Elisa is love, a different kind of love than how she feels for Alec. When this thought burns, searing, she tells herself the only salve is remembering the one true thing—her baby girl gained a better life.

But then what does Émilienne have left?

Why, you have yourself! You are Émilienne. And you have Alec's love.

At last, this brings a smile.

CHAPTER TWENTY-EIGHT

PARIS, 1912

Alec is home when Émilienne returns from the afternoon of tea and shopping with Liane. Lily takes her packages and sends her out to the terrace, where she says he waits.

Delighted by the surprise, she heads out to the terrace. Stopping at the doorway before he spots her, she smiles at the sight. Alec slouches in the chair, arms crossed, legs sprawled, cap pulled low over his eyes. Even a stranger would know this man is a jockey.

Her shoes click on the stones, and he starts. Sitting up, pushing back the cap, he gives her a strange look. "Hello, beauty," he says, rising. Tossing the hat onto a table, he comes toward her. But there is something in his face that warns her. A flash of something in his expression—is that fear crossing his face?

"What's gone wrong, Alec?" She sucks in her breath as she asks the question.

"I have received a summons from the 23rd Dragoons."

She clasps her hands together, as if in prayer. Watching

him, she rests her chin on the tips of her fingers. "What does this mean?"

"I've been called to duty—"

"Duty?" In the instant, she recalls a conversation some time ago at Royallieu. Étienne and Boy Capel discussing the possibilities of war. They talked of nothing else but war in Europe that night.

Reaching out, she holds his arm. "Does this mean war? Please, no!"

He pulls her close, surrounding her, it seems, as she starts to cry.

"This is not war, Émmy. Only garrison duty." She pulls back, and he holds her eyes. "Please don't cry." He dips his forehead, touching hers.

She nods, gulping back tears. "If not war, then . . . why?"

"I don't know. Who knows how great minds work?" He shrugs. "But France is not at war. This is only an old rule—conscription. And like every other man called to duty, I shall obey."

Alec steers her to the settee, where the cups of tea and coffee wait. Here he sits down, and she does too. She leans against his shoulder. On the other side of the terrace wall, the world rolls by—voices on the pavement, motors, the rough sounds of lorry wheels. Down the street a dog barks. She fixes her eyes on the gardenias blooming even in the late summer heat. Above, the sun is high, spreading light over Paris. All should be well.

She turns to him. "What does this mean for us?"

He looks off. "I'm required to stay in garrison at Lunéville, but—"

"Live there? No!" She pulls away, watching him. "We must part? How shall I ever see you? Why, Lunéville is just a village, a small town, and so far away, near Strasbourg!"

"About three hundred eighty kilometers from Paris," Alec says.

And so close to the German border. She thinks of the mad kaiser, of his disdain for what he sees as a frivolous view of life in France. Things she saw for herself as his mistress for a short while, long ago. But she keeps the thoughts to herself. A courtesan must always keep her secrets.

Shaking her head, she grasps Alec's shirtfront in her fists. "You must refuse to go, Alec. You are British by birth. Not a born Frenchman, why should you have to fight?"

With a sigh, he looks at her, surprising her with his frown. "Enough, Émmy," he says in a quiet tone. "I am French now through and through. Dragoons are only light calvary. And this is not a call to war. You must not worry. And we are together *now*." Releasing her grip from his shirt, he shifts back.

"But we shall live apart!"

"Listen to me." His eyes pierce hers. "Garrison duty is only a means of preparing, if ever war should come. A country must stay prepared. The Germans have kept soldiers on our borders for the past few years. We must protect France by showing strength. That's all this is—a show of power."

She crosses her arms, fighting tears. Everyone knows Germany maintains masses of troops along the French border, ever since they took Alsace–Lorraine in the Prussian war years ago. Feelings are still raw in France over that. Swallowing tears, she gulps. "How long will you be gone?"

"I have no idea how long this will last, but the good news is that I will be permitted to continue racing." He smiles, tipping up her chin. "We shall be together on most weekends, Émmy. Do you understand?"

Again, she nods, listening.

He slips his hand around to the back of her neck. His voice turns gentle now, the tone one would use with a frightened child. "I have no choice. I was chosen because I ride. And . . . I report to the garrison next week."

Anger replaces her tears. Pushing him away, she stands up. "If you are right, you're protecting France from nothing more than ghosts."

"Look here, this is the law . . . the rule." His voice turns teasing. "Let us go inside. Surely in France, the rules allow for afternoon love."

On one sunny day in early autumn, when the air is crisp and cool, Liane and Émilienne sit together at a small round table on the sidewalk outside of Café de la Paix. Cups of hot chocolate steam before them.

Waving to someone passing, Liane turns back to her. "Where is Alec these days?"

"He has been in training at Lunéville the past four weeks. But he's coming home this week. He rides on Saturday at Longchamp."

"Will you join him in Lunéville?"

She looks off. The past month seems a year. After a moment, she adds, "I don't know." How could she leave Paris? How could she leave the lights and music, the shops and cafés, and her friends?

Liane gives her a look, then picks up her cup. "Alec is a good man, Émmy. I would not let him out of my sight if I were you."

She tosses her head. "I never worry. He loves me."

Truth is, she has other worries right now. Yesterday a notice arrived from her banker, the obsequious young man with the thin mustache. It seems she has exceeded some threshold in her bank account and may no longer withdraw funds until the fault is cured.

Threshold. She has no idea what this means.

But she shall visit the bank shortly and straighten things out. She is in the luck now, she knows. She feels it, and Brevard's last tip on a horse running this weekend confirmed. He almost never gives a tip, surely not unless he feels certain. Brevard knows Longchamp and the horses as if it and they were his children. If he says a horse is set to win, one way or another, the matter is set in stone.

Émilienne studies three well-dressed young ladies sitting nearby. The one nearest her table wears one of Coco's hats. She recognizes the dress designer, too, an expensive but onery gentleman she avoids. She watches the girls for a moment, so young and pretty and comfortable, so certain of their futures and places in the world. So certain of their due.

"Have you seen Mata Hari's newest show?"

She turns her eyes back to Liane, shaking her head.

"We thought your Bal des Quat'z'Arts was modern . . . Émmy, this girl takes it too far, strips to her skin."

Émilienne laughs. "Yes, I hear she finds it hard to find a place to dance these days. But, look here, do not compare my dance to Mata Hari. I wore a pink undergarment, long sleeves, and down to the ankle the old-fashioned way—remember? Nothing like this woman's nude show."

Smiling, Liane nods. Émilienne curls up a corner of her lips. "Mata Hari leaves nothing for a gentleman's dreams."

"Things are not the same now, Émmy." Liane's tone holds a touch of sorrow. "Paris changes—electrical lights, motorcars with the smoke and noise."

Émilienne ducks her head, lighting a cigarette and watching smoke curl toward the blue sky. "I prefer the old days too. Our carriages were more comfortable." With a glance at Liane and thinking of Alec, she asks, "Does your prince ever speak of war in Europe?"

"Only mutters about the Germans now and again. But we don't see each other much. He is old, you know. Not well." She looks off. "Émilienne, it seems everywhere is talk of war. Everyone is frightened . . . including me."

"I worry too. But Alec says the rumors are false."

"Then why was he called to duty?"

"He says for the Dragoons, conscription is just routine." After a beat, she says, "Now the training is over, they say they will let him off for racing most weekends, so I suppose he must be right."

Liane's voice turns harsh. "Let us not talk of war."

She nods. Liane is the only one to whom she could admit that she also has fears.

❦

Two weeks later, from below, she hears Alec's voice, back from Lunéville. Smiling, jumping from the bed, she hurries to the dressing table and her comb. She must look her best when he walks through that door.

And, just in time, he appears. She turns about, staring at him, struck by how handsome he looks in the uniform—dark blue with gold braid—and Alec so fit and trim and young and bright. Elegant. He stands in the doorway, preening, then opens his arms wide, and she runs to him.

"Darling, how did you escape!" she cries. "If ever you face the enemy wearing this uniform, they shall be blinded by your beauty!"

Releasing her, he steps back, snapping his legs together, and salutes. They both laugh. Why, this is her same old Alec. He still belongs to her.

"I've missed you, Émmy." They walk into the bedroom

together, and he sits on the edge of the bed. "It has been so long. Now, we are together." Smiling up at her, he adds, "You see? This is not so bad."

So long as France is not at war. But she promised herself to be good, to be brave and not complain. She steps close, tipping up his chin. "As you said, we have no choice."

He tosses his cap in the air, and, hands on her hips, he pulls her onto the bed, burying his face between her breasts. Alec's kisses, his touches are fierce at first, as hers are hungry—until they reach the heart of the storm and come together. Then, at last, sated, she rests her head on his chest, listening to his heart-beat while he strokes her hair.

As they lay together in the quiet late afternoon, Émilienne tells herself that, after all, their love is strong. Things are not so bad. He trails his fingers down her arm, dissolving the reverie. She moves aside; still he holds her in his arms.

"How is Lunéville? Was it a terrible bore?"

"It's a nice little place." Releasing her, he turns, resting on his elbow and looking down, tracing her jawline with his finger. "I think you might like it, Émmy. I like the others too; the men are friendly, all good riders."

When she does not reply, he adds, "We could be together more often . . . have you thought of this? You must visit me there."

Leave Paris now? She stares, then pushes up from the bed. Walking to the dressing table, she sits down, facing him, crosses her legs and lights a cigarette. Surely, he is not serious. But, yes, sitting up now, Alec goes on.

"The town is a friendly place. We garrison in an old castle." He watches her with care as he speaks. "I think you might like it, if you try."

Impossible. "You just came home, and still you speak of Lunéville?" She shakes her head. "Let us talk about this later,

Alec. I have waited so long for your return . . . let's enjoy this day. Besides, we don't have much time together since you ride this weekend at Longchamp."

He says nothing.

Rubbing out the cigarette, she rises, moving to the armoire. There she flings the doors wide. "Now, let's go out somewhere— to a park, perhaps? Or . . ." she says, turning to him, "perhaps we shall find a café and friends on this fine day."

She pulls a dress from the armoire—pink, a color Alec likes, one in which she was often photographed, when she was young—one of her favorite dresses.

With a glance over her shoulder, she sees that he has not moved.

She spins around. "Come, Alec. Let us make the best of the day. Why, I will send around for Liane and her latest gentle- man and have them meet us later on for dinner too." But even to herself, her voice sounds shrill.

Alec merely stares. "What bug has bit you? I've just come home."

Move to Lunéville! What is he thinking?

She waves off his words. Still holding the dress, she rings for Lily, then carries it to the bed. Suddenly, flinging her hand to her head, she turns, looking about. "Please, don't turn strange, not with me. Not today when you've just come home."

With a loud sigh, he stands up, stretching. "I had hoped for a quiet day. If this is what you want, I shall change clothes and call for the motor."

He strolls from the room just as Lily arrives.

"Émmy, I'm here." Lily's voice is light as she breezes in. "I was caught in the kitchen with cook."

"Never mind, just help me dress. And please tell the cook that Alec and I shall dine out this evening."

Lily helps her into the dress, then runs through the buttons in back. No more thoughts of Lunéville, Émilienne vows. Nor of the Dragoons. She must concentrate on Alec this evening. And on the coming weekend. And the horses. This Sunday shall turn the trick, she is certain, having followed three thoroughbreds in the field for several weeks. She has won some bets, replacing her withdrawals from time to time, although she does not recall the amounts.

When she is dressed and Lily gone, Émilienne goes to the armoire. Peering in, she pulls out the small safe and carries it to her bed. With a quick look at the door, she turns the dial, unlocks the box, and lifts the lid.

The jewels shine up at her. She has sold some over the years, including the tiara. But what is left has value. Although, perhaps not as many high-quality jewels remain as she had thought—perhaps she shall sell some of these for her bets this weekend, since her bank account is blocked. Reaching in, she pulls out a small box containing earrings. A moment of uncertainty strikes, and she eyes the little box, feeling a tightening in her stomach, remembering last year when she finally sold the best earrings, the blue diamonds that Étienne had given her years ago.

She should have kept records, of course. But must a girl really think of things like that? Still, gazing at the jewels, it seems impossible she has sold so many in just one year.

Taking a deep breath, she opens the little box, a pair of emeralds given to her by George when he was Prince of Wales. Holding these up to the light, she admires the clarity, the cut, then wraps them in her fist. Yes, these will do. She shall sell them tomorrow before the weekend races. And, she vows, her winnings shall go straight into the bank.

CHAPTER TWENTY-NINE

Yesterday a note arrived from Monsieur Robard, requesting a meeting this afternoon at two, in his office at the bank. Émilienne frowns, thinking of the short notice. But then she smiles because Alec comes again this weekend. He's managed to race at Longchamp, or nearby at Deauville or Chantilly and others, quite often, lessening the pain of their parting by the Dragoons.

This weekend he races at Longchamp. Spring is here. The weather is wonderful, and nothing, not even Monsieur Robard and his bank, shall spoil these days.

She picked a well-fitted though somber dress for her meeting with the banker. Upon arrival, she was shown into an empty office by one of the bank clerks, and now, it seems she must wait for the banker who is attending to other business, according to the clerk. *Do they not know who she is?* Here she waits in an uncomfortable straight-backed chair, facing a large desk with a window behind. The scenery—another wall across an alley.

She shifts in the chair with a sigh. Really, she has thought all along that Robard is an odious little man. Lighting a ciga-rette, she takes a deep draw of smoke.

On this May weekend, Alec rides Gal Fem for Hennessy stables. Such an exciting few days ahead, with Alec home. And he is certain to win.

The only dark cloud on the horizon is his growing insis-tence that she leave Paris, move to Lunéville. Of late he seems obsessed with this idea—there, his duties are light, and they could have more time together. She understands, of course. But Paris is her home, and Émilienne cannot imagine leaving the city for such a small town where a garrisoned castle is the center of interest. For a year, she has avoided visiting. She is a girl of the city. A city keeps one busy, keeps one thinking, on their toes. There's no time for rummaging through wor-ries over such things as war, while German soldiers stand only miles from the border. And if war should ever come—and she thinks not, but if so—she shall not be found in Lunéville. Better Paris.

No, she shall not leave Paris, she vows. Not even for the love of Alec Carter. How does one survive in a town so small? Royallieu was bad enough, and there she had good friends, and parties on the weekends.

Just then the door opens behind her. "Good afternoon, Ma-demoiselle d'Alençon." She watches in silence, blowing smoke while Robard removes his hat, hangs it on a brass stand beside the door, and turns. "I apologize for keeping you waiting."

She plucks the cigarette from her lips, holding it between her fingers. What is there to say to such a greeting? She has waited long enough. She watches in silence as he lowers him-self into the chair.

"Thank you for coming this afternoon. My note was sent on short notice, I realize . . ."

"Yes, it was. This is a busy afternoon for me, Monsieur Robard. What is the nature of this summons?"

He exhales a deep breath, moving the chair closer to the desk. Leaning forward, resting on his elbows, he clasps his hands before him.

"The subject, as you put it, relates to your loan and your account with us, mademoiselle. It seems you are delinquent on your loan, and the balance in your account is now below the threshold allowed."

"Yes, the threshold?"

He frowns. "The threshold is the amount you must always maintain in your account, mademoiselle, until you repay your loan. A reserve, security for the bank when you borrowed funds."

When she says nothing, he goes on. "As you know, despite our usual requirement for the signature of a woman's husband or father to extend credit, we made an exception for you, an unmarried woman." He peers at her. "Our governing board made the exception in your case, given your fame and success."

He leans back, drawing his brows together. "However, you have not made payments on your loan in several months, Mademoiselle d'Alençon. And you have not responded to our letters. Therefore, I must inform you that your loan, being overdue, must be paid in full by Monday, or we shall be forced to place a lien on your home and foreclose."

She shakes her head. "I don't understand. The loan is separate. Money in my account is my own." Gripping her reticule, she moves to leave. "I shall withdraw my funds at once."

With a sad look, he shakes his head. But his voice is cold. "Not until you pay off our loan, mademoiselle. The funds in your account will be used to reduce your loan, if not paid by the date due, on Monday."

His words spin in circles in her head. Clasping her hands,

she lifts her chin. "What is the amount required for full payment of the loan?"

Glancing down at papers stacked before him, he says, "With interest, one hundred and ten thousand francs, mademoiselle."

"Are you certain?"

"Interest adds up, mademoiselle."

Smoke curls between them in the silence. Such a large number. She swallows. Then, making up her mind, leaning forward, she rubs out the cigarette in the tray on his desk. "I shall have my lawyer call at once."

He nods. "Good. Better for us to deal with him. I understand business is difficult for a woman alone. Perhaps he can explain."

Fury simmers as she stands. "I understand all too well."

He rises with her. "Let me help you to your carriage."

"I do not need your assistance. Stay where you are." Her voice trembles, and she blushes but does not look away. "I shall return with one hundred and ten thousand francs, monsieur. And then I shall withdraw every sou I own from your bank."

"As is your right, once you pay."

Turning away, she pushes through the door into the big hall. Not until she has crossed the entrance, head high and steaming along, not until she passes through the doors and finds herself standing alone on the pavement, does the truth sink in. There, she stops, just for one moment, closing her eyes.

She has no means of paying back the loan. And no means of obtaining her own money, locked away in the bank, until she does.

As she is handed into the carriage, it occurs to Émilienne that ten years ago she could have paid off this debt after one night with a wealthy gentleman.

CHAPTER THIRTY

The light wakes her. In the soft bed she turns, feeling for Alec, confused. Of late, she often feels confused.

"He arrives on Friday, Émmy." Lily, passing through the room with laundered clothing, smiles at her. "It's Wednesday morning."

Émilienne shifts to her elbows, squinting, remembering that conversation with the bank. "Close the shutters," she grumbles, falling back onto the pillow. "What time is it?"

"Half past twelve." Lily's tone is pert as she moves about the room, ignoring the shutters and the sunshine. "You asked me to make certain you woke by this time today."

"I did?"

"Yes, you have business today."

Sitting up, remembering, she tosses the quilt aside and swings her feet to the floor. Lily hands her a silk robe the color of a lover's blush, a new one Alec especially likes, and she covers herself. "I must have a bath. And something to eat, here in the room while I dress. I have no time to waste today, Lily."

Lily nods. "I will attend to breakfast and return."

"Oh, and I shall wear the dark blue dress this afternoon." Stopping before the dressing table mirror, she stares at her reflection. "My hair is beyond help, Lily! Just look at this." Shaking her head, she sits down before the mirror. "Impossible to fix."

Behind her, in the mirror comes Lily's smile. "I shall bring breakfast right away. After your bath, we shall comb out your curls. It's not so bad, others would pray for hair like yours."

The moment the door closes behind Lily, Émilienne hurries to the armoire. With both hands she spreads the hanging dresses apart, reaching for the safe. She has memorized the numbers, and now she runs them through her head, turning the dial this way first, then that. At last, with a heaving sigh of relief, she hears the light little click. Pulling the safe door open, she peers inside.

There, the velvet boxes are all in place, but not as many as she recalled. Each box contains earrings, necklaces, pearls, bracelets, all gifts—a few left from Georges. Most from other lovers, saved over the years. She reaches for the earrings first, then draws back. No, she has sold too many of those, she thinks. Staring at the boxes, she struggles to remember which ones she sold, but cannot.

She reaches instead for the necklaces. Those sell well. Still, it is difficult to believe she must find one hundred ten thousand francs within days. And that does not count funds she planned to use on a good bet. The bet is safe, she is certain. Opening the box containing necklaces, she makes an instant decision.

She lifts her three-strand diamond choker.

Perhaps she shall take along some earrings too. She draws back—only one pair of quality left here. She lifts the ruby earrings from the box. *How can this be?* These were given her by Étienne, the last of his gifts. Her throat tightens at the thought of selling these jewels.

But there is no time left to think.

Holding onto the choker and the earrings, she closes the safe and returns it to the hiding place. Suddenly she feels faint. She stands before the armoire, clinging to the door while the room seems to spin. She stands very still, pressing one hand to her forehead, then down over her eyes, until at last the spinning stops.

Despite sunshine, she pays no attention to the weather, nor to passersby. On this afternoon she feels numb as she hurries along sidewalks toward the jeweler. There are no drivers around to see, to cause talk down in kitchens. The only person who knows she sells her jewelry is Lily. And Lily, she trusts. Holding her reticule containing the jewels close, she grips it tight. The shop she has in mind on rue Royale is not so far away.

She halts on rue Cambon, across the street from Coco's shop, gazing through the glass. Several young women mill about. Coco must be doing well.

Just then the door opens, and two girls come out onto the pavement. Touching her hair, Émilienne draws in a deep breath. Hairstyles seem to have changed. And their skirts are shorter than her own, by two inches perhaps. How has she not noticed before?

She used to set the styles. Now, it seems she is out of date.

The two girls swing along, talking and laughing as if they've no worries in the world. Just then, a rowdy group of young men push past Émilienne, swarming around her as they hurry on. A flush rises at the indifference they show, sweeping past without a glance. Someone in the crowd spots the two girls ahead, and they cross the street, following them.

For a moment Émilienne stops, resting her hand on a hitching post on the street, feeling unsteady. Not one man glanced back. Not one had recognized her and called her name. She smooths her hair and looks about. *Why, only a few years ago . . .*

But she has no time for thoughts like this today and hurries on.

On the pavement outside the jeweler's shop, she pauses again, gathering her wits. This shop understands quality; she used to sell her jewelry here. She was fond of the elderly owner but moved to others for better prices years ago. Now, she has returned to those other shops too often. Best not to push that luck.

Taking a deep breath, she opens the door. A bell rings as she enters. Inside, the light is dim. No other customers mill about. Despite the displays, this is not that kind of shop.

She feels a presence, although the old man has yet to appear. Eyes watch through a peephole behind the register set in a window to the back room, she discovered years ago. Now, adapting a casual look, she half turns, waiting, glancing back through the glass to the narrow street. Dust motes dance in sunshine streaming through the window while she waits, arms folded over her chest, jewels well hidden. Outside, a motorcar's engine spouts black smoke. Behind it comes a carriage.

At last, she strolls to the long counter near the register. Under the glass are diamonds, emeralds, pearls, jade, rubies—all displayed on a black velvet cloth. Inferior jewels, compared to her own, she decides. Small and poorly cut.

As she straightens, the door to the back of the shop opens. She looks up, startled to see a young man enter the room. "Good morning, madame," he says. "How may I help you today?"

"Where is Monsieur Chastain?" The old man with whom she usually bargains.

"Ah, you knew my father. I am sorry to say he is gone, madame." As he speaks, he walks toward her behind the counter.

Unsettled, she tips her head, moving closer, inspecting the somber young Chastain across the counter. His features are sharp. His eyes, green, too close. Hard, like marbles. The son is nothing like the father, a man who knew his business but dealt with a bit of humor too.

"I offer my condolences, monsieur. I knew your father, not well, but we did business together over the years. Over many years."

The young man nods. Spreading his hands on the counter, he glances at the reticule. "And what may I do for you today?"

With one pull she unties her reticule from her waist and pulls out a velvet pouch, placing it on the counter. The young man does not move, watching as she opens the pretty embroidered pouch, pulling out the necklace and then the earrings, each wrapped inside a velvet cloth. One of the cloths she places on the counter, arranging the jewels on it to advantage.

When she straightens, the younger man moves close. "May I . . . ?"

"Yes, of course."

Pulling out his glass, he places it over one eye and bends, studying first the necklace, then the earrings, holding them up to the light. She leans on the counter and turns aside while she waits.

At last, he straightens, removing the glass. He taps the tips of his fingers on the counter, calculating one last time, before looking up at her. His eyes are flat, devoid of emotion. His father was hard too. But fair.

"We are not purchasing rubies this season." She frowns, watching him. "And I am afraid the diamonds in the necklace are inferior."

"Impossible. Why, they are small, but there are no imperfections on these stones, nor within. I am certain of this, monsieur."

He nods in agreement. "They have a few inclusions, perhaps,

but otherwise you are correct." He sets the diamonds down. "However, they have a faint yellow hue. And look for your-self—do you see the slight glaze on these stones?"

She pulls the cloth to her, bending, studying the diamonds. Then she looks up. "I do not. I see no fault in these diamonds. They are magnificent."

He pushes the cloth closer to her. "The color and dullness indicate a shallow cut, madame. This diminishes the quality. Less sparkle with a shallow cut."

With a glance at the necklace, she looks up, confused. His father was never so particular.

"I can offer twenty-five thousand, madame."

"Certainly not," Émilienne says right away. The boy's tone is cold and flat, as are his eyes. In his eyes, not a spark of shame at the value he offers.

Remembering the banker's threat, she lowers her tone and softens her expression as she speaks. "This . . ." and she lifts the neckless, dangling it in the light, "is a gift from the German kaiser, Wilhelm, young man. These stones are of the finest cut."

Her throat tightens as she speaks. She longs to flee but holds her place. This shop is her best choice right now. In the past, here she has usually found at least a fair price. And if she leaves now, she cannot return. "Why, it is just luck for you that I came to your father's shop first."

When he shrugs, his bottom lip juts out. "This is my price."

"You are not your father's son."

His face flushes. "Good day, madame. I wish you luck, but I believe you will find my offer stands, compared to others. Even those more lenient than our shop."

As he starts to turn away, she places a gloved hand over his. "Wait."

The clock is ticking toward Monday morning. A desperate

feeling grows inside. She'd not realized how many jewels she sold over the past few years, not until opening the safe this morning.

A quick decision is required. With her best smile she looks into the boy's eyes, and, leaning on her elbow, chin in hand and curling her lips, she says, "Your father and I got along quite well. Let us think more about this beautiful necklace."

His eyes travel to her cleavage. He stares, then turns his head, fist to his lips as he coughs.

"I ask only for your best price."

Their eyes meet, his have warmed a bit. "Ah, under the circumstances I cannot . . . well, you see . . ." With a glance about, he lowers his voice. "Unless, perhaps, you would care to discuss this subject under more comfortable conditions. May I offer you an afternoon aperitif?" He eyes flick to the closed door behind him and back.

She straightens while freeing a strand of curls from under her hat. "I must have some understanding of the value of such discussion. Should we come to an agreement over the price of my jewels in our negotiations, by what amount should I expect an increase in your offer?"

He spreads his hands on the counter again, looking down and tapping one finger. Good, he is a bit nervous. "That is up to you, madame." But when he looks up again, she sees it in his eyes. The hunger.

She looks across the countertop from beneath lowered lids. She cannot afford to lose this chance. She must be practical now—no time for pride.

"This is a good time for an afternoon sip." Her voice turns husky, and the boy turns red. She shall get her price, and this should not take long. "Let us discuss the problem and find a solution."

The boy smiles, and she glides around the counter toward

the back room door while he locks up the front. She can endure this boy for an hour or two—and Alec need never know.

At home, she closes the door softly behind her, wanting to be alone. She tiptoes up the stairs, and there, Lily waits in the doorway, watching her ascend. Something about the girl's expression strikes her deep inside—could that be pity on her face?

Before she can summon a smile, Lily rushes to her. Flinging her arms about Émilienne's shoulders, the girl holds her tight while she weeps. Lily knows her well.

Wiping Émilienne's tears, Lily steers her to the bed. There, Émilienne sits at the edge while Lily unbuckles her shoes and pulls them off. Like a blind woman she responds to Lily's instructions, standing, turning for the unbuttoning of her dress, untying of the corset, removing petticoats. Lily slips a silk nightgown over Émilienne's head, then pulls back the bedcovers.

With a sigh, Émilienne slips thankfully between the sheets. Lily places a cool cloth on her forehead. She pulls pins from her hair, easing tension, then steps back. "Rest now," she says.

Her soothing voice brings a faint smile. "How long have you been with me, Lily?"

The girl turns, puckers her lips, looking off. Then she shakes her head. "Too many years to count, Émmy."

She closes her eyes. It seems forever since that long-ago time when she was new to the stage, and Lily came around. Lily stood by her when the last bank took her first home. And, again, when the duchess took Elisa.

Now she stands by her even as she struggles to find a way out of this hole. He had tricked her, the young jeweler. He paid only thirty-five thousand francs for the necklace, and what could she do but accept!

Thirty-five thousand . . . only a drop in the hat compared to her total debt.

Still, she has the ruby earrings. Tossing and turning, staring at the ceiling, she tells herself that tomorrow will be a better day. Tomorrow she shall sell the ruby earrings. Tomorrow, she will rest.

CHAPTER THIRTY-ONE

She trembles as she walks. But she has sold the ruby earrings and the money is in her pocket, and now she strides through the 6th arrondissement, down rue Bonaparte, back toward the river, turning over a new idea in her mind. She received nine thousand francs this afternoon for the earrings from a lesser jeweler. Sales from the jewels—forty-four thousand francs in all—are not even close to paying the bank.

She could sell more jewels, but that takes time.

And she has got enough to make one solid bet on Sunday.

If she uses the money this way instead of handing it over to the bank, she could win the fortune she needs. She could close her accounts, find another banker who understands her worth. The more the idea turns in her mind, the better it feels.

Just then, someone calls her name. Turning, she spots Étienne sitting at a table on the terrace of Les Deux Magots in Saint-Germain-des-Prés. He lifts his hand, waving, and sitting there, too, are Boy Capel and Coco.

She weaves her way through tables, most empty this time of the afternoon. Étienne and Boy rise as she approaches, Étienne holding out his arms, greeting her with kisses. After they settle down again with Émilienne among them, Coco takes over, ordering for her a glass of good red wine.

Oh well, it is late enough. Besides, when one has no control over circumstances, all a girl can do is sit back, relax, and hope for the best.

"Why, it has been forever since we four were together," Coco says. "What a pleasant surprise." Her voice has lost some of those high notes, that almost tipsy sound girls not yet women sometimes have. She appears quite stylish in her new look—the fitted suit, white gloves. And, of course, her hat. Long gone are the jodhpurs and old shirt for this one.

"Where were you going?" she asks.

"I have just come from the Luxembourg Gardens." Neither Coco nor the men shall ever know her secret—that she is selling jewels. "The weather is lovely today, and Alec is out of town."

As she talks, she decides she shall put her new plan to work at Longchamp on Sunday. There is risk, but that has never stopped her before. Especially not with the possibility of such a high reward. Besides, giving the money to the bank is throwing it away, since she cannot meet their demands with what she has.

Now, feeling better, she gives her friends her best smile. "What news goes around?"

From across the table, Coco frowns. "We were discussing the state of the world when you came along, Émmy. And, with these two men, it is always war."

"Hold up!" Boy shakes his head, turning to Coco. "You speak too free, Coco. Nothing is certain, after all."

But his words come too late. War, and Alec conscripted, living so close to the border—now starts that trembling again.

Émilienne folds her hands in her lap to hide this, turning to Étienne. Étienne Balsan is the one she trusts.

Just then the waiter sets a glass before her. Forcing another smile, crinkling the corners of her eyes, she watches Étienne as she speaks. "War in France? Whatever does Coco mean?"

He gives her an airy look and shrugs. "Nothing to worry over, Émmy. It is the Balkans again."

"And Queen Victoria's grandsons," Coco adds, smiling. "The czar, the king, the kaiser. As always, the cousins."

Russia, Britain, and Germany. But again, what of France?

Boy nods. "The Balkans are at war, and Russia holds interests there. Austria, as usual, causes trouble, belligerent as they are. And, of course, Germany sticks with them. As you may know, the kaiser is close to Franz Ferdinand, Austria's archduke."

"The archduke must be his only friend," Coco says.

"And England, what of George?"

"The king believes he is the peacekeeper." Boy shakes his head.

"While they strengthen the navy," Étienne adds.

Boy Capel is a diplomat of sorts, Émilienne knows. He knows everyone in power, all through Europe, Russia, Asia.

Émilienne shudders, watching him, remembering what Alec once said—near Lunéville and Strasbourg, Germans patrol their side of the border. "Is war possible, then?"

Boy glances at her. "It is possible, yes."

Émilienne, looks off, feeling the tremor. Alec! Sunlight filtering through the leaves above form dancing spots of light in shade. If she had known the course of conversation at this table, she would never have stopped.

"Enough talk of war," Étienne says, shooting Boy a look. With a little laugh, he adds, "The Balkans are always at war. This is nothing new."

"Europe is too small and close to laugh," Coco snaps.

"Well then, shall we take a trip? I have property in Brazil."

Étienne's tone is laconic, but Émilienne knows him well enough, conscious of a strange undertone beneath his words.

Picking up her glass, she sips, unsettled, thinking of Alec in the new silence. This is an old conversation, she tells herself. Going nowhere, meaning nothing.

The month is May, the year 1913, a time of peace. All is well. Turning her eyes to the pleasant scene from the terrace, she concentrates on the beauty around them. The sun slants on the sidewalk now. Tables on the terrace slowly fill, voices chattering around them. On the street motorcars race past, engines snarl, as always these days—capturing the streets of Paris, replacing carriages, like her own.

Étienne reaches into his vest pocket, pulling out a cigar.

Coco, watching, suddenly demands one too.

He looks at her and grins.

"Just light one. I shall try it."

He clips it, hands it over to Coco, laughs when she puts it in her mouth and immediately spits it out.

But the laughter slightly turns the mood, even as Émilienne worries. It is all too much, worrying about money, placing the bet, and Germans on the border, war. But France is at peace! *Peace.*

No one wants to think of war, or passing time, nor even of the clouds above, turning dark over the horizon.

Early the next morning, no later than ten, at best, voices from downstairs wake Émilienne. Pushing up against the pillows, she rubs her eyes then the back of her neck. Suddenly, she hears Alec's voice, then his boots clapping up the stairs.

She sits up straight, running fingers through her curls, wishing she had time to comb them out before he arrives. Just then the door flings open, and Alec walks in. Spotting her, he stops, standing legs apart, arms dropping to his sides, eyes on her alone.

Ah, how good looking her man is—and her eyes sweep his blue uniform, his muscular thighs, arms, shoulders, and even with the shutters still closed, she sees his knowing smile. Worries of the past few days fade away.

He comes to her, sitting on the edge of the bed, leaning down, kissing her long and hard. Then, pulling her up to him, he slides her into his lap, wrapping his arms around his girl. She feels his strong heartbeat as she leans her head against his shoulder. How she loves this man.

He rests his chin on the top of her head, and she melts against him.

And, just like that, the day ahead fills with joy.

"Darling . . ."

"My love." He cradles her, lifting her into his arms, then in one smooth motion placing her down onto the mattress.

"Only you, Émilienne." His voice is thick now, just a whisper. "I think of you every minute of every day when we are apart." He slides his hands down her arms and looks up. "What is this? You are trembling, my love."

"It is nothing," she says, brushing back her hair. He watches her for an instant, then cupping her face in his hands, he bends to kiss her. As his tongue explores, her tears come.

"What, again?" He lifts up, watching her.

"These are happy tears. Tears of joy."

In the cool, shuttered room, they make slow, languid love as the world outside disappears and only the two of them exist. Once, she turns her head, kissing the palms of his hands, telling how she loves him, how she misses him during the weeks, and then again, their bodies join, moving as one, and a song inside carries her to new heights of love and joy, to a place where words do not exist.

In these few minutes on a blissful morning, nothing exists for Émilienne but Alec and their love.

CHAPTER THIRTY-TWO

PARIS, 1913

Alec spends Sunday morning taking Gala Fen through his paces, preparing for the race. He left in the early hours, leaving Émilienne asleep.

Liane picks her up in her motor—with her driver, of course. At the racecourse they make their way through the gates. The main race, Alec's race, is last, so Émilienne shall sit in the stands with Liane this afternoon. Liane, married to royalty now, has a pass. As they enter through the gates, they pause for a moment, admiring the flags of France—blue, white, and red set against the broad white sky. Émilienne turns to Liane, squinting against the sun.

"What do think about the chatter of war?"

"I never think of unpleasant things, my girl." She links arms with Émilienne. "What good does it do to worry about things like that ahead of time? It's not as if we have a say in the matter."

"But where would you go if war comes? What would you do?"

Liane purses her lips, looking ahead. "Get out of Paris first,

I suppose." After a pause she adds, "I should go to Monte Carlo until it is over. No one cares a whit about Monte Carlo." She laughs. "You must come with me. If we are parted in the mob in Paris, meet me at the tables."

Just then a crush of young grisettes entering the gate push them aside, swishing their skirts. The grounds today are crowded, much more than on most weekends at Longchamp. Already the stands are packed.

"Caroline is with a picnic," Liane says as they enter the stream of people again. "Just on the other side. Shall we meet over there before the races start?"

Émilienne agrees. But when they part, she feels Liane's eyes following her. She knows where Émilienne goes, and if she loses, Liane will scold. Other than Lily, Liane is the only friend who knows the side of her that places bets.

Parasol overhead, Émilienne walks on. She has glanced at the morning line, checked the odds, and feels certain now of luck. She struts through the crowd wearing a new Jacques Doucet, a rose-colored gown, and on her head, pink silk fashioned into flowers, resting in a fluff of net, ribbons, and lace.

Styled by herself, she shall say when Coco asks. She smiles at this thought.

The air is thick with perfume as she slips through the crowd. Why, the place is electric this afternoon. Just ahead she watches the bookmakers amid a constant circling crowd. She shall not bet on Alec, and, as usual, a stab of guilt slips through at the thought. She argues with herself. Alec almost always wins. The odds are with him every time—though, as always, a bet on her lover reaps little reward.

She shakes off the thought. He need never know.

The transaction is brief as she places her bet, handing over forty-four thousand francs, on Morgan Bluff, a thoroughbred she has won with before. Out of win, place, or show—she bets her horse will place or win, giving her two chances, with the odds six to one right now. Although they still could slip. Despite the odds, Brevard gives the nod. It's not a tip, but he agrees.

When Morgan Bluff wins or comes in second, she shall have enough to please the bank, with a good sum left over as well. Relief swells as she hands over the notes, giving away as well the sordid memories they bring forth.

Now, the dirty notes are gone; the bet is placed. Soon she shall rid herself of Monsieur Robard. Perhaps she shall even replace the jewels she sold.

She tucks away the ticket, this time slipping it inside her bodice. No sense running about with a fortune in a reticule, which a pickpocket could easily steal. Turning about, she stands still, scanning the pretty scene—the milling crowds, the lovely grassy field, the first horses heading now for the gates with their escorts. Her race is third. And last comes Alec and his almost certain win.

Tonight, they shall celebrate—his win, her freedom from the problem of finances. Though the last, he shall never know.

Caroline's voice rises, leading Émilienne in the right direction. There across the way she spots Liane and Caroline with a group of young men standing around, all talking and laughing in the shade of a tree. When she calls out, Caroline turns and, lifting a bottle of champagne, calls out again, "Best hurry, Émilienne!"

A gentleman beside her turns, watching her approach. Ah yes, she thinks, swaying across the grass, she still attracts the eyes. Liane hands her a glass, and the gentleman pours. Then the three friends—Émilienne, Liane, Caroline—all begin the toasts. The first, of course, to the Lion.

Just then a booming voice interrupts. Turning, she recognizes the man, the artist, one of Toulouse-Lautrec's great friends. He is also a reporter for the press. Holding up a sketch pad, he says, "Mademoiselles, I must have your picture."

He is well known, drawing for the best papers, capturing the news following the demimonde in Paris. A sketch comes fast, a photograph takes too long.

He gestures, and they move close together. "Time stops," he calls as he begins. Feeling grand, smiling now, Émilienne holds still. Five minutes, at the most.

"Perfect!" he proclaims at last. They gather around, the three, gazing at the sketch. Just then, announcements come from the starting gates. Soon, the first race is called. Two more to go. And suddenly, the trembling returns. A chill cuts through her now—perhaps excitement or joy? Or fear?

"*The Three Graces*," the artist says, gathering his belongings. "Watch for this tomorrow, mademoiselles. We are in time out of time, like magic. This is one for the ages, a portrait for the future."

❧

Caroline departs with a gentleman, while Liane and Émilienne decide to use her husband's pass for the stands. The announcer calls the second race. The horses burst from their chutes as they walk along, and his voice turns louder, then urgent as the field rounds the turn, and then they're on the homestretch.

Listening no longer, Émilienne and Liane pass through the enclosure entrance gate—Liane showing the pass.

Émilienne must stop this trembling. She must stay calm. She returns a gentleman's smile as they head for their seats—the familiar man over there—but only while his wife is turned to someone else. Following Liane, she walks on with an air, she hopes, of nonchalance.

As they take their seats, Émilienne glances at the winning horse in the second race prancing to the circle, then down at the tote board just below. She leans forward while a man changes the odds now. Almost holding her breath, she waits.

Five to one, on Morgan Bluff. Less money, but better odds.

Liane turns, asking a question, but the clamor around them drowns her words. Émilienne merely nods. Gabrielle Dorziat walks past, and she and Liane wave. *Stay calm, Émilienne. Stay calm.*

But the trembling continues.

Somehow, some way, which later she does not recall, she hears the third race announced. It seems to take forever, jockeys edging their mounts into the chutes, escorts close behind. She closes her eyes; now all she must do is survive.

How free she shall feel when this race is over and she wins. The noise in the stands is deafening now. The crowd beginning to cheer before the start. She closes her eyes, bones and muscles locked in place, her thoughts spinning.

Now comes the announcer's voice—"And they are off, Dancing Girl and Best Luck, nose to nose, and here comes Morgan Bluff, with Green Fields moving up . . ." Leaning forward, she strains to hear.

This is it—her big chance. All Morgan Bluff must do is place. Soon she shall be free of worries, of this trembling.

They round the turn, heading for home, and then . . . "Best Luck in front, now Dancing Girl, Morgan Bluff, and Green Fields, and now it's Best Luck in front, with Morgan Bluff moving up. Morgan Bluff now second by a hand, Dancing Girl third . . ."

Yes, he is second! Blood rushes to her head as she freezes. First or second place, she needs first or second.

"And Dancing Girl flying . . . moving up for the challenge,

and now . . . over the line, it is Dancing Girl—Dancing Girl, first! Best Luck, second—Morgan Bluff, third . . ."

Just like that, everything is gone.

Émilienne stares straight ahead as, in the instant, time slows, and then the world turns silent.

Black and cold.

She floats in the dark. Forever in the dark.

And later, in a wink, she hears a noise, causing her to stir.

Sharp light, a blinking star. Sounds of the universe, high and shrill.

And then a voice.

"Émilienne! Wake up, Émmy!"

She hears. She knows the voice. Something warm touching her, something sweet.

Slowly, she opens her eyes.

Alec looks down at her. He smiles, the light of the star. "Hello," he whispers. "Thanks to God, you are here now, with me."

Without moving, she stares at him. "Alec?"

"Yes, my love."

"Why aren't you racing?" Clouds fade, the blinking light is gone. She looks past him, where Lily stands, then back to him. "What happened?"

"You fainted." As he speaks, he presses something cool to her forehead. "At the racecourse."

The race. Liane beside her, the noise, the crowd.

"The good doctor says you're not injured. Liane was there, you fell into her lap." He smiles. "You had good luck today."

She starts at the word, and memories roar. Luck. "Forgive me, Alec." She turns away.

He touches her chin, turning her eyes back to him. "I already know. Liane told as much. You bet heavy and lost." He shakes his head, then seems to catch himself.

She nods.

He takes her hand, kisses the back, then holds on. "Do you think that matters right now, my love? We shall talk later, but know you are not alone. I am here with you. I shall care for you."

A tear escapes. He wipes it off. "Now you must sleep." She looks past him again. But Lily is gone.

With a kiss on her forehead, he crawls into the bed, lying down beside her. She opens her mouth but cannot speak. He lays beside her, his arm over her, and slowly, she closes her eyes.

"The only thing I care about is you, Émmy."

She longs to confess, but this he won't allow.

His fingers close her eyelids, a gentle touch. Again, she falls asleep.

※

The next morning, they have breakfast on the balcony. The month is May, still May, she muses, though it seems more time has passed, a lifetime in a night of sleep—and Alec is still here.

She turns to him. The time is now. This is how she begins, this is how she explains. From the beginning to the end—she tells of her need to place those bets, despite the risks. She tells of the money lost, the jewels sold, the bank, the account, her loan.

Lost. All lost.

"What will happen now," she wonders aloud. "With our home." But already she knows. Again, a bank will take her home.

Alec shakes his head. "Never."

She stares at him.

"You shall sell."

Still, she stares. "As simple as that—just sell?"

He picks up the coffee and takes a sip. "Of course. What else? You must sell, pay off the bank, and keep the rest." And, after a pause, he adds, "And move with me to Lunéville."

Before she can answer, he says, "You will find peace and quiet there. No more trembling. No more fear . . ."

Setting down the cup, he turns to her. "No more worrying about the theater, *Gil Blas* and the new dancers, your fame, your security, all of that. Did you think I didn't know?"

Seconds pass. And then she looks at him. "Are you finished?"

"No."

"Then what more?"

With that, he comes to her. Kneels before her. Wrapping his hands around her hips, he looks up. "You are my only love, Émilienne. I wish to marry you. To care for you. I want only you, to love you forever." After a beat, he asks, "Will you have me?"

His voice softens with each word he speaks, a soothing balm.

Standing he pulls her up. With his arm around her, they walk back into the bedroom while he talks of Lunéville. Of a small stone cottage with a garden, up for sale—just a short walk to market or visiting friends. There are few motors in Lunéville, the air is clear, the water fresh. You can still hear the birds there. At night you will hear owls, the fox's howls.

"But . . . what would I do in such a small place?"

"Live with me, in peace."

When she says nothing, he sits her down and tips her chin. "I can give you a leg up, Émmy. This is what two people do when they love."

She studies him. Is this the man she thought she knew so well?

He paces before her, back and forth, talks on and on of plans and ideas.

No one has loved her this way before. Already, he seems a part of her. But he has stopped talking now, and he looks down at her, as if waiting for her to speak.

"Will you marry me?" he says again.

She smiles up at him. "Yes, Alec Carter." And as she speaks, the words fill her heart with peace. "Yes, yes! I love you. I shall be proud to be your wife."

CHAPTER THIRTY-THREE

Near the River Marne and surrounded by forests, the town of Lunéville—about four hundred kilometers east of Paris as the crow flies—draws her into an embrace at once. At the town center is the castle, an enormous château similar to Versailles in proportion and beauty and situated near a lake. It is there the 23rd Dragoons are garrisoned.

And it is there, in the formal gardens, where Émilienne d'Alençon and Alec Carter are married.

In the months she has lived here, Émilienne is surprised to find she has come to love the pretty town. Here the sun is bright, the air fresh and pungent, the people are calm and friendly. As Émilienne heals, returns to herself, her own natural joy returns, and she finds friends easily enough—shopping in the marketplace, in the outdoor cafés, strolling through the castle gardens, the pretty shops. Many, like her, are wives of garrisoned Dragoons.

Every morning, as today, she awakes at six o'clock, watching the sunrise through the windows. The cottage is small, built of stone. Three large windows in the bedroom pull color and light inside, expanding the room. Then she turns over and falls back asleep. Life is slow in Lunéville, but she does not miss Paris. Time does not rule in Lunéville. It just rolls on, like the waters of the Marne.

She treasures the leisure, the quiet.

Now with a wife and a home, Alec returns to her almost every night. The men of the Dragoons are also often given time off for families on the weekends. Alec still races on certain weekends, although he chooses the meets carefully—now Émilienne is here. Lying in bed with him at night, she feels comforted, surprisingly free. Lovemaking is gentle and sweet, fulfilling her, a woman who knows the tricks.

While Paris rumbles with each rumor of war, Lunéville, so near the German border, is quiet. Alec and his friends dispel her fears of war. In Paris, everyone feeds on rumors, he says. If true, would not the entire garrison at Lunéville be abuzz with the news?

Why, she can see this for herself. Dragoons and commanders are well settled in routine. All soldiers marking time, like him— like the German ones at the border, young men with families, with hopes and dreams. No one wants war.

Alec's voice soothes Émilienne each night.

She is safe now. Alec will keep her safe.

Alone this morning, she lies in bed, watching colors fade into clouds. No, she shall not return to sleep. Life changes, and she shall too. She must rise early as the other ladies do. She must dress right away, as Lily has gone. No more morning and afternoon gowns for Émilienne, she thinks, with a wry smile.

How she misses Lily. She has had two letters of late. She stays with her sister and the husband, for now. But Lily writes she is still in love with her accountant. They shall marry soon, and Émilienne and Alec must come to the wedding—she insists! Already he owns a small cottage big enough for a wife and a baby or two.

She, too, has started a new life.

With a sigh, Émilienne flings back the quilt.

She wanders into the kitchen alcove, just off a room that she calls the Grand Salon, a sliver of the space in her old bedroom in Paris. But she thrusts the thought away. Here is her home. In the kitchen she lights a fire. The first thing she learned in the kitchen was to make hot chocolate, coffee, and tea. And simple meals, as her first friend in Lunéville, Madame Jeanne Gallienne, has taught.

She laughs, thinking of those beginnings.

Sitting at a small table for two in the kitchen, she sips coffee, surprised each time she reflects over how her life has changed. She thinks of Coco's little shop, Chanel Modes, and the plans that girl has dreamed up for the future. Who would have known that young girl at Royallieu would hold such determination inside? She chose her direction, created a plan, and followed it step by step all the way.

Years from now, Émilienne will be forgotten, she supposes. Just another pretty girl, struggling to survive. That is the road she chose.

But Coco—the girl is now a woman, carves the way for girls who follow. Perhaps Coco has started a revolution for women in France this time. She is the one who shall be remembered years from now, looking back. Boy Capel will hurt her, she is certain—that is just his way. But no matter; Coco will succeed.

And who cares about the past or the future? Still, a smile comes, remembering—the cheers, the curtain calls, the night Georges and the Princelings pulled her carriage through the streets, entrances at Maxim's, led by Hugo through the crowd. Lover's gifts—worth fortunes.

Gone, now. Just like time.

She lifts a shoulder. After all, what should one expect from a dancer, someone used to the bright lights onstage, going out to play, sleeping late, wearing diamonds and emeralds and sapphires and pearls as if they were simple baubles.

Now she has Alec and his love. This change, moving away from Paris, was easy on the inside when the time came—because of Alec.

The other things she needs to know—how to keep a home, how to cook and clean—she is learning over time. Jeanne takes her to market, shows how to find the best fruits, the freshest vegetables. How to cook, how to make a meal. How to plant a garden.

Now, as the bells toll eight o'clock, she rises, moves to the sink and washes her cup, still surprised at her new duties. Placing the cup carefully on the shelf, she hurries into the bedroom. She pulls on a light blouse, a long skirt—no corsets now—and slips her old dancing slippers on her feet.

Émilienne sits down before a table and mirror, which Alec bought, and she pulls a small jar of pink paint from the drawer, paint salvaged from her days onstage. With a finger she smudges it over her lips. Pressing her lips together, she regards her reflection. Strange, those lines at the corners of her eyes seem almost invisible now. Why had she worried so before?

She braids her hair, wrapping the braids around her head. No fancy pompadour here. This is Lunéville, not Paris. With a last look at the mirror, she fingers the black pearl hanging around her neck, always a reminder of Elisa. The only jewel she did not sell before moving from Paris. Perhaps one day, it will be Elisa's.

Then, picking up a big straw basket holding a shovel and

packets of seeds, she heads out through the door to the garden in back. Outside she pauses—already fall has come. The air is cool and sweet. She takes a deep breath, remembering the smoking automobiles in Paris.

At the edge of the garden she sits, placing the basket on the grass beside her. The soil is turned, still slightly damp, good for planting. Flowers grow lush. Her seeds will sprout quickly in this fine earth.

Kneeling in the grass, she looks about for a moment. Never has she felt this happiness before. The sun, above the horizon, spreads golden light over the field before her and through the trees further on. Sitting back on her heels, she looks up.

She looks up into the light.

My candle burns at both ends;
It will not last the night;
But ah, my foes, and oh, my friends—
It gives a lovely light!

—Edna St. Vincent Millay, "First Fig"

A NOTE FROM THE AUTHOR

Famous courtesans flourished in Paris during the Belle Époque, the beautiful era, a time of relative peace in France—after the French Revolution, the Napoleonic Wars, and the Commune riots—beginning in the year 1871 and ending with World War I in 1914. Émilienne d'Alençon, Liane de Pougy, and Caroline Otero were known as the last and greatest of the courtesans, the most beautiful and scandalous—"*The Three Graces*," they were called. But, by the end of World War I, the seemingly frivolous lives of the courtesans, the butterflies, disappeared into history.

A courtesan was much more than a mistress, who was usually hidden from her lover's family and the public. Instead, kings, princes, and wealthy aristocratic lovers were proud to be seen in public with dazzling courtesans on their arms. In addition to spending a fortune on the girls, gentlemen gifted them fabulous jewels—diamonds, rubies, emeralds, strings of pearls—often along with a coach and horses, a furnished home and servants, sometimes great estates. Evenings were spent promenading the Grands Boulevards of Paris; at the Folies Bergère, the Moulin Rouge, Les Ambassadeurs, and other cabarets and theaters; or making an entrance at Maxim's, where courtesans reigned and society ladies were not welcome. Often such gentlemen entered into legal arrangements with courtesans, providing them with wealth and security for life, even if they should part.

Courtesans were often referred to as the *Grandes Horizontales*—a tongue-in-cheek, irreverent way of calling them prostitutes. But in France during the Belle Époque, neither Émilienne nor other courtesans were considered just prostitutes. Courtesans were the glittering stars of the demimonde. Yet many, if not most, rose from impoverished lives, learning the secrets of beauty and charm on their own in order to survive in a sometimes-brutal world. A courtesan was also prized for her wit and humor, her fashionable and trendsetting attire, and her manner—different from ordinary women to such an extent that she seemed almost magical, her very presence crackling with an ephemeral force of energy as she walked by.

On the surface, despite her highs and lows, Émilienne was known for her joyful spirit and passion for living a free life. Here in Émilienne's own words, reported by Victorien du Saussay in an interview in 1893: "I am a girl who doesn't give a damn. Say it in these words, it's important to me. And as for my artistic career . . . I do this for fun. I don't have any pretensions, I just play. By the way, it bothers me to work, a woman isn't made to work." This interview and other stories about Émilienne's life can be found in *Émilienne d'Alençon: vivre d'amour en 1900*, written by Carole Wrona.

If you are interested in reading more on the Belle Époque and the courtesans, in addition to the above, I also recommend *The Book of the Courtesans* by Susan Griffin.

It is interesting to me that Émilienne and Coco Chanel were such good friends—Coco so practical and cool, and Émilienne such a passionate dreamer. Although at the beginning of her career, Coco was dependent on wealthy men—Étienne Balsan and then Boy Capel—through her friendship with the older Émilienne, she seemed to observe and change. While Émilienne continued life, as always, dependent on her men, Coco eventually chose another path, earning her way, even as Émilienne sank into despair, at least until she met Alec Carter and her life changed.

Alec Carter was one of Europe's greatest jockeys. In the last year leading up to World War I, he won a second Grand Steeple-Chase, riding Lord Loris for James Hennessy. But, in the same year, on June 28, 1914, after an explosion of tension in the Balkans, a Serb nationalist assassinated Archduke Franz Ferdinand of Austria and his wife, igniting the events leading to World War I.

One month later Austria-Hungary declared war on Serbia. Russia, having interests in Serbia as well, mobilized. With this, Germany declared war against Russia on August 1, 1914. And, to protect its southwestern border, the country declared war against France on August 3, invading through Belgium, not far from the city of Nancy and the town of Lunéville. The strategy as declared by Wilhelm was "Paris for breakfast, St. Petersburg by lunch." In turn, Britain declared war on Germany, as it was bound under a treaty to protect Belgium.

The moving forces here were all grandchildren of Queen Victoria—Czar Nicholas II of Russia, Kaiser Wilhelm II of Germany, and King George V of Britain. As predicted by Étienne and Boy in the novel, the cousins' war was underway.

When the war began in France, Alec is known to have fought valiantly with the 23rd Dragoons regiment, a French cavalry unit. Sadly, he died within the first three months of fighting, leaving Émilienne once again alone.

Alec was the only enduring love of Émilienne's life. In reality, they were unable to marry because of an earlier marriage by Émilienne to another jockey, Percy Woodward. That inconvenient marriage lasted only a few weeks, but it appears Émilienne merely went on with life, never filing for divorce.

Facts concerning Émilienne after the war began are vague, although it is known that near the end of her life she resided in Monaco and Paris. She wrote three books—an autobiography, now lost; a book of poetry; and one on secret tips learned backstage during her dancing career about beauty and makeup. After the war and Alec's death, she turned to women for love, finding intimacy with new friends and old ones, like Liane de Pougy. Émilienne was a free spirit who never allowed herself to be limited by social mores.

Émilienne had a daughter, although the father remains unknown. Circumstances around the birth are vague. A birth certificate in London indicates she bore a child in 1887 at the age of seventeen, a daughter, although Émilienne refused to recognize the child until 1904. Even after that date, however, history does not record any interaction between the mother and child, with a few possible exceptions. *Gil Blas* reported that Émilienne was once seen at the Opera in Paris with a young girl who was believed to be her daughter, although no one else reported this. And one biographer reports that someone unknown provided the child with an expensive education in England. Another report online describes an impoverished woman claiming Émilienne as her maman.

Other than this, the child remains a mystery.

Georges-Auguste d'Ange, a young and wealthy aristocrat in France, did fall deeply in love with Émilienne. He was real, although I changed his name. Their romance was well known throughout France, followed avidly by the press, much as the lives of celebrities are reported today. When his powerful and politically charged mother learned of the liaison, however, she pulled the lovers apart, sending Georges to fight a lost cause in the Congo of Central Africa, where he died.

Details of the immediate aftermath of Georges's death concerning the babe, Elisa, and Émilienne's war with the duchess rose from my imagination.

Last, but not least—Charles Desteuque, the man with sad eyes who helped Émilienne, Liane, Caroline, and many other courtesans rise to fame. The "Empty Bottle" died a horrific death, out of his mind and in a lunatic asylum. He always carried around photograph cards of the three courtesans in various poses, pulling them out to show to others.

But, when he did, he's said to have kissed the image of Émilienne, whispering, "I made her!"

In writing this novel, I changed some dates and played with the flow of time to keep the story moving. Although Émilienne is thought by some to be one of the most beautiful and intelligent courtesans of the Belle Époque, she has not received as much attention in history as Caroline and Liane. It is my hope that this book will rectify that and bring her life story and joie de vivre to the pages of history in a new way.

Émilienne died on February 14, 1945, in Monaco, it's said, although again the facts are vague. Some say she was buried in a family tomb in Paris. Some say she rests in peace near Alec Carter.

Well, dear readers, I prefer to believe the latter.

ACKNOWLEDGMENTS

So many fine, talented people are involved in creating a book that it is difficult to know where to begin to write these words. So, I shall begin first by thanking my husband, James Craft Lott—Jimmy, to me—for his love, understanding, and support, never complaining when I disappeared into my writing room for days at a time. Émilienne's was a difficult story to compress into one book, covering so many years in such a busy life. But Jimmy, my alpha reader, read each of my many final drafts of the book with sensitive, loving grace.

In this beginning I also thank my good friend and agent for over twenty years, Julie Gwinn, vice president of the Seymour Agency. Always optimistic, always ready to help solve problems and celebrate happy occasions, she radiates joy. Thank you, Julie, for your friendship through the years and for your encouragement and support. Without you my books would be manuscript drafts sitting on a shelf.

Big thanks are due to the team at Blackstone Publishing for

turning my story of Émilienne into one more beautiful book. I so enjoy working with them and consider them friends. Special thanks go to Rick Bleiweiss, head of new business development, a writer, himself; Ananda Finwall, managing editor; and Deirdre Curley, line editor, for once again polishing the text so it shines. Thanks also to the graphic design team, for their beautiful cover evoking the mood of the story and the Belle Époque.

I cannot say enough about the amazing talent of Corinna Barsan, my editor with Blackstone. Like poetry, for me at least, a great editor like Corinna expands an author's thinking during the editing process. Corinna's sensitivity to every nuance of the manuscript made the final editing of *Émilienne* a pleasure.

Last, but not least, I thank Elisa Houot for her assistance. Elisa, the French representative for the Seymour Agency, was invaluable. The best and earliest sources of information on our girl Émilienne are published only in French. Elisa not only interpreted the primary source book from "old" French to English for me, page by page, with explanatory footnotes where needed, but did so while battling through the recent pandemic crisis in France. More amazing, while under fire—so to speak—she managed this work at a pace that allowed my own to flow as it should.